# Barlowe Pride

## *Eden Monroe*

## *Print ISBNs*
Amazon print 9780228626077
Ingram Spark 9780228626084
Barnes & Noble 9780228626091

*BWL Publishing*

*Books we love to w*
*Authors around the world.*

http://bwlpublishing.ca

# Dedication

*To my late mother, Faith Edwards*

# Table of Contents

# Prologue

Duke Barlowe sat comfortably in his saddle as the sure-footed stallion picked its way up the steep rock-strewn path to the highest point above the valley, a ride both he and Champion had enjoyed countless times.

It was late May and the sun that had warmed the land during the ever-lengthening daylight hours, was now making its gradual descent toward the horizon in a spectacular golden sunset.

At the top of the rise, they rested by a stand of hardwood trees fresh with new leaves. Duke settled back in the seat to survey his ranch, flung like a quilt of vibrant patchwork green, far below. It was the second-biggest spread in the valley, yet modest in size when compared to much larger outfits elsewhere. Hayden had called the Summer Vale Ranch his grandfather's kingdom. Indeed, it had been in the family for generations, built on a generous land grant from the British Crown in the late 1700's to Josiah Barlowe, a decorated army officer who'd fought on the side of the Loyalists during the American Revolution.

Summer Vale continued to flourish under Duke's management until age began to catch up with him. The ranch was still stocked with prime beef cattle although not in the same numbers as it once was because the fences needed mending or in some cases, replaced entirely. A brutal winter had helped pull down the last of those on the south pasture and at eighty-one he could no longer swing a hammer like he used to, especially with his health declining. Otherwise, he doubted younger men could keep pace with him. But his barns still stood straight and strong and he was proud of that.

Because there were no sons, it had always been understood that his grandson, Hayden would inherit Summer Vale Ranch. However, that dream had died through necessity twelve years ago, and the decision still weighed heavily upon Duke. Now there was no one to follow. No Barlowe, other than his daughter, Peggy, Hayden's mother, and she had absolutely no interest in ranching in Bloomfield or anywhere else. But what choice did he have? Never had he felt more alone, abandoned, which was absurd upon reflection because he was the one who'd done the banishing. Hayden had called him the king of Summer Vale. He supposed it was an accurate description although it had been said in anger; meant to be disparaging. So be it, but you didn't cross Duke Barlowe. There was a price to pay for those who did, and nobody knew that better than Hayden.

Duke raised his hand to massage his chest in the classic cardiac salute, the discomfort almost constant now despite medication. He had a bad heart, had for some time although Hayden had told his grandfather, the day he threw him off the ranch, that he didn't have a heart. He knew he did though because of the unrelenting pain and the doctor had warned him it could give out at any time. He'd felt all day long this was probably that someday. Hence the ride to his favourite spot tonight while there was still time. He wanted to have one last look at the old place and think about better days, certainly happier ones when his Martha had still been alive. He'd lost her much too soon and still mourned her after all these years. He'd paid her a visit this afternoon in the small cemetery behind the church. Soon he'd see her again and that warmed him considerably.

The pain in his chest grew worse, the massage providing no relief. Let nature take its course, he thought reasonably. Why fight the inevitable? The end would come and it did, not a minute later as he slowly slid out of the saddle and collapsed heavily onto the ground beside Champion. The old horse nosed his master then raised his head and stood vigil.

Walt, the one remaining ranch hand, found Duke and Champion there early the next morning just as a gentle spring rain began to fall and he quickly removed his hat out of respect. The king was dead.

# Chapter One

Hayden's cellphone rang just as he was about to latch the gate on the round pen holding this morning's round-up animals from the north pasture, a solid looking bunch of two- and three-year-olds although nothing truly outstanding about any of them. The horses at Paradise Hills Dude Ranch were for pleasure-riding dudes who signed on for one of the ranch's several vacation packages. They thought anything with four legs, a mane and a tail was beautiful, as if flattery and a positive attitude would compensate for their lack of experience. But a horse didn't care if you thought it was good looking or not, they just lived to get their day's work done and get another greenhorn off their back. Whatever. He'd learned managing a dude ranch was a calling, one he didn't necessarily have. The money was good though and he'd become religious about salting what he could of it away for a place of his own someday.

He ignored the phone while he finished securing the gate and was not quick enough to catch the call. It started ringing again.

"Hello!" He sounded impatient, unfriendly, but he was just naturally brusque, matter of fact. He didn't mean anything by it.

"Hayden? Is that you?"

"Yes, Mum, it's me. Good to hear your voice! I haven't heard from you in a while, what's up?"

"I have bad news, honey," she said with a catch in her voice. "Daddy died."

There was a moment's hesitation. "Whose Daddy?" It took another moment for it to sink in. It couldn't possibly be Duke Barlowe, the man who acted as though he was going to live forever. "Your father you mean?"

"Yes, my father. Your grandfather."

He swallowed a flash of irritation, the scab torn off the bad memory in an instant, a wound that hadn't even begun to heal after all. "I'm sorry for your loss, Mum."

"Your loss too, Hayden. He was your grandfather."

"He was my grandfather, but there's nothing I can do about that," he said, trying to keep the bitterness out of his voice, and failing. "When did it happen?"

"Last night I understand. He went for a ride up in the hills and apparently just dropped dead while he was sitting in the saddle. Walt found him. Daddy died alone, just him and his horse."

"I'm not surprised. He couldn't get along with anyone other than that horse ... and maybe Walt."

She sighed. "I understand what you're saying, dear. Daddy could be difficult."

"Try impossible."

"Okay impossible at times, especially when things didn't go as he hoped they would."

Hayden laughed harshly. "You mean didn't go his way. Period. Look I'm not going to trash my grandfather but he made it pretty clear how he felt about me twelve years ago. Everything I felt for the man died the day I left there. He killed it."

"You two used to be close."

"As long as I did everything exactly as he wanted me to we got along fine, yes. When I started thinking for myself it was a different story. Anyway, like I say I am sorry for your loss, but it's no loss to me. I won't be coming home for the funeral."

"There won't be a funeral. When I spoke with Wynn over at the funeral home today he said Daddy had made all of his own arrangements. No viewing, no funeral, just cremation and burial beside Mum in the family plot."

"He probably knew no one would come to his funeral anyway. Cancel everything ahead of time to save face I guess."

He could hear his mother exhale; see the inevitable smoke rings because she was rarely without a cigarette in her hand. He'd encouraged her to quit for her own good, begged really, but there was that Barlowe pride again, or should he say contrariness.

"I don't think it was as bad as that," she reproved him gently, "and I did love him very much in my own way. I would certainly be there, but as it turns out everything has been taken care of. So at least I don't have to make that long trip to New Brunswick. But we do have something that needs to be seen to, immediately."

"What's that?" he asked.

"Summer Vale Ranch."

"What about it?"

"It's yours."

"Oh no it's not!" was his immediate reaction. "When I left that day I never even looked back. That place is history to me. Let's talk about something else, please."

"We have to talk about the ranch, Hayden."

"If you say he left the place to me I won't believe you. No way would he do that."

"I'm telling you it's yours, lock, stock and barrel. I'll call the lawyer as soon as we finish speaking and start the ball rolling."

"Aren't you listening, Mum?"

"I am, I'm just choosing to ignore your protests is all because I know you love that place." More smoke rings. "You always have."

"Used to love the place. Past tense."

"It's not the ranch you don't love, honey, it's the man who owned it, although I don't believe you hate him as much as you think you do."

"First of all I don't think for a minute he would have left the ranch to me. It isn't something he'd do. The man kicked me out of his life because I married a woman from a family he didn't like, as though that was any of his business. He disowned me, Mum. You know that. Even when you tried to talk to him about it later he wouldn't change his mind. Who does that to their own flesh and blood? I didn't murder anyone. I just picked the wrong woman as far as he was concerned."

"You know how much he hated the Sutherlyns. They were a thorn in his side his whole life. Besides, I wasn't crazy about your choice of bride either."

"Fair enough, but you didn't disown me over that mistake. I'm a grown man. I made a bad decision and I corrected it."

He thought about Mary Rae, his now ex-wife. He hadn't seen her for a few years and yes, she'd been hell on wheels, a really bad choice in the matrimony department. Nevertheless it had been his mistake to make, not his grandfather's.

"I'm just saying that's why he got so mad at you."

"So are you telling me he changed his mind about Mary Rae?"

Her brief pause was enough to tell him that no, Duke Barlowe had not changed his mind. He would never bend, completely unrelenting. His back too stiff with pride to try to undo the damage he'd done.

"You know, Daddy."

"Yeah, I know, Daddy."

"But the ranch is still yours, Hayden. Come home, dear and run it. Make it great again."

"Soooo help me out here. He wouldn't forgive me for what he called the ultimate betrayal; for taking up with the Sutherlyns as he put it ... but he changed his mind and decided to leave the ranch to me anyway. I think you're mistaken. I don't believe he left the ranch to me. I can't see him doing it. You actually think that's what's in the will?"

"I'm telling you the ranch is yours. Haven't you always wanted to own your own spread?"

It was true, he did, but getting that kind of operation going took big bucks; big bucks he didn't have at the moment although he'd made some pretty sound investments over the past few years. He'd also earned a decent living running other people's ranches. Alberta had beckoned when he'd lost his home in New Brunswick. He and Mary Rae had packed up what little they owned, stuffed it into a van and headed west. It wasn't hard finding work, not with his ranching experience. In truth though it had taken him a long time to get over losing Summer Vale and the plans he'd made for when he owned it someday, just as his grandfather had always promised.

"There's something you're not saying, Mum. Gramp never left me the ranch, did he? I think you're telling me it's going to be put up for sale and I should come home and buy it."

"No, that's not what I'm saying at all."

"Well what then?"

She took a deep breath. "I'm saying he left me the ranch, Hayden, and I'm not interested in ranching. Even if I was interested I can't pull up stakes here in Maryland at this stage of my life for any reason. I'm married now and this is our home, so what do I want with a ranch? When I left Summer Vale I too never looked back, just like you although not for the same reason. The difference is you like ranches, I don't."

Now it was his turn at thoughtful silence before he finally spoke. "I don't want it, Mum. If he didn't want me to have it, just sell it and keep the money. I'm doing fine on my own."

"Hayden! You know you and your grandfather have a lot in common. You're both as stubborn as a mule. I believe he wanted you to have it but he was just too pigheaded to make things right between you. In any event you are the rightful heir, you've certainly put enough work in on that place over the years. I am simply correcting a grievous error on his part. You have to take over the ranch, there is no other way."

"Still...."

"Listen to me! Brian Sutherlyn is chomping at the bit to get Summer Vale and if I put it on the market, and I will, he'll buy it in a heartbeat and annex his own spread. I know things went terribly wrong between you and your grandfather and that was heartbreaking, but he did work his whole life to keep that place going, even through tough times. The last thing he would have wanted was to see it pass into Sutherlyn hands."

"You know, it would almost be poetic justice to see that happen and him not alive to control it."

"I've never known you to be spiteful, Hayden. It doesn't suit you, dear."

"He thought he was king of the valley. He wasn't."

"Many thought he was."

"Yeah well he's not anymore, and if I did come back I can see the animosity they felt for him being shifted to me."

"Not necessarily. You've always been your own man, Hayden."

"You said Gramp and I acted the same."

"No, I said you had a lot in common. There's a difference. My father suffered through many disappointments in his life and it made him bitter. But you're wrong in saying no one would come to his funeral. Actually he was well respected in many circles."

"Name one."

"You know he was president of a local service club at one point. He not only found time for that in addition to everything else but gave it a lot of energy."

"Okay, that's right. Sorry."

"You're bitter, Hayden, and I don't blame you. Maybe you're angry because he was right."

"What, about Mary Rae?"

"Yes, about Mary Rae. She ended up making your life miserable."

"That's my business. Like I said, my mistake to make and nobody else's."

"That's true, dear, and you made a doozy, but I'd be the last one to judge anyone in that regard. Not after the mistake I made with your father."

He heard her light another cigarette, the top snapping back into place on the metal lighter as she inhaled.

"Do you ever hear from him?" he asked.

She chuckled sarcastically. "Not since I was five months pregnant with you. I've tried to talk to you about that many times but you always tell me you're not interested. Have you changed your mind?"

He looked out across the summer meadow under a periwinkle blue sky, snow-capped mountains the perfect backdrop. His horse was becoming antsy under him, wanting to get back to work. There'd always been a degree of curiosity about his father, but maybe not enough to want to meet him. It wasn't something that kept him awake at night. It had always been an instinctive feeling that he should leave well enough alone. He'd always wondered though if his mother maintained any sort of contact with the man. His mother had not married until she was fifty, and he was happy for her. Barry Snow was a great guy.

His grandfather was the only father he'd ever known so when he'd turned against him, it had been a long sharp knife to the chest. It was a wound that would never heal as far as he was concerned.

"No, I haven't changed my mind. Let's save that story for another day. I don't judge you for having me, never that, because I love you. You've been a good mother to me and even though Duke Barlowe was your father, whatever that meant, please don't defend him to me."

"I'm just saying...."

"Please, Mum. Don't."

"All right, you win, but that brings us back to the ranch. It's yours, son, all we have to do is change the title into your name. Please don't walk away from what was always meant to be yours because of what happened between you and your grandfather."

"I wouldn't feel right about taking it, not under the circumstances. Can't you see where I'm coming from?"

"I can see where you're coming from. I know you've always wanted to own your own ranch, not work to make another man rich. Not that ranchers are rich, but you get my meaning. You're meant to run Summer Vale and call it your own. You're a Barlowe, that's where you belong."

He'd thought from time to time about returning to his home province. He still missed it, even after so many years in the west. Maybe it was time to go home. But he didn't see how he could swallow his pride and move back to that ranch, a place he swore he'd never set foot on again. Now here it was being offered to him on a silver platter.

"Hayden? Please tell me you'll go home and take over Summer Vale."

"I don't think I can, Mum. I have my pride you know."

"I guess you do, but maybe you could do with a little less of it. It seems to me that Barlowe pride has caused quite enough problems. Maybe we need to let some of that pride go, take a big step back and look at the bigger picture. And speaking of pride, son, when you come back why don't you look up Naomi Martel?"

"She's still not married?"

Sweet Naomi Martel, now there was a prize, but the timing just hadn't been right way back then. She'd only been seventeen when they'd met, to his twenty-two and they'd gotten serious much too quickly. They'd met at a grocery store in Franklin where she worked part-time and he'd been smitten right away with the beautiful teenager. And that's what she was, a teenager, and those five years had seemed like a lot at the time. Their birthdays were only a month apart so when she turned eighteen, there was still that five-year age difference one month later. She'd been the first to bring up marriage. In fact it became all she talked about and because he didn't want to lose her, he'd saved and bought a diamond ring he couldn't afford. But he'd increasingly felt that things were moving much too quickly in their relationship, like he was on a runaway train, one that was quickly gaining momentum. The deeper they'd gotten into the whole engagement thing the more obsessed she became with it, always with a different bridal magazine to show him until he became thoroughly spooked. Another issue was intimacy. He respected her for wanting to wait until their wedding night, but he was tired of being held at arm's length until the whole thing started to feel like a death sentence and he'd bolted. It seemed as though everything was too cut and dried to suit him at the time. He'd loved her, but the timing wasn't right. He'd felt suffocated and so initiated the break-up as gently as he could although he'd left her in tears that awful night. Maybe if she just hadn't pushed so hard....

Mary Rae Sutherlyn was as wild as a hawk and generous with her favours. At the time she'd seemed like a breath of fresh air, the girl of his dreams. No endless details to work out. She provided exactly what he was craving after the past few months, spontaneity. She let everything happen in the moment. So throwing caution to the wind one day they'd up and got married. That's when everything had blown up at home. He'd never seen his grandfather more furious. That Hayden would dare to marry the daughter of his sworn enemy, the no-good Sutherlyns, had been too much. Hayden might have gotten the girl and all the sex he could handle, but he'd lost everything else in the bargain. He could only imagine how devastated Naomi must have been when he walked away.

His mother broke into his thoughts. "Did you hear me? I said I don't think she's married. I saw an Internet ad for her company the other day. She's a computer programmer; still living in Franklin and her last name is the same. I also didn't see a wedding ring on her hand, which I would say is a pretty good indicator she's single. Now she's the one you should have married, Hayden. You should have just slowed things down a little bit if you were uncomfortable, asked for more time; not break up with her. She would have made a wonderful wife for you. I agree with Daddy on that although he shouldn't have done what he did. That was very wrong as I've already said a million times, both to him and to you."

"I can't change the past, any of it. What was the name of her company? Do you remember?"

"Not right off hand, but search computer programmers and her company will likely come up because she's running that ad right now."

He made a mental note to do just that the first chance he got. He'd thought of her many times over the years and wondered what she looked like now. She was even more beautiful probably.

As if his mother could read his thoughts she went on to supply the necessary information. "She's a good looking woman; really quite beautiful. I assume it was a current picture in the ad. There was no mistaking it was her, and then I checked the name. Bingo!"

He didn't want to appear too interested, although he definitely was now that his mother had brought it up. "Yeah, I'll check it out sometime for old times sake."

Peggy laughed, not falling for his nonchalance. "Sure, like as soon as we get off the phone. You don't fool me, Hayden. I suspect you still feel something for her. The two of you were going hot and heavy until you went and called everything off. You probably broke the poor girl's heart. You know she called me one night not long after you ended things with her."

That got his attention as he reached ahead to give his horse's neck a reassuring pat to settle the animal down. "She called you. I never heard anything about that. What did she want, other than to trash me? Not that I didn't deserve it."

"She was crying; asked me to intervene on her behalf. She said she wouldn't beg you to come back; just wanted me to tell you the breakup was a mistake. Of course I couldn't do that."

"She was just too young if she thought that would work. Naïve. You can't talk a man into doing something he doesn't want to do."

She chuckled. "Well certainly not a Barlowe."

He saw his opportunity and smiled as he spoke. "Then why are you trying to talk me into going back and taking over the ranch?"

She took another long pull on her cigarette. "Because I'm a Barlowe too. Honey, I've never interfered in your life. You know that."

"Until now," he said without malice.

"Until now, and you have to listen to me."

"What do you care what happens to the ranch? You couldn't wait to get off it as soon as I was old enough not to need you as much."

"I only stayed as long as I did because I had you and that's where I wanted you to grow up. Don't get me wrong, I think Summer Vale is a really beautiful place and a big part of me loves it. But I was never a country girl at heart. I wanted to get away, do more, see more."

"You were born country. What happened?"

"I was a throwback is all I can think. Grandmother Nancy grew up in New York City but when she met and married my grandfather Wendell, they settled on the ranch. She loved him so she stayed, but it couldn't have been easy. Anyway, the ranch, do you want it or not?"

"Not."

"Hayden! Stop trying to play hard to get. I don't believe for a second you aren't jumping at the chance to get back there and have at that ranch … among other things."

"What other things?"

"I should say another someone. A certain triplet who may or may not still be available."

He glanced at his watch. Time to get over to the office and meet the latest batch of dudes about to take on the Wild West for the weekend. "Don't even think about playing matchmaker," he warned his mother with humour.

"I won't, this one is entirely on you. Besides, what's to say she'd even have anything to do with you after what you did to her? There probably aren't any matches to be made but you never know, do you? Soooo … what about the ranch?"

"Come on, Mum, stop. Besides, when was the last time you saw Summer Vale?"

"Last month as a matter of fact. I was home to see Daddy, both Barry and I."

"Was he any nicer to Barry?"

She hesitated. "Well ... they still didn't exactly hit it off."

"Big surprise there."

"It doesn't matter now anyway, Barry wasn't bothered by it. He's a very easygoing guy. So, about the ranch...."

"What did the ranch look like when you were there?"

"Daddy was eighty-one and he had a bad heart so the place had slipped a little."

"A little."

"Okay a lot, but nothing that can't be fixed. The way you work, you could bring it around in a hurry. Honestly, Hayden, it's not that bad. Anyway, the land alone is worth holding onto."

"Sounds like a money pit to me. I don't have a big bank account, Mum. It sounds like it needs a lot of work."

"Have you been following the market? The price of beef has gone up so now would be a good time to get back into it."

"I'd have to buy up a bunch of feeders and sell them in the fall. By then the price could be down again. Besides, I'd need the money now, especially to restock it."

"There's already a good-sized herd on it, and a good market. There's the money you need right there to get everything back to where it needs to be, mostly fencing from what I could see. That's what was bothering Daddy the last time I spoke to him, the condition of his fences."

"There's already a herd you say?"

"I'd say about a hundred head. That's good isn't it?"

"It's not bad."

"Lots of new babies this spring too, all walking around enjoying that nice fresh new Bloomfield grass."

He chuckled. "You're painting a very tempting picture, but I don't know. Maybe there are just too many bad memories that go with the place now."

"You have to let the bad stuff go, Hayden. Move on. What happened to you wasn't right. We both know that, but it's not going to do you any good to hold onto it and let it eat you up inside. Did you ever think your grandfather regretted his actions? That may have very well been the case, but he was just too proud to say so; to admit he was wrong."

"I was pretty easy to find if he'd wanted to make an apology, but that call never came. I would have come back if he'd done that."

"That Barlowe pride again. He couldn't swallow it and look what it cost him. He lost out on twelve more years with you. I know he loved you, dear, he just couldn't get past his pride to tell you so."

"I've tried to get over all this. I honestly have, but it's still hard. I thought we were tight, had the best kind of relationship but he turned on me in a heartbeat and turfed me out. He also called me a bastard, which I am I know, but to hear him say it was something I'll never get over. Even if I did want to come back I'm afraid just seeing the place will dredge everything up and I'd have to deal with it all over again."

"So make it your own. Tear down the ranch house and build a new one or renovate if that's what's bothering you. Change whatever you want to, it's up to you. Besides, seeing the land again will probably bring back really good memories. That's possible too isn't it? Glass half full, Hayden. Think positive. So what do you say?"

"I still think if he'd wanted me to have it he would have left it to me himself. I don't like going in the back door to get it, which is what this feels like."

"Who cares! We're correcting a gross injustice if nothing else. Allow me to do that for you, honey. That ranch has your name written all over it, we just have to get the necessary paperwork done to make it official."

"I've been thinking about it as we've been talking and the only way I'll take it is if I can buy it from you. Those are my terms, take them or leave them."

"Fine. I can live with that and do you agree to whatever price I set?"

"Absolutely but set a fair one. It might take me some time to pay if off but I think you know I'm good for it."

His mother was relieved, he could hear it in her voice. "Excellent and take all the time you need. I think you know I will be fair about it "

He adjusted himself in the saddle and glanced at his watch again. He had to wind this up or he'd be late to welcome the guests and that was a definite no no on this ranch. There was just too much competition to take customer satisfaction lightly. A warm, timely welcome helped kick off a positive visitor experience.

"I know you wouldn't try to rook me, Mum."

"Great! I want one dollar for the ranch. That's my price and you just agreed to pay what I asked."

"One dollar! Come on! No way!" he told her, turning his horse in the direction of the main office and cueing the gelding into a lope to get there in time.

"One dollar to make it legal and Summer Vale is all yours. Those are my terms."

"You're sneaky."

"No, I feel that's a fair price. Are you going to be a man of your word?"

He sighed, knowing his mother had won. She always did, but he couldn't deny the excitement spiking through him as he slowed his horse to a walk for the final few metres to where guests had already begun to assemble.

"Sold!" he said, chuckling, "now I've got to go, Mum. I love you."

"I love you too, honey. Congratulations! You are the new owner of Summer Vale Ranch."

# Chapter Two

It was with reluctance that he said good-bye to Paradise Hills Dude Ranch, not because he would necessarily miss his job, but he had become very good friends with the owners, Jinx Dooley and his wife Elaine. They promised to stay in touch, as people always intend to, but seldom do once separated by time and distance. They'd had some good times together.

And now he stood in the front yard at Summer Vale Ranch. A tsunami of emotions threatened to swamp him as his gaze swept over the old ranch house he had called home for twenty-three years; the corrals, barns and other assorted outbuildings, the pastures, the hills that surrounded it. He looked at the river, a shimmering silver ribbon that sneaked past the ranch a short distance away. His mother had been right. There was a large herd of beef cattle in the main pasture, confirmed by Walt on the drive up from the airport in Franklin.

He'd thought about Naomi when the plane's wheels finally hit the runway, but that was another matter for another time. It had been good to see the ever-faithful Walt who was now a grey-haired sixty-two year-old, although still robust and able bodied. He'd wasted no time explaining to Hayden he had no wish to stay on full time now. He had only done so up until this point out of loyalty to his grandfather, but he'd help Hayden whenever he was needed and that was very good news indeed. He and Walt had always gotten along well despite their age difference. He was one of the main reasons why it was good to be back at Summer Vale as memories of happier times slowly began to resurface.

Once they'd arrived at the ranch Walt dropped Hayden off with the two suitcases he'd brought with him. What little he'd left behind would be delivered via courier in a day or so. He bid Hayden good day and left for home. Walt was nobody's fool, he knew Hayden's return to the ranch would be an emotional one and he'd want to do it alone. He was right.

After giving the place a once over Hayden headed for the barn to see Champion. His grandfather's horse had to be at least twenty-five years old now if he was a day. His mother said Duke had been found with his horse, so at least he knew the old chestnut stallion was still very much alive. The horse barn was the smaller of the two front livestock buildings, but generous enough in its dimensions to house six good-size stalls. His grandfather still believed cowboying should be done from the back of a horse, not on something with a motor. Hayden figured Champion could use a little company seeing as how horses were herd animals and he'd be alone in the barn. However, when he unlatched the door the first thing he saw was Aries, a darker chestnut gelding. He'd been a frisky three year-old when his grandfather had given the horse to him on Hayden's eighteenth birthday. A lump immediately lodged in his throat. His grandfather had kept his horse all these many years. It had just about killed him to walk away from Aries that terrible day, but he'd had no choice, no money to trailer him all the way to the west. And by the time he could afford to do it, he'd reasoned the horse had probably been sold and he'd been too stubborn to call and ask. The horse nickered, recognizing him, bobbing his head excitedly.

Duke and Walt had taken good care of him because his coat was shining and the barn itself was showroom clean. Wiping his eyes with the backs of his hands he hurried to the box stall where he wrapped his arms around the horse's neck, laid his face against his, and cried like a baby. His mother hadn't told him Aries was still on the ranch. Maybe she thought it was too painful for him to hear, and knowing his mother, hadn't thought to tell him about the horse when she was trying to sweeten the pot to get him to return. But now he was back to stay and bolstered by the warmth of three old friends, one human, two equine, he was already starting to feel like he had done the right thing.

It was after he'd carried his cases inside and done a walk through the house that he pulled out his cellphone and called his mother.

"Just wanted to let you know I'm back on Summer Vale, Mum. Got in about an hour and a half ago."

"Great! How does everything look? Pretty bad, right?"

Hayden smiled. His mother could best be described as quirky, a little off the wall and most certainly she danced to her own drummer. He couldn't help but guess it was a highly unusual tune but it didn't matter. Growing up she'd made him laugh, a lot, and he idolized her. He'd always been proud of how pretty she was and the circumstances of his birth had honestly not mattered to him. He had her and that was all that mattered. He'd even understood when he was fifteen that it was important for her to go back and finish high school. She'd gone on to get her business degree and subsequently carve out a nice career for herself in online marketing. Those years had been an adjustment, but he'd loved her enough to understand it was what she needed to do. It was an adjust for them all when Gram got sick and his mother had set up an office at home so she could help look after her until she died. Then she'd met Barry through her work and moved to

Maryland to be with him. Even though it meant he saw her even less, he was happy for her.

"I don't know where you get that this place is in terrible condition. The fences need work but the buildings are in good shape. All in all I'd say it was kept up pretty well."

"Oh well that's good. I just saw a bunch of posts lying on the ground, and besides it was a while ago now and all of the snow wasn't quite off. You know how ratty everything looks until the land dries off and starts turning green. But that's good news for you. Did Walt drive you up from the airport? He said he would when I called him."

"Yep, and another thing, Mum. Why didn't you tell me that Aries was still here? I loved that horse and it was hard to leave him. I can't believe Gramp kept him. He was right there waiting for me in the barn."

He heard his mother light a cigarette and he felt that old familiar drop in his spirits. He lived and died with every cigarette she smoked. The thought of losing her to some terrible disease actually kept him awake some nights although he understood he was up against the formidable enemy of her addiction. He tried not to take it personally, but why would she risk her health, her life with him in it, for a drag on a cigarette? He tore his mind away from that constant worry and waited for her answer, then decided to change the subject if only for a brief aside.

"I hear you're still sucking on those things. You told me you were going to quit three years ago."

"Hayden, I don't want to hear it."

"I worry about you, Mum."

"Well don't do that. I'm fine. I found these new ones with a double filter so that's better, right?"

He sighed, gritting his teeth. "Come on, Mum, you're smarter than that."

"Okay, the subject is closed," she said, expelling smoke as she spoke. "Now you asked me about a horse?"

"Right. You didn't tell me my old horse was still here on the ranch."

"It's just a horse," she said with a smile in her voice. "I knew you liked him but I guess I didn't realize how much he meant to you. Anyway I didn't know he was still in the barn because I never go in there when I'm home for a visit. You know how I feel about animals. We don't exactly get along. If they leave me alone I leave them alone, but I'm so happy the horse you used to own is still there. That must have been a really nice surprise, was it?"

"The best. I'm going for a ride once we're through here."

"I can't tell you how happy it makes me that you got the ranch, and it won't be long before you're right back into the swing of things."

He hesitated. "It's hard, Mum. It was all right here waiting for me as soon as I stepped out of Walt's truck. It was like it had happened yesterday; I expected him to come marching out the back door asking me what I thought I was doing, putting a foot on his property. I keep trying to relax, but I feel him here. I suppose it'll take time to get over that."

"At least now you're facing it and you will get over it. That's one thing I've found about life, Hayden. We constantly surprise ourselves as to what we can overcome. We just have to keep on pedaling. It really is as simple as that. If we stop for any reason or God forbid give up, life goes right over top of you like a steamroller. You have to stay strong, no matter what anyone says or does."

The conversation ended with that sage advice and he wandered into the kitchen, pulling out a chair from the substantial wooden table. He settled into it, his elbows on the table. He remembered his grandmother's molasses cookies, she must have baked a million of them just for him and he ate every one. He'd even steal them out of the cookie jar, placed conveniently within reach on the green Formica counter. Of course he wasn't supposed to be having sweets before a meal and even though he knew she knew, she'd never said a word about it. His grandfather on the other hand was much stricter, but always loving. To lose his love had been wrenching. Nevertheless he decided to take his mother's advice and move on; try to remember the good times and there had certainly been plenty of those.

A movement out in the yard caught his eye and he watched a shiny red half-ton roll slowly to a stop beside the corner of the house. There was a decal on the door but he couldn't quite make it out in the glare of the sun. He watched to see who would get out. To his consternation it was Brian Sutherlyn, his ex-brother-in-law and a loudmouth just like his old man. He'd wait for him to come to the door and see what he wanted, as if he didn't already know. Minutes passed with no knock. And then he realized that Brian likely thought there was nobody home, what with Duke dead and the place probably standing empty. He was about to get a surprise.

Glancing out the window again he saw no sign of his visitor, so opening the door he went out into the yard; still nothing. And then he heard the horses nicker in the barn so he headed in that direction. When he walked in he was astonished to see that Brian already had Aries on the crossties and was placing a saddle blanket on his back.

"Can I help you with something?" Hayden asked as he leaned against the doorframe.

The other man whirled around so quickly he almost lost his balance, his eyes blazing. "What are you doing here?" he demanded, obviously not surprising well.

"I might ask you the same question. Why are you saddling my horse?"

"Your horse! I thought you were still a saddle bum out west."

"Obviously not. Put the horse back. Now."

Brian appeared as though he was trying to disguise his discomfiture at being caught in the barn. "Walt told me I could ride here whenever I wanted."

Hayden continued his unblinking stare. "He said no such thing and you know it. A Sutherlyn would never be welcome on this ranch, now I said put the horse back. You're trespassing."

"Weren't you thrown off this place years ago?"

"Yeah well now I'm back ... to stay. Have you been helping yourself around here since Duke died?"

"What difference does it make what I do here, this is all going to be mine very soon anyway. It's just a matter of writing a cheque and getting the paperwork done. Then it will be me throwing you off this ranch. Summer Vale isn't your home anymore, so get lost."

Brian Sutherlyn had more gall than any man he'd ever met, a real chip off the old block. His father, Wilbur Sutherlyn, the victim of a stroke ten years ago, would never be dead as long as his only son was alive. He could see why his grandfather hated Wilbur. He was not only mouthy and opinionated, but as greedy as they came. He was also quarrelsome, loved to fight, and sued the Barlowes over every tiny thing he could think of just to be miserable. From water rights to a slight error in the Barlowe deed that saw Summer Vale encroaching a miniscule five feet on the Sutherlyn's Triple S, Wilbur Sutherlyn had dragged Hayden's family through the courts on a number of occasions. He wouldn't exactly call it a feud between the two families but there was a grudge that went back many years, although his grandfather would never say what it was about. His mother had told him though. Wilbur and Duke had both been in love with Martha Raymond, and she had chosen his grandfather over Wilbur. There had never been any love lost between the two men anyway, but after losing Martha to Duke, Wilbur had done everything he could to antagonize his rival. Many thought Wilbur would soften when he married the much-younger Eunice O'Neil, and her money, but no. It appeared Eunice couldn't stand him either. She'd eventually left him and their two children, Brian and Mary Rae, behind, obtained a divorce and was never heard from again.

"You're wrong about that," Hayden told him. "This is my home and you're not welcome here."

Brian sneered. "Don't tell me your grandfather left it to you because I won't believe you. I have it on good authority the ranch is going up for sale and unless I miss my guess, you don't have two nickels to rub together to buy it. Am I right?"

"No, you're not right. Summer Vale is my ranch now."

"Show me the deed."

"I don't have to show you anything, now get off my ranch."

"You're pretty highhanded for someone who had the nerve to dump my baby sister. You Barlowes are good at getting rid of people you don't want around, isn't that right?"

Mary Rae was indeed the baby of the family, several years separating her from her older brother and both were spoiled rotten. What he'd once found so exciting about the wild, entitled girl he'd married, had quickly soured and divorce was the only solution that would give him any peace of mind. Now he couldn't stand the sight of any of them.

"I'm not going to stand here and discuss my personal life with you, Brian. It's none of your business. And I changed my mind. You don't have to put the horse back, I will. Just get out. Do it now."

Brian folded his arms in a false show of bravado when in fact he was a wimp who ran for cover when anyone called his bluff. "You're a pretty big talker for a prodigal son, or grandson. Throwing your weight around on a place you yourself were thrown off of because the old man had enough of you. Now you're back after he turns toes up, but then again vultures don't waste any time do they?"

Hayden held his temper, never taking his eyes off Sutherlyn. "You've got no right to be on this property. Like I said, you're trespassing."

"And like I said, show me your deed and I'll leave. Face it, junior, you've got no right to be here either, so back off and get out of my way while I saddle this horse. When I sign on the dotted line this whole thing will be part of the Triple S. These horses will be mine and so will everything else. In just a matter of days you'll be standing on my property and it will give me great pleasure to throw you off, bodily if I have to."

Hayden laughed out loud at that one, knowing he outweighed the older man by at least forty pounds and was half a head taller. He took a step closer but Sutherlyn didn't budge an inch although there was fear in his eyes.

"Brian, you've got exactly one minute to walk away and then I'm calling the police."

Brian shrugged, still attempting nonchalance. "Go ahead. It seems to me my friend Stephen is working today. I was out with the boys last night, and he was one of them. I was telling him how I'm buying this place and he's already looking forward to dropping by for a ride sometime. He'll ask to see your paperwork of course when he makes the service call. When you haven't got anything to say it's yours, and therefore have no authority to throw anyone off it ... or be on it, guess who'll be walking away then? Certainly not me."

Hayden smiled, grateful the property transfer had indeed been finalized, expedited at his mother's request. The registered documents had reached him by courier a day before he flew back to New Brunswick. He was tempted to let Brian play his hand, enjoy his embarrassment when his police buddy showed up. That was probably just a lie anyway, but he had no desire to let things go that far ... if he could avoid it.

"Brian, I'm just going to say this once. The property is now in my name, and registered. Check it out online if you don't want to believe me. It will not be going up for sale. Get over it."

"You're telling me your crazy old grandfather who kicked you off this place and told you never to come back, actually left everything to you in his will? No way. I did check. Your mother owns it."

"I own Summer Vale Ranch, Brian, and none of you Sutherlyns are welcome here."

Brian was flushed and it had little to do with the warmth of the day. "You're lying through your teeth. I've already been in touch with your mother and made her an offer, which she said was very generous. That tells me she's the one who owns it and not you. It's just a matter of time before she grabs the dough."

"She told me she talked to you."

"So she owns it, not you, sonny boy."

Being called sonny boy at thirty-five was meant as an insult, but it was actually a backhanded compliment. Glass half full his mother would say.

"My mother told me you offered her more than it was worth, to her anyway. So?

"So, I can't imagine she'd turn it down. After all she's a Barlowe too, greedy, and in her case, easy. Which reminds me, did you ever find who your father is or was that too hard to figure out?"

"You're about two seconds away from a body cast if you don't tuck tail and hit the road right now. Get into that expensive rig of yours and make some dust. I'm not making idle threats, Brian, and you know it. I'm not going to stand here and let you trash my family, besides you've got enough skeletons in your own closet to be sticking your nose into ours."

Brian stepped away from the horse. "You're bluffing Barlowe, there's no way your mother would turn down what I offered her. She told me herself she had no interest in ranching so this is a no-brainer, even for you. You're trash, a man with no father, a man whose own grandfather disowned him."

The Sutherlyns played dirty, nothing was too low for them and Brian had learned his lessons well. Wilbur Sutherlyn had been lower than a snake in a rut. And to think he'd married one of them; thought at one time that Mary Rae was different. He'd told himself he was rescuing her when they'd gotten together, but as they say about a snake, no matter how pretty it can still be lethal. He'd learned that lesson the hard way.

Hayden held onto what was left of his patience with an effort. He might have a healthy helping of pride, but unlike his grandfather he was slow to anger. It took a lot to push his buttons but once they were pushed, look out. But he'd never been a man to strike first before asking questions, doing everything in his power to avoid violence. Some men would take that for cowardice but he saw the strength required to be that way. Brian Sutherlyn was now taking him even beyond that constraint, deliberately, but even he seemed to know when it was prudent to pull back and he wisely did so.

Stepping aside to allow Brian a clear path to the door and the older man headed slowly toward it before turning to face Hayden again. "You may have won this round but I'll be speaking with my lawyer today. Your mother made a verbal contract with me for the sale of this property and I intend to enforce that. It's every bit as binding and I'm willing to spend whatever it takes to win that litigation. You might want to buy a suit to go to court, but then again what am I thinking? You Barlowes like to show up to court in your wrangler gear. So be it. This isn't over."

"Oh yes it is. You'll be wasting your money if you file any stupid lawsuits. My mother never agreed to sell this property to you. That's an out and out lie."

"Prove it."

"I intend to."

With that Brian turned on his boot heel and strode away. Seconds later Hayden could hear the truck fire to life, the tires chewing gravel as he reversed in a hurry all the way to the main road. He stood and listened until he couldn't hear the motor anymore. And then since Brian had been kind enough to put Aries' blanket in place, he finished tacking him up, took him off the crossties and led the gelding outside. A ride into the hills was just what he needed at the moment. He'd made that trip with his grandfather countless times. There was no better way to clear his mind.

He let the animal have his head through the open fields where there were no fences to hold them back. He gave him a fine ride until Hayden slowed the pace and walked the rest of the way up onto higher ground. A path through the trees took him to the spot where his grandfather had died. It was where they'd always stopped to look out over the valley and so he stopped there himself, feeling his grandfather's spirit beside him. Had he regretted what he'd done to his grandson? He'd been hurt when Hayden announced he and Mary Rae had gotten married. He knew his grandfather suspected he was hanging around the Sutherlyn ranch since he'd met Mary Rae and while he might not have approved, he'd wisely kept his feelings to himself. He was likely hoping it was only infatuation and would pass. It hadn't. He could see now he'd blindsided his grandfather with the news of their marriage and he'd taken it badly. That much was history.

Duke Barlowe had hated the Sutherlyns, and having just had that encounter himself with Brian Sutherlyn, he could understand why. He knew there'd been lawsuits, but he hadn't drilled down too deep on the subject with his family. He understood now they'd kept the worst of it from him while he was growing up. And not just lawsuits, there'd been plenty of mischief done to hurt Summer Vale Ranch. He'd heard them talking about the gate of the enclosure holding the bull that had been mysteriously propped open one night, although they'd been fortunate enough to get the animal back before it had done any damage. And the night the chicken coop had been pulled down on top of a whole flock of laying hens. It'd killed them all, but no arrests were ever made because of lack of evidence. That had been retaliation, pure and simple, he now realized because the Barlowes had prevailed in a lawsuit brought by the Sutherlyns over water rights. The Sutherlyns would stop at nothing to get their way or do pay back if they didn't. It now appeared it was going to be a generational thing.

When he got back home he'd have to call his mother and give her a heads up about the accusation made by Brian Sutherlyn. He didn't want to upset her although he knew that didn't happen easily because she was one lady who knew how to roll with the punches; had never given a whit about what other people thought. He certainly admired her for that. Things didn't go a mile deep with her the way they did with him, but to each their own. The bottom line though was more legal fees for the family to defend a baseless accusation. It was something the Sutherlyns were very practiced at, and they were about to try to be very good at it again.

When he got back to the barn and finished cooling Aries, he let both animals out into the large paddock in back. Pasture fences were his number one priority, and that included for the horses as well as the cattle.

Back at the house he was surprised to see a casserole dish and what looked like a foil-covered pie plate sitting on the back step. They couldn't have been there long because they were still warm and smelled delicious. There were cards on each of them. One was from Sadie Pickens, a widow up the road a bit who used to buy eggs from him on his egg route. The other was from Joanne Conley. She and her husband ran a dairy farm a mile or so away. He'd drop by to say hello tomorrow and thank them for their thoughtfulness. At least now he had

48

something to eat for supper. He'd go for groceries tomorrow and while he was there he'd drop into the Service New Brunswick office and have his grandfather's old pick-up changed into his name. First though he'd need to insure it. There were so many things to get done, but he'd get to them one at a time.

Next he pulled out his cellphone and had that conversation with his mother. She laughed at the allegation and a possible lawsuit. Given the Sutherlyn's penchant for frivolous litigation, documents would in all likelihood be served within the next day or so if they were coming at all.

"Don't lose any sleep over any of this, Hayden," she said. "He's just blowing smoke, as usual. They operate on the theory that if you throw enough mud at someone, some of it's bound to stick, but this won't. I often tape conversations, like in meetings, and the tape was running when Brian and I had our conversation. I told him, as I do everyone else, I was taping but I doubt he paid any attention to that. So I've got this. Don't give it another thought."

He rang off feeling better. He was very protective of his mother; actually they were fiercely protective of each other.

He was putting his cellphone away when a knock came to the back door. He doubted it would be Brian again, but if it was he might not find Hayden as accommodating as he'd been in the barn. You could only poke a bear so many times.

Pulling the door open a wide smile creased his face when he saw who it was. Minnie Warden, his late grandmother's best friend stood there holding a basket with a dishtowel draped over the top. The woman had to be in her mid-eighties but she was just as nimble as she had always been. He wasted no time inviting her in.

"I can't come in because Purdy's waiting for me in the car," she explained, turning to indicate the older model vehicle idling in the front yard. Hayden waved hello. "I was so glad to see you with Walt earlier, Hayden, so I figured you were back home to stay. I'm sorry about your grandfather. I called Joanne and Sadie to tell them I'd seen you and they said they'd whip something up for your supper. I said I'd make biscuits to go with whatever they were bringing." She passed him the basket. "There's some butter in there too in a plastic dish in case you don't have any. Knives I know you have."

"My mouth is already watering. Thank you so much. You sure you won't come in?"

"No, we're off to the church to get ready for that yard sale on Saturday. Enjoy!" she said cheerfully as she turned to go. "And don't be a stranger."

He glanced at the clock after the Wardens left. Four o'clock. Close enough to suppertime and it was a shame not to dig in while everything was nice and warm. The macaroni and cheese casserole was beyond delicious, Minnie's biscuits some of the best he'd ever tasted, next to his grandmother's, and the apple pie hit the spot. The best supper he'd had in a long time. And since Walt had made sure the hydro had stayed hooked up, he had a nice cold refrigerator to store the leftovers in. He was starting to feel even more at home.

He put the horses back in the barn just before dark, spending extra time with them, brushing their coats until they were as shiny as copper pennies. After settling them in for the night he went back to the house to try to find something on the antiquated television set. His grandfather didn't believe in cable TV, so he had to make do with the one local station. Still he found an interesting talk show. He hadn't watched it long before he drifted off to sleep. A knock at the back door woke him and squinting his eyes to come fully awake, he went to see who was there.

He was tempted to slam it shut just as fast as he'd opened it when he saw who was standing on his doorstep, wearing a big smile and little else.

"What do you want Mary Rae?"

# Chapter Three

"Hayden! Is that any way to greet your wife?"

"Ex-wife."

She smiled, resting a hand on either side of the doorway, arranging her body in a provocative pose. "I was your wife at one time and that should count for something."

"All it counts for is that we used to be married, but we haven't been for seven years. We've been apart now longer than we were together."

"And speaking of together, that's what I think we should do, Hayden, get back together."

"No. Uhuh. No way. I like being divorced from you, just fine."

She affected a playful pout. "Come on, Hayden. We had a good thing at one time, a very good thing. We weren't divorced for very long before I changed my mind, but I couldn't find you anywhere to tell you. You certainly did a disappearing act. Where did you go?"

"I wasn't trying to hide," he said, disgruntled after being awakened from his nap for ... this. "I got a job on a dude ranch in British Columbia. That's probably why you couldn't find me."

It was as though she didn't hear him. Clearly she had a much different agenda. "I couldn't believe it when I heard you were back here. Don't you ever think about me?"

He stretched. "Honestly, yes I do but not in the way you might think. Look, Mary Rae, we had our time together. We were young...."

"And in love."

"Ahhh, looking back, maybe not. We were just a couple of stupid kids who thought we were in love. You said as much yourself. I asked for a divorce because it wasn't working, but we both agreed it was time to go our separate ways and so that's what we did. I'm surprised we stayed together for five years. It was crazy and besides, you jumped the fence, remember? We were barely speaking at the end if you recall."

She shifted position, slipping her hands onto well-shaped hips. "I'm not trying to pretend it was any other way, especially how it was at the end. What I am saying is now we've had some time apart, like about seven years. We've had a chance to put things in perspective and I find I still have feelings for you. Come on, Hayden, can you honestly say you don't have any feelings for me?"

"Honestly?"

"Yes, honestly. You're not made of stone. You can't have forgotten all of the good times we had. I know you're human under that tough facade."

He nodded, still tired. "I am that and I admit there were good times when we were first together, but our relationship ran its course. I don't hate you, if that's what you mean but I'm not in love with you either. Not like I thought I was; not like I should have been as a husband. I don't feel too much one way or the other. The truth is we never should have gotten married. We didn't know each other well enough."

Now her arms were folded. "Ouch! That wasn't very nice but I'll say one thing, you're still one sizzling hot hunk of a cowboy. I thought you were sexy when we first got together but now.... Whew! You're smoking hot, Hayden."

He studied her with a sardonic grin. "Have you been drinking or something?"

She laughed, and he liked the sound. It was impossible not to. Mary Rae had the most infectious laugh he'd ever heard in a woman. She was usually the life of the party, but there was also a dark side to her that came into play very quickly when she did not get her own way. He did not want to mess with her and there was no way he wanted to go down that road again. She wore him out with her mercurial moods, her tantrums ... her ... unacceptable other behaviour; there was just no end to it all.

"No I'm not drinking ... or something. I don't take any of those pills anymore if that's what you mean. Besides, I wasn't into them to the extent you thought I was or accused me of, but I got rid of those things a long time ago. It's just me, Mary Rae, clean as can be."

"Good for you. I mean that. So how did you know I was back at Summer Vale?"

"News travels fast in Kings County. Besides, I'm staying on the Triple S at the present time. I've been there a while contemplating my options shall we say, enjoying the laidback pace of country life again."

"Can't find a job?"

"I don't have to. My trust fund has kicked in and that will keep me very nicely for the rest of my life. No nine to five for me, Hayden. You know I don't like that. I go to bed when I want to, get up when I want to and in between I do exactly what I want to."

"So what are you over here bothering me for? Can't imagine, going by what you just said, you'd want to sign on to be a rancher's wife. Wouldn't that be too much work?"

She chuckled. "What do you care? I'll take care of the bedroom, hire someone else to take care of everything else."

"Hire someone? Uh, my name's Barlowe, not Sutherlyn. I'm not made of money."

"Of course you're not, sweetheart, but I have enough money now for both of us. My father didn't have any either until he married my mother and she paid big to get him to sign the divorce papers, but I digress. We all got a good share and with mine you could turn this ranch into a real money maker. Just think what the two of us could accomplish. The possibilities are endless. You'd have a tiger in your bed every night and no more money problems ... ever. Isn't that what every man wants?"

He folded his arms loosely in front of him, shifting into a spread legged stance as he watched her. Mary Rae was a fiery redhead. He could still appreciate the beauty of her flaming red hair and milky white skin, and those emerald eyes were treacherous for any man. And she was built; make no mistake about that. She was also a wildcat between the sheets and he was sorely tempted as she stood on his doorstep clad only in the briefest of thong bikinis and stiletto heels. What would one more night hurt, a tiny inner voice taunted him. But his more rational side countered that it was just too easy. The consequences also had to be considered. She was lethal, and he reckoned this was the part where he'd have to stay strong because Mary Rae had gotten his number a long time ago. She knew the fastest path to his heart ... to any man's heart really, although to the best of his knowledge she had been faithful to him during their time together. Well most of it anyway.

He took a deep breath and expelled it slowly. "I'm afraid I'm going to have to take a pass on that, but thanks for stopping by."

She dropped any semblance of a smile, now apparently ready to play hardball. "Hayden, I'm dead serious. I want us to give it another try. I think now that we're more mature we could make a go of it. At least let's talk about it. We don't even have to get remarried right away. Maybe the best thing is to live together and see how things work out, which I know they will. I've grown up a lot since we broke up. Matured."

"Matured? How mature is it to come to a man's door in a thong bikini after dark? Who does that!"

"Well you're not just any man, Hayden. I still think of you as my husband so what's the big deal? It helps to get the juices flowing, doesn't it?"

"From where I'm standing you're still the wild, unpredictable, entitled woman you've always been."

"You say that like it's a bad thing. Life with me was never boring. Come on, admit it."

He chuckled, his face pulled tight. "Life with you was never boring, but there's something to be said for sailing calm waters too. Your behaviour always kept me knocked off kilter, trying to get my head around what stunt you were going to pull next. I got tired of living like that."

"Name one stunt that knocked you off kilter. Come on I dare you, Hayden! Just one!"

He was in no mood for these games. He was jetlagged for one thing and was planning to go to bed early, alone, and get plenty of sleep for tomorrow when he'd start at this place with a vengeance. Now here was his ex-wife standing on his doorstep trying to get him into bed. If successful she wouldn't rest until she'd wormed her way back into his life using sex as the leverage. She could be very persuasive and she was not above using her body to get what she wanted. It was her currency and she kept it in very good shape he begrudgingly acknowledged, now that it was standing before him practically laid bare.

"There were so many of your crazy stunts it was hard to keep count."

"Aha! You can't name one, can you?"

"Okay, how about the time you brought eight dogs home from the shelter? Eight big dogs."

"Since when don't you like dogs?"

"We were living in a small apartment! You got us kicked out! It was just another stupid thing you did. Or how about the time you stayed out half the night and then brought at least a dozen people home with you and they tore the place up? Another eviction because of you. You just fly off on whatever airhead idea you happen to have at the moment. You never really think anything through because you were allowed to do whatever you wanted when you were growing up. No rules and no consequences."

She smirked. "What's wrong with that? I like to have fun. You know, since we're pointing fingers, you can be a little stuffy sometimes. No make that very stuffy. But hey, I'm prepared to overlook that because I still love you."

"Mary Rae...."

"And that brings me to my next question. How is it that you're even back here? I know your grandfather just died but he hated you so he wouldn't give you the ranch. Do you actually own it now?"

"If you've come to get information for Brian, you've wasted your time."

"I don't work for my brother, but you know I know it was because of me you got kicked off this place. But I for one am glad you're back because it puts us right back to where we started. We planned to live here and raise babies, remember? Well here you are and here I am. Let's get started on those babies, we don't have a moment to lose."

She was so off the wall it was laughable at times. "May Rae, it's time for you to go." He looked past her into the yard. "How did you get over here?"

"I rode my horse. You remember Silver Dollar? Well he's twenty years old and better than ever, but I'm afraid he picked up a stone in his left front foot on the way here. I won't be able to ride him home like that."

"You rode over here at night in a bikini, wearing those high heels? You don't have a car?"

"Of course I do, a very nice one. I just felt like riding a horse, kind of like the Lady Godiva thing although I don't have blonde hair." She shook out her long hair that did in fact tumble well past her shoulders. "I came the back way, not on the road. I didn't want to dazzle everyone, maybe cause an accident. Seriously though, Hayden, you need to look at his front foot. He's really on the limp and I don't want him to be permanently injured."

"It's pretty hard to see anything in the dark, not with that old outside light," he said, pointing to the poorly lit front yard.

"Can't you take him down to the barn and look there? That's not too far for him to walk. I'll just wait in the house while you do that. Thank you."

She tried to step past him into the kitchen but Hayden reached behind him and pulled the door closed. She had no choice but to go down the steps. He followed her to where he saw the horse tied to the oak tree beside the driveway.

"When did the gelding start to limp?"

Mary Rae squatted down beside him. "Just before we got here so I don't think it'll be bruised too bad if you can get it out right away."

He sighed, knowing when he was beaten ... almost. "I'll go turn the barn lights on, you lead him down and I'll take a look."

She did as he asked and sure enough, under better lighting he could see the horse had indeed picked up a very small stone under his shoe but it was barely pressing on the frog. He easily dislodged it with a hoof pick then led the horse slowly around the yard. The animal was not at all reluctant to put any weight on the foot so it didn't seem the frog was bruised. He noticed saddlebags on her horse and hoped she'd brought something more substantial to put on for the ride home. It was warmer than usual for this time of night but there was still a chill in the air. He couldn't imagine she wasn't freezing in that getup. She might as well be naked.

"Your horse is fine, but I'd walk him back though, not ride him just to be on the safe side."

She looked at him, surprised. "Walk back, at night?"

"It's not that far, Mary Rae," he spoke over his shoulder. "It'll only take you a few minutes."

"I'm nervous being out after dark alone."

"Now you're nervous. First of all you won't be alone, you'll be with your horse."

The pretty pout was back but he wasn't going to fall for it. "Don't you remember how nervous Silver Dollar is? Especially at night? Every little sound spooks him."

"Then why ride him over here in the first place? If he spooked you could have gotten thrown and hurt."

"That goes to show you how badly I wanted to see you, Hayden. I didn't even think about my own safety, I just came. I did all that and you're not even happy to see me which I don't think is very nice."

"Wearing only a bikini."

"That was your welcome home present, well part of it. You get the other part when

61

we get back to the house, and the fun part is it won't take you long to unwrap it."

"There isn't going to be any fun part back at the house. You're going home. Period. We don't need to start all of this up again and complicate our lives. We were married once and it didn't work. That's why we got a divorce. That's why they created divorce."

She stroked Silver Dollar's long neck. "What I'm saying is we should have only gotten separated and thought things over before we went ahead and made it final. Now that I've had a chance to think it over, I shouldn't have agreed to a divorce at all."

"But you did and it is final. It takes two to make something work, and I am not interested in trying again."

"So are you still into women? I can't imagine a man would turn down a night with me if he were. I'm just saying."

Hayden chuckled as he leaned against a stall door. "I'm still into women, Mary Rae, but I'm not looking to go another round with you. Sorry but there it is."

"You don't think I'm beautiful?"

"I think you're very beautiful. Any man would, but you already know that. So why the fishing trip?"

She folded her arms, still not used to being said no to. "What can I say that will change your mind?"

"Nothing. I'd like us to be friends, I don't need an enemy, but it's a no to us as a couple."

"You mean another enemy."

"Any enemies at all."

She changed tactics, he could see the look pass over those incredible green eyes of hers. "How is your mother?" she asked cheerfully. "I really liked her."

"Mum is doing just great. I was talking to her a little while ago and she's very happy with where she is in her life."

"Still married to her second husband?"

"Still happily married ... and Barry is her first husband."

"Oh yes, right," she said, those cat eyes of hers narrowing maliciously.

"There's no need to be mean, Mary Rae. I made peace with my life a long time ago. Besides, people aren't as hung up today about such things as they once were. There are some things that can't be changed, it's only those who resort to nastiness who are to be pitied. I think my mother is the best woman in the world and I find no fault with her at all."

"You've never told me how you came to ... be."

"How I came to be?" He threw back his head and laughed. "I think I came to be the same way most people do, the old fashioned way. If you're hinting at the details, I don't figure they're any of your business any more than they are mine."

"You don't even know who your father is?"

"Nope, and I'm fine with that."

"I think you're telling a big ole whopper, Hayden Barlowe. You're just too proud to let on you care. If it were me I'd want to know. Oh wait a minute, I do know. Wilbur Sutherlyn was my father and I'm proud of it."

"Do you enjoy being purposely mean, Mary Rae?"

"I do if I don't get what I want, you just chose to overlook it because you didn't want to see it."

He sighed heavily. This sort of cat and mouse game could go on for hours. She was good at it whereas he wearied of it quickly. If someone had something to say, spit it out. Don't play stupid games; poke those silly little darts in here and there. He had chosen to overlook that side of her, not only in the early days, but also during their entire time together. She was dead right. She could be spiteful, but then again after all she was a Sutherlyn and they knew how to take cheap shots. But they had plenty of skeletons in their own closet. The difference between the two families was that the Barlowes refused to get down in the gutter.

She closed her eyes, which he knew from experience was her attempt to collect herself because her strategy was failing. In a moment she'd try another approach. He was right, but he wasn't going to buy this one any more than he bought the others.

"I'm sorry, Hayden. I was out of line. You deserve better than that but I've never been a good loser. But then again I don't believe I have lost yet. When I love somebody I never give up, you should remember that about me too."

Right. He remembered she'd signed those divorce papers fast enough because she'd been smitten with rodeo cowboy, Gil Furlong. He wasn't sure what happened there, but it hadn't ended in marriage like she'd been counting on.

"What about Gil? You had the big love for him the last I heard. What happened to that? Why aren't you on his doorstep wearing your almost there bathing suit?"

She gave an unladylike snort. "Gil! What a loser he turned out to be. He told me he loved me and then I caught him with more than one buckle bunny."

"So much for true love."

"It wasn't the real thing as it turned out, not like what you and I had."

"I'm sorry you keep getting disappointed, but I don't think what we had was the real thing either, not when you look back on it. We didn't have anything in common when the infatuation died down."

"We were great together in bed."

"Yes but you can't stay in bed your whole life. If memory serves me, we had plenty of arguments in bed too."

"But we're different people now."

"We're the very same people, Mary Rae, just older and hopefully wiser. What we had wasn't strong enough to stand the test of time. It actually fizzled out fast."

She gave him a long look and he couldn't guess what she was thinking when she turned on her heel to face Aries' stall. The horse, still reacting to the presence of Mary Rae's horse, allowed her to pet him. She did have a way with animals. He had to give her that, a real soft spot that sometimes got her in trouble as in the great dog shelter caper.

"I'd give you a treat, big fellah," she told Aries, "but I guess you can see that I don't have any pockets to keep them in." She turned to face Hayden momentarily. "Is this Aries?"

"Yes, that's my horse."

He'd never brought her home to meet his grandfather or his horse, otherwise he would have been told to leave a lot sooner. No, he and Mary Rae had kept their relationship a secret until they up and eloped, and then the expected explosion had occurred.

"I remember you telling me how much he liked peppermints," she said, her attention back on Aries before moving to Champion. "Was this your grandfather's horse?"

"Champion, yes."

"Do you miss him? Your grandfather I mean."

"What do you think?"

"I think you hated him."

"I didn't hate him, I hated what he did."

"That was because of me?"

"You already know the answer to that."

"Because he hated the Sutherlyns."

"With good reason."

"He was a hateful old man."

"I don't want to talk about my grandfather. I'd think you'd know that by now."

"I heard he killed himself."

Hayden puffed an exasperated sigh. "You heard wrong. He did not kill himself. He had a bad heart. He dropped dead."

"Are you sure about that?"

"I'm sure about that. They found him lying beside old Champion here. My mother told me the doctor said his heart could give out at any time, and it did. Apparently. End of story."

"Oh."

"Oh is right."

She turned back to face the horse and he couldn't fault the view of the thong bikini bottom, or the top for that matter considering her figure. But Mary Rae didn't seem to mind, she wouldn't even give that a second thought considering the swimwear she'd bought to wear to the beach when they were together. He'd had to put his foot down on more than one occasion. He hadn't wanted his wife to be looked at in that way. She enjoyed the gawks, no matter how much sunscreen she'd had to slather on to keep from looking like a lobster.

She whirled around and caught him looking. "Hayden, why don't we go for a moonlight ride? It's such a beautiful night and it would be a lot of fun. We'd leave Silver

67

Dollar here of course because he's got a sore foot, but you could ride Aries and I could ride Champion. Wouldn't that be great? Come on!"

The thought of her saddling up wearing that bikini would be mighty interesting, but the ride would not be the end of it. True, he'd planned to go riding first thing in the morning just like he always had, but a moonlight ride would be even better. The problem was there was always more with Mary Rae. She would not be content to leave it at that, she always wanted more and then more again. That would be her toe in the door. He knew her too well and unless he was prepared to sign up for another round, he had to say no. She was not the type of woman to do things by half measures. When she wanted something, aggression, with a capital A, was her middle name. Still, his traitorous body reminded him, it had been a while since he'd been with a woman and a night with his ex-wife held exotic promise. He certainly remembered that well enough.

The view from the ridge where he'd gone today would be really nice in the moonlight, and romantic he had to admit although he was not often accused of being romantic. His body, reacting to the sight of her was urging him to say yes. Hell yes! She wasn't stupid either. She could tell when she was gaining ground; knew exactly what he liked....

Covering the distance between them she didn't stop until she was smack dab up against him, his back literally against the wall. His hands hung at his sides, still getting the message from his brain that this woman was off limits. However they too were sensing the shift as apparently with a will of their own they found soft warm flesh to slide across and his heart gave a leap when she brushed her lips against his before he had a chance to pull his head away. But who was he kidding? It was a half-hearted attempt at best. This shouldn't be happening, but he'd been lonely too long and Mary Rae was a whole lot of woman to try to resist. If it were just for one night, he'd sign up immediately, but no, there was still the more part. He didn't want more. He wanted only tonight.

His hands reluctantly found her shoulders and set her away from him even though every fibre of his being was calling out for what she promised, a night of bliss. But then he'd wake up in the morning and Mary Rae would be in bed beside him and he would have lost all the precious distance he had managed to put between them. He did not want to wake up next to Mary Rae again, ever. She was in the past. Them as a couple was in the past and he intended to leave all of it there.

"Why would you deny yourself this?" she asked, her voice husky with desire and that alone was having an effect on him. "You know you want to be with me."

"Because it's a bad idea is why."

"You have to be more specific. I'm not thinking straight at the moment."

"There's a mouthful, Mary Rae. I've already told you why there isn't going to be an us anymore. It didn't work out before and it won't work out again. There is no future for us. I have moved on and I would suggest you do the same."

"Don't tell me you're going to go back with that Naomi Martel in Franklin!"

"Who said anything about Naomi? Leave her out of this."

"So you are going after her again. Well don't waste your time. It's been what, eleven or twelve years? She's probably happily married with a houseful of kids and forgotten all about you."

"Probably."

"So why even bother checking?"

"Mary Rae, keep your nose out of my private life. Now, it's time you went back home. I'll get the keys to the truck and drive you over."

She stepped away from him, doing a sexy pirouette in the middle of the barn as if he'd missed anything about her body in the past hour. "I think it's a little early to turn in and besides, I'm not the least bit interested in going back home. How am I supposed to sleep when there's a big sexy cowboy only a few minutes away?"

"Right."

"You like to play hard to get but I'm guessing when you turn in for the night you won't be able to get to sleep either. You'll be thinking about me, and how you'd wished you'd taken me up on my offer. Think about it, Hayden, it's been a few years since we've been together. I'm a mature woman now and I know all sorts of new ways to love you."

He groaned inwardly, darned if that woman didn't get to him and she certainly knew it. Even if she didn't, he was a red-blooded man with only so much self-control. He'd bet she wouldn't have to beg any other man to get him where she wanted him. But he'd been born with an extra helping of common sense, well at least he'd grown into it given his past mistakes where Mary Rae was concerned, and was still able to say no. Now where was she going?

Smiling back at him she strutted toward the stairs to what she correctly guessed was the haymow and began to climb, swaying her bottom enticingly.

He'd checked the mow for hay this afternoon and was pleased to see there was still plenty in stock, full bales, broken bales and loose hay.

"You go up there, that's where you'll be spending the night," he warned her, but she didn't pay heed as she continued to climb until she reached the second floor. He could hear her heels clicking on the bare boards above him until she found the loose hay in the far corner. "Good night!" he called out, but she only laughed that laugh of hers that told him she was enjoying this sexy adventure.

Good, well she could just spend the night in the barn; see if he cared. He'd stable Silver Dollar for the night, turn out the light and go back to the house and get some sleep. He headed for the door but when he reached the light his finger hovered over the switch. He couldn't do it, turn out the light and leave her up there in the dark. This was the only light switch and that meant she'd have to make it down those stairs in the dark and with the heels she was wearing she could easily turn an ankle and have a bad fall. Of course he didn't want that to happen. No, he'd have to go up there and get her and bring her down, get her to the truck and drive her home. That's all there was to it. This game had gone far enough.

Taking the stairs two at a time he could see her reclining on the hay, her legs crossed, stilettos still strapped in place. She had every intention of getting her way. He strode toward her, just as intent on removing her from the barn. That was until she laughed and threw her bikini at him, both pieces.

# Chapter Four

He caught the two miniscule bikini pieces with a quick snatch of the hand, never taking his eyes off the beautiful woman posing in all her beauty on the hay. She smiled. He smiled, then reminded himself yet again that despite the fact he was as unattached as she was, a roll in the hay with her was a really bad idea. But he couldn't argue with the view, and then something else caught his eye through the small window at the end of the mow. Flashing red and blue lights.

"What the...." he said, but before he could cover the distance to the window he heard a man's voice on the first floor of the barn.

"Hello, anybody here? We've got cattle all over the road."

He tossed the bikini back in her general direction then glared at her. "Nice work," he said before he hurriedly descended the stairs where a Mountie stood just inside the doorway.

"Our phone is ringing off the hook," he told Hayden. "Some of your neighbours are already out there trying to get them back into the pasture. Apparently there's a fence down. So they're going back in the way they got out, but some have gone across the road into the fields and a few are in people's yards."

Perfect! Hayden was already reaching for his cellphone to call Walt as he thanked the Mountie who headed back out, promising Hayden before he left they'd keep an eye on his property from now on. Walt promised to be there in minutes. Hayden quickly saddled Aries then rushed to tack up Champion for Walt so they could round up the more errant escapees on horseback.

Hayden and Walt had their work cut out for them, the wily cattle making the most of their unexpected freedom. Hector McMillan, who lived not far from Summer Vale, guarded the damaged fence, leaving it down so the unaccounted for ani33mals could get back in and the ones who were still in the pasture would stay where they were. It was nearly three hours before the last of the cattle were rounded up and herded back into the pasture. The moonlit night was certainly a blessing to help them find the missing strays, but it was difficult to do any kind of headcount in the dark. They searched as thoroughly as they could and once all appeared to be accounted for, Hector, Walt and Hayden patched up the fence. It should hold until they could do a more thorough job in the morning. It was apparent, even by flashlight, the wire had been purposely cut and two fence posts broken off. Hayden took pictures of the damage with his phone in case he needed it to show the police, but he knew exactly who was behind the whole thing. So this was the way it was going to be. Fine. Bring it on.

In any event the decrepit state of fencing at Summer Vale would have to be addressed immediately. Walt agreed to help fix fences where they could and replace those in the worst shape. Hayden would order a load of fence posts in the morning from the mill up the road, and they should be good for a speedy delivery. Another item of immediate concern was getting a handle on current beef prices. So he'd also study the market reports in the morning and get this herd sold off as quickly as he could, except what he'd hold back for breeding stock. Then he could do what needed to be done to get things rocking and rolling here before he brought in any more livestock. Anyway that's what was waiting tomorrow, which was only a few hours away.

He and Walt were both tired clean through to the bone when they finally put their horses up for the night and Walt left for home. He on the other hand headed up to the haymow where he had a pretty good idea Mary Rae was still waiting for him. And she was, sound asleep, now dressed in sensible jeans, sweater and sneakers. It had been a good-looking bikini but any desire she'd been able to kindle between them had long since evaporated, his anger still burning like a freshly banked bonfire. As if sensing him standing a few feet away, her eyes fluttered open and she looked up at him. Her earlier sass was missing in action, replaced by righteous indignation. In that regard it was as though the intervening hours had not passed.

"Nice work?" she repeated. "What's that supposed to mean?"

"You know damned well what it means. You come over here and try to seduce me, distract me while your idiot brother cuts the fence and lets my cattle out of the pasture. So that's what you've stooped to? Doing Brian's dirty work?"

"You're crazy, Hayden. I don't do my brother's bidding. I never have and I never will."

"Right. Every cow on this ranch is a major investment, Mary Rae. I don't have to tell you that. Losing even one hurts my bottom line. I know you don't care, not with all your bags of money, but you know what I'm saying is true so that's why you helped him do it. To ruin me; drive me out. Well I've got a newsflash for you, lady. I'm not being driven off this place, not ever again."

"I have no idea what you're talking about. How did your cows get on the road?"

"As if you didn't know. Actually, I thought better of you. I never thought you'd stoop to the same tricks your father used to play, being so small-minded. And while you're laughing behind your hand, think about the people who could have gotten injured or killed tonight had they struck one of those animals. It doesn't bear thinking about, does it?" he shouted. "You just live in the moment, don't you? You said you were mature, but you're still that self-centred little girl I had the misfortune to be married to."

Somehow getting gracefully to her feet and looking regal despite having been sleeping in a haymow, her redheaded temper kicked into high gear. Kicked was the operative word as without warning she hauled off with everything she had and let him have it. She caught him just about his cowboy boot, scoring a painful blow that served to further inflame his already boiling temper, although he was glad she was wearing sneakers rather than those hard-soled stripper shoes.

He resisted the urge to vent the full force of his temper on her, say things in the heat of the moment he'd later regret. Temper outbursts were common for Mary Rae, so he wasn't surprised, but he had never ever laid a hand on her. Not even when he was provoked, such as now. Instead he'd walked away and if he intended to walk this one off, he wouldn't be stopping until he got to the tip of South America.

"Not cool, Mary Rae!" he managed through gritted teeth, still in pain. "I don't put my hands, or my feet, on you so don't do it to me."

"You're a heck of a lot bigger than I am. You can take it."

"It doesn't matter. It still hurts."

"What you said hurt me," she flung back at him. "I had nothing to do with your stupid cows getting on the road. And what makes you think someone let them out? Everything is falling down around here, maybe they just leaned a little too hard on the fence and it let go. Maybe it's like everything else around here, old and decrepit."

"Anything else?"

"Yes, plenty, but I doubt you'd let me get it said."

"Why did you come over here tonight anyway, dressed like a hooker?"

"It was only a friendly visit and you'd better be kidding about the hooker part if you don't want a matching lump on the other leg. You were my husband for five years, you've never seen me dressed like that before? You always liked me best when I had nothing on at all if memory serves me. Now it's like you've never seen a naked lady before. I think maybe you have changed what you like if you're so offended by a woman in a bikini."

"You and I are divorced, Mary Rae. It's not any woman in a bikini I don't want to see, it's you."

She folded her arms, her eyes still sparking. "You're in a terrible mood."

"Really? You picked up on that did you? Very perceptive!"

"And you're sarcastic when you get pissed off. It doesn't take much does it, a few cows running around where they're not supposed to be and you come unglued. And I'd still like to know why you think I had anything to do with it. I haven't got magical powers to do something out there while I'm lying in here waiting for you. Or maybe you think I did it when I first arrived, found which pasture the cows were in, then ran over there in stilettos and cut the fence. Does that sound even the tiniest bit ridiculous to you?"

Hayden's leg was still on fire and he was trying to shake it off. "Funny how things just happen, eh? Isn't it a coincidence that your brother is over here a few hours ago shooting off his mouth, acting like he owns the place; making threats. Then before the night is out my fence is damaged and my herd is out on the road. I'm not saying you did the cutting, I'll just hazard a guess he did it while you were at my door distracting me with that scrap of a bathing suit."

She smiled a full-on Mary Rae megawatt smile that at one time had made him weak in the knees. A willing young man she had easily been able to dazzle. "So I was able to distract you. I'm flattered."

"Any woman who shows up naked or nearly naked at a man's house at night is a distraction, but that's all you are anymore, Mary Rae, a slight distraction. Now, I see

79

you're all dressed for travel, so go, and don't come back."

"Walk all the way over there in the dark? No way."

"You'll have your horse for company."

"He's lame, in case you don't remember."

"He's not lame and he's been resting that foot now for hours."

"He's very special to me, Hayden. I don't want to make him walk anymore tonight. I'm serious."

He swore under his breath. "Fine, I'll get the keys to the truck and drive you over on the back road. It's not licensed yet and with my luck if I used the main road  I'd get stopped, even just that short distance. The last thing I need is a fine. Everything I've managed to save has to go into this place. Come on, let's go."

"Hayden, if you and I get back together you never have to worry about money ever again."

"I'm sure your brother would love that, you helping me finance this ranch. In case it escaped your notice he's trying to run me off, just like your father and Brian tried to run my grandfather off. It didn't happen then and it's not going to happen now."

"I'll say it again, since I can't seem to make you understand. What my brother does is his own business and what I do is mine. The money I have is in my bank account, not his. My father left it to me fair and square. Brian can do what he wants with his share and I'll do the same with mine. Brian and I are barely on speaking terms at the best of times. Maybe I'd enjoy building this place up just to spite him."

Hayden shook his head. "You and Brian are barely on speaking terms, yet you live in the same house," he challenged her.

"It's a big house. We don't really ever have to see each other."

"And Brian's wife?"

"Didn't your mother tell you? They split up a couple of years ago, so there's two divorcees in residence now. Brian likes the women though. I've gotten to meet quite a few of his conquests, although I haven't liked any of them. Let me see, the last one was Chickie and I'm not kidding, that was her name, or a nickname. It doesn't matter because she's history now anyway. The latest is Penny and her I like, although I doubt they'll last because she's financially independent and has a son. She's probably too good for him, but I digress. We were talking about us getting back together, which I think is a really good idea and you'd be smart to consider it. Don't get all macho and reject me because your nose is still out of joint about things I did when I was much younger. I'm pretty sure I've already apologized for all that stuff anyway. So come on, admit it, you still have feelings for me. If you could stop being angry with me long enough, you could channel those emotions into something more positive."

He sighed and taking off his hat, ran a hand through his dark hair. It could use a trim; he half expected her to say so, but he'd never cared much about being fashionable, haircuts or otherwise.

"I'm not going to lie to you, Mary Rae. I still have feelings for you, but not the way you think. Not enough to rekindle our relationship. We got divorced because it was the right thing to do and we have to leave it at that."

He could see her face was beginning to cloud over, a storm brewing behind those eyes and he sagged where he stood, completely bone weary. What he wanted was to get some much-needed sleep. If he'd ever thought all of this was waiting for him back in Bloomfield he might have taken a pass on returning to this ranch. Nevertheless he knew in a quick second he'd have come anyway while dreading something like this could happen. Not that he gave Mary Rae much thought now. He'd figured she'd moved on, not waiting to pounce as soon as he got back. She hadn't changed as far as he could see; she could still be exhausting.

He was not prepared for her tears. "I'm not playing games, Hayden," she said quietly. "I thought I wanted a divorce. I agreed when you said it was what we should do because we weren't even sleeping together at the last of it. But I've had time to think things over, plenty of distance to put things in perspective. I even thought I was in love with somebody else, but when it came right down to it he couldn't compare to you. No, I want my husband back. Why can't I have my husband back?"

"Because I'm not your husband anymore."

"The divorce decree is just a piece of paper."

"So was our marriage certificate but you seem to think that's important enough."

She turned her back to him, her shoulders hunched as she cried noisily.

He knew he should put his arms around her and offer comfort, but this was a tricky situation. Comfort could easily turn into more, much more than he was bargaining for.

She turned toward him again and indeed her face was wet with tears. She pointed to the hay, which by now had been flattened into an inviting nest. "Can't we sit down together for a few minutes and talk this out? I can't say the things I was planning to say when I'm being rushed out the door. Can't you at least spare me a few minutes?"

He sighed tiredly. "Mary Rae, I'm exhausted. The last thing I want to do is talk about something like this, especially when it's already been hashed out six ways from Sunday and officially ended. I know it was ended because I have the document that says so. Final! Complete."

She swiped at her eyes. "Okay then, at least sit down while I apologize. Surely you can give me that much."

Throwing up his hands in exasperation he plunked himself down on the hay, sitting with his knees bent, his hands resting loosely on them. "Okay, you've got exactly five minutes to say what you want to say. Let's have it, and then you're outta here."

She settled down beside him, sliding her arm as far as it would reach around his shoulders and leaned her head against him. "Hayden, I am sorry about tonight. I made a fool of myself, but as my father used to say, don't regret how you won, just be glad you did. So I pulled out all the stops, wore my new bikini, saddled up Silver Dollar and rode on over here. I think I should at least get some points for moxie. Right? When was the last time you opened the door to find a pretty girl there, ripe for the taking?"

He had to chuckle. "Not lately."

He thought about Molly Brunholdt who'd also worked on the Paradise Hills Dude Ranch in British Columbia. She had tried everything in her power to turn his head, from a fake fall off her horse to calling him in the middle of the night because there was a mouse in her apartment. He'd seen no reason to string her along though because he wasn't in the least attracted to her. Why pretend he was? He could have had what she was offering, most of the other men on the outfit had, but he didn't see any point getting

84

mixed up with the wrong woman. He still felt that way, although Mary Rae was different of course. He'd been married to her. She was complicated, he'd found that out in a hurry once the fairy dust had settled, but she was a desirable woman. Just thinking about her in that silly little bikini was still working on him.

Maybe it was knowing she was still wearing it under those jeans and sweater that made it all the more interesting. Or had she taken it off? Maybe he was overtired but the fact that while offering her apology, which he had to admit sounded genuine, she was breathing a little too close to his right ear. She knew that was one of his buttons and now she was kissing his ear. Mary Rae could be relentless, even about sex, and she'd worn him down in those early days ... brought him around to her way of thinking. Was tonight one of those occasions? He lay back on the hay, knowing when he did the floodgates were sure to open and they did, the water level rising quickly.

It had simply been too long. He had no intention of getting back with his ex-wife, and he'd make that doubly plain ... in a few minutes, right now he was being swept away. His defences were clearly down, but for now maybe he would take what she was so intent on giving him. A one-off; there'd be no repeat performance.

It wasn't the most romantic of interludes; perhaps an itch that had to be scratched for both of them and it was over within minutes whereupon after righting himself, he promptly fell into an exhausted sleep.

* * *

Mary Rae lay luxuriously in the hay, stretching like a languid cat. How she had missed Hayden. In her eyes he was still her husband. All it would take was undoing the divorce and while she'd never tried to do it, how hard could it be? She'd made a mistake, okay a lot of mistakes while she and Hayden were married, but there had been good times too. If they'd tried a little harder to fix what was wrong maybe they'd still be together today and not lying in some haymow, although it was a sexy place to make love. Instead they'd be in their own four-poster bed; probably have children.

Realistically though she wasn't the ranch wife type, but they could easily get around that with hired help. She could certainly afford it. But she'd be with Hayden and that's all that counted. She cursed ever meeting Gil Furlong, it's what had finished off her marriage, although at the time she hadn't cared. Gil was a major rodeo star and she'd been caught up in the glitz and glamour of his celebrity. It hurt badly that as soon as her divorce was final and she was available, Gil had quickly lost interest. That had been brutally obvious. She'd tried every trick in the book to keep him, but she didn't stand a chance against the never-ending parade of buckle bunnies. Eventually she'd given up. Bitter over how things had turned out for her in the west, she'd returned to New Brunswick to lick her wounds.

She'd started going out with Arthur not long after she'd returned to Bloomfield, a doctor she'd met while golfing with a friend of hers in Moncton. Dr. Arthur Prescott, handsome, successful, but not interested in marriage because his mother's apron strings would stretch only so far. She'd wasted five years waiting for the good doctor to propose. She eventually understood it was never going to happen and ended it.

Now, at thirty-three she was starting to feel as though life was passing her by and her interest in Hayden was given new life. When Gil Furlong had turned her head all those years ago, she hadn't realized she was overlooking the real gem in her life, her own husband. But that was then and this was now. She desperately wanted to give their marriage another shot and she would have to say that round one had definitely gone in her favour. Was it love she felt for Hayden Barlowe? He was a hunk, a sexy, laid-back cowboy any woman would give her eyeteeth for. She'd seen that plainly enough from the interest other woman had shown him whenever they'd gone out together. Well, maybe it wasn't love she felt for him, in the traditional sense, but she wanted him back. They could work out the rest from there.

She shivered despite the warmth of her sweater and jeans, the night growing chillier by the minute. After all, it was only May when despite the warmth of the daytime hours it could still get mighty cold after the sun went down. She could see through the window in the loft that the lights were still on in the house, so slipping quietly out of their impromptu nest she tiptoed to the stairs, descended soundlessly and once free of the barn, quickly covered the distance to the house. Too bad Hayden hadn't suggested they make love in a real bed, but she knew it was a spur of the moment thing so she'd have to accept the venue at hand, a true roll in the hay. So be it, because if he woke up now he'd have her out of here within minutes.

Reaching the house she went inside, immediately spying a hand-worked quilt folded neatly on the end of the sofa. Scooping it up she headed back, switching the kitchen light off behind her. Retracing her steps to the barn, having already memorized the direction to the haymow stairs, she turned out the lights and carefully picked her way up to the second floor. The moonlight shining through the window provided ample light to guide her to where Hayden was sound asleep on the hay. Lying down carefully beside him she pulled the quilt into place. He grunted and shifted in his sleep.

Holding her breath she waited for the inevitable, but he didn't waken. Waiting another minute or so until his snoring resumed its regular cadence, she settled in against him under the quilt. His snoring sputtered to a stop as he shifted yet again and her heart leapt hopefully when he pulled her against his side. Eureka! She was finally home; back in Hayden's arms where she belonged and she vowed to not stop until she was permanently back by his side.

* * *

Early-morning sunshine flooded the haymow in a golden light falling across the sleeping couple. Hayden slowly opened his eyes, squinting against the impossibly bright sunlight, his brain still foggy after only a few hours of sleep. Seconds later a bolt of lightening illuminated his tired brain as he realized that not only was he sleeping on a pile of hay, but the woman in his arms was also Mary Rae. He sat bolt upright, apparently with little regard that his abrupt movement woke his sleeping partner. Her head bounced unceremoniously onto the hay. She sat up sleepily, more than a few strands of hay tangled in her hair. He probably had as many or more in his own as he continued to take inventory. He spied his boots a few feet away and then he remembered taking them off, and why, as last night's debacle pierced his brain with

89

even greater accuracy. What had he done! Stupid! What was worse he hadn't used anything, but he remembered again just as quickly that Mary Rae wasn't the type to not protect herself. Since she'd engineered this entire thing he likely had no worries there. She might be flighty at times but she was responsible in many other ways and that was one of them, thankfully.

"Good morning, sleepyhead," she said softly. "Lay back down, it's early."

"No, I've got to get up. Come on, get up and get that hay off you, off both of us, and then I'll drive you home. You can get a drive over tomorrow or something and pick up your horse. Or you can walk him home this morning. Your choice."

"I can't believe you're being so rude to me, not after last night."

"Last night was a mistake, Mary Rae. One I'd just as soon forget. Come on. Let's get out of here. I can't believe I slept in the haymow, like some teenager. I've got a kink in my back."

She tugged on his arm. "Lay back down, silly, don't always be in such a rush. I'll work that kink out of your back. I've got very talented hands. I can't imagine you've forgotten that."

"Nope, you're right. I haven't forgotten, how could I since it's only been a few hours? But it's not going to happen again. Come on, up and at it. Let's go."

She stretched out luxuriously. "This is really very comfy. It's early morning and no one's around so nothing says we can't make love again. What's the difference anyway? We're practically still married."

He pulled the cover off and tossed it aside. "Where did you get this quilt?"

"I went up to the house last night and found it on the sofa. I turned off the light and came back here. You were dead to the world so I didn't want to wake you, you being so tired and all. So I covered you up and decided because it was so nice and warm I'd crawl back under here with you. I could stay up here all day."

Just then they noticed a very large spider dangling on an invisible string just above their heads. With a shriek she was up off the hay, dodging the spider and dusting herself off.

Hayden chuckled and if he'd been able to, would have thanked the spider for its timely visit. He was sure nothing else would have worked the same magic because she was now quickly descending the stairs. He caught up, brushing off the back of her sweater and picking strands of hay out of her long wavy hair, then resumed dusting himself off.

She was waiting at the bottom of the stairs for him. "Why don't I go up to the house and cook a nice breakfast for you, that is if you've stocked up on any supplies yet."

He shook his head. " No, I...."

"No supplies? Okay, I'll take my horse home and filch something from our fridge and come back and make breakfast. Bacon and eggs, right? Orange juice? White toast with butter and marmalade? See? I remember."

Mary Rae was an excellent cook as he recalled, a natural, given she'd really had no formal training. A bona fide foodie, she was always trying new recipes she knew he'd like, and he had. His mouth watered just thinking about one of her delicious breakfasts. But no, he had to pass it up. It was all the other stuff he had no intention of signing up for again. As if his body might be considering it, his mind reminded him of things he should take into consideration. Her moods, her games, her flirting with his friends to make him jealous; not speaking to him for days when he had crossed some imaginary line and offended her. She'd even disappeared one time for three days and told him she'd do it again because he didn't deserve her and she'd done it to make him mad. Well it had and he'd nearly walked out over it, but he'd given her one more of what amounted to dozens of second chances. And then there was Gil. No, she could cook him a breakfast fit for a king and his answer would be the same. She'd used up all her chances.

"Thanks, Mary Rae, but I'll pass. Look, I've got a full day planned. Walt invited me over for breakfast at seven with him and Alice and then we're going to come back here and get busy assessing the damage to that front pasture fence; get it fixed. There still might be some strays out too, so we have to get some kind of handle on numbers. No, you go on home. Thanks anyway."

She shrugged, apparently determined to be good-natured about his rejection. Saying no to Mary Rae could trigger something really awful. He still had the psychological scars to prove it.

"No, problem," she said sunnily, "I'll pick up some groceries while you're busy, stock your fridge and then cook supper for you."

"The answer is still no."

"Oh! Are you eating at Walt and Alice's tonight too?"

"No, but I've got leftovers in the fridge that need to get eaten. I'm all set for supper, thanks."

"So are you inviting me to come and have supper with you? I'll bring the wine."

"No wine, no invite. Look, Mary Rae, last night, us together, should not have happened. It was a mistake I was trying to avoid making, but it ended up happening anyway. It won't again. I meant what I said. I have no interest in getting back with you. I'm not trying to hurt you, but I have to be honest. We are through and it has to stay that way."

She went pale, even for her. He could see it and it didn't make him feel any better. He didn't like saying things to upset people, but he wouldn't be forced into anything.

"So do you plan to remain celibate for the rest of your life? You're only thirty-five."

"No, I don't intend to do any such thing."

"Given your enthusiasm last night I would say that's a smart move. Do you have someone else lined up then?"

"Mary Rae, stop this. What I do is none of your concern."

Her expressive face hid nothing and he'd learned to read it well, especially the unmistakable flame of jealousy that flared in her eyes. "Don't tell me you're going to try to find that Naomi Martel again. It's been twelve years, Hayden. I doubt she waited for you. You broke her heart once when you chose me over her, it wouldn't be nice to do it again. Even if she was still available after all this time, I'm not giving up on you ... on us."

# Chapter Five

Naomi shut her computer off and rolled her chair away from the desk. It had been an especially busy day ... night, because she usually started coding after she finished supper and worked well into the wee small hours. Not always, but more often than not.

She enjoyed her work as a computer programmer, writing and testing code for computer software programs and applications in order for them to function as they were designed to do, turning software program designs into computer compatible instructions. It sounded complicated to the uninitiated, but she loved the challenge. She realized not everyone was interested in testing a computer to the full extent of its capabilities, but it was something she had gravitated toward at a young age. True she had received the requisite training, but she'd also had the aptitude and knew early on she wanted a career in the technology field.

It had been a number of years now since she'd gone into business for herself after working at home for a multi-national corporation, and she'd done well. Her latest online ad bumped her workload up considerably, and she'd then had to stop at what she could comfortably handle. She was actually now turning business away. She couldn't imagine a better way to make a living, and she earned a very nice income as a programmer. However, as with any stationary job she had to be mindful to push herself away from the desk more often, keep a good exercise routine. The long hours of sitting were beginning to bother her lower back, the ache reminding her to get up and stretch; walk around a bit. She knew she'd soon have to invest in one of those desks that would allow her to stand while she worked.

Hmmm, two o'clock in the morning. She padded into the kitchenette of her upscale apartment on Franklin's east side and stood in the living room where a large picture window provided a sweeping panorama of the bay. Some would say it wasn't the best view in the world, not compared to real estate that overlooked the much more picturesque harbour, but she enjoyed watching the ships come and go. She liked the hustle and bustle of the bay and the causeway that ran through it. There was always traffic there no matter what time of the day or night.

Her cellphone rang, startling her, and she crossed the room to pick it up off the coffee table. She saw it was Ritchie, her boyfriend, so she pressed TALK and went back to stand in front of the window. She needed stand time.

"Hey, honey, sorry to call so late but I took a chance you'd be up. Busy night?"

Ritchie was one of the nicest guys she'd ever met, dependable, punctual, ever at her elbow as though trying to anticipate her every need. She knew he was in love with her, had known it for a long time. As a matter of fact he'd said as much a week or so into their relationship, and now five years later he remained just as devoted.

She felt comfortable with Ritchie, safe somehow. She'd vowed never to be hurt in love again, which at times seemed silly now that she was a grown woman of thirty. She knew she withheld a large part of herself, and that included her heart.

"No worries," she responded pleasantly. "I just finished my last job for the night and let me tell you, coding that one really kept me on my toes."

Ritchie, a contractor, had a healthy respect for computers ... from a distance. He was not at all comfortable with technology, wisely hiring others more adept at it for the paperwork side of his business.

"I can't imagine how you figure all that stuff out," he said with a smile in his voice. "It sounds to me like the biggest headache in the world."

"I love the challenge of it actually. I'd be bored without it, but hey, you know I'm not one of those techie snobs who looks down on anyone who's not computer savvy. To each their own. Besides, I could never do what you do, create all that beautiful cabinetry and what not. I personally could not hammer two pieces of wood together and make it look like anything. You don't even use blueprints or plans. You're gifted, Ritchie, a true artist."

"Gee, I would have called sooner if I was going to hear all that flattery. Thanks, honey."

"So you just called to say hello?"

"Yes."

"You get up with the birds, so what are you doing up in the middle of the night?"

"I couldn't sleep."

"Oh? I'll bet it's that Renshaw project again, isn't it?"

He sighed. "Yes, the Renshaw project. Marlina Renshaw was put on this earth to make the lives of other people difficult. She's had me rip those kitchen cabinets of hers out twice now because she keeps changing her mind. Of course she's willing to pay for all of the extra work, but it's hard on the head. I have other jobs waiting and they're starting to get impatient."

"Have you already installed the new cabinets? I mean the third set of new ones?"

"I'm about to and I'm keeping my fingers crossed they will satisfy her. If they don't I'll have to make a decision. It's fine she's covering the cost overrun, but if I tell her these are the last set I'm willing to install and she doesn't get her own way, she's already told me she'll give me a bad review online. That'll negatively impact my five-star rating and hurt my reputation. Of course I don't want that."

"That's not fair. Can't you sit down and have a meaningful conversation with her? Maybe get a little clearer picture of what she has in mind?"

"She's very clear because she gives me a picture and says she wants her cabinets to look exactly like that, but the problem is she keeps looking online and seeing something she likes better. And away we go again. She's driving me crazy. But if I can manage to give her what she wants and make her happy, supposing that's even possible, I'll get referrals from her. I know I will. Anyway I didn't call to dump all over you, Naomi. I really did just want to hear your voice. It picks me up, you know?"

She always felt guilty when he said things like that because she couldn't respond in kind. And if she couldn't say it from her heart, she didn't believe she should say it at all. She'd been up front with Ritchie right from the start, only touching briefly on her previous letdown. She'd made it very clear to him she wasn't shopping for a husband but would love to have him for a friend. A special kind of friend, a friend with benefits as the modern adage went. Pushing those ground rules as far as he knew he dared, he'd asked her on more than one occasion to move in with him but she didn't even want to take it that far. No, she was comfortable with things the way they were and after almost five years together she assumed he had accepted the nature of their relationship. That it would never be more, and she was relieved he'd stopped pressing her about it.

She'd met Ritchie Jamieson at a benefit dance for a local couple whose child required expensive medical treatment out of province, and she'd been flattered when he'd asked her to dance. In fact, if she'd had a dance card he would have quickly filled it because he monopolized her attention for the entire evening. He was good looking, oh yes, and well mannered, polite. She could tell that right away too. She had entertained more than one fool during the few dates she'd gone on in the space of twelve years and she liked that he was the strong, quiet type. She felt he would not demand more from her than she was prepared to give, and so she'd instinctively felt safe with him.

It was her distinct misfortune, she often thought, that she had met Hayden Barlowe when she was only a girl of seventeen and fallen hard for the tall dark cowboy. Even at such a tender age she'd known he was the man of her dreams. He'd been the one. And when he'd returned her affection she'd thought their future together was secure, marriage, babies. She was a city girl through and through but was fully prepared to make the transition to country life if it meant being with him.

He'd even taken her home to meet his mother and grandfather and in her naivety, she'd believed that sealed the deal. She only had to wait for the giving of the ring; the formal request for her hand in marriage and she'd schooled herself to not blurt out yes too quickly. For her part she would save herself for their wedding night, and oh how spectacular that promised to be. He'd told her he loved her, she'd said the same to him, so wasn't the rest the stuff of fairy tales? No.

She'd pushed too hard; she could see that now. He had indeed produced a ring and popped the question, so why wait? A born organizer, she'd applied herself in earnest to arranging the perfect wedding and felt there was no time to be lost. Looking back she guessed she had more of her Grandmother Bridger in her than she cared to admit, but the problem was that Hayden had felt pressured by the never-ending wedding chatter and fled. And married someone else within a ridiculously short time.

She still felt the pain when she thought about that awful time in her life, the suffocating agony when she realized there would be no wedding; that Hayden had actually walked away. The night he'd told her it was over between them was like a nightmare and she could honestly say she was in a state of shock when it began to sink in. He'd been kind when he told her, but the fallout had been agonizing. It was as though the bottom had fallen out of her world and she swore as she struggled to rise above her personal devastation, she would never allow another man to hurt her in that way again. She'd finally managed to get a white-knuckle grip on reality, and that had set the tone for her life.

She knew any woman in their right mind would grab Ritchie Jamieson with both hands and hold on tight. He was perfect husband material, but when she compared any man to Hayden, they never measured up. She had long ago accepted the fact she would never love again, not like she had loved Hayden Barlowe.

"Have you gone to sleep, Naomi?" Ritchie asked reasonably.

She snapped her attention back to their conversation; embarrassed she'd fallen into an all-too familiar daydream. "I'm here." She chuckled. "Maybe I'm just tired. And you should try to get some more sleep too since you're supposed to be up and at it in less than three hours."

"I wish you were here," he said softly, seductively, "then I could probably sleep better. Maybe someday you'll change your mind about marrying me and we can have the same civic address."

"Ritchie...."

"What? A man can dream, can't he?"

She chuckled, trying to soften her tone. "It wouldn't matter anyway in the long run. I work all hours, most often late into the night or early morning, so I wouldn't be in bed with you even if we did both get our mail at the same place. Some things wouldn't change. I'm a night hawk and you're an early bird."

He smiled. She could hear it in his voice. "But you'd be in the next room and I would be content with that. I could sneak in and give you a kiss every once in a while. I'd settle for a little more closeness, but don't worry, I'm not going to go down that road again, I promise. I love you, Naomi, and I will take whatever I can get. And I know you can't say that back to me right now, but I believe someday you will. People don't always love each other equally when they get together, one's often ahead of the other but they usually catch up. It just takes time."

Tears blurred her vision. Good old faithful Ritchie, he never planned to give up. She felt guilty, as she usually did. She should just break things off and free him up so he could find someone who wouldn't make him wait, someone who could be there for him right now. But he'd always insisted he could handle the way things were between them and so she'd allowed it to continue. She did have feelings for him, but not strong enough to be called love.

"Ritchie, you are so sweet and I don't deserve you. Friends?"

"The best," he said. "And now I'm going to take your advice and try to get some more sleep. I think you should try to do the same. You say you've been tired lately, so I think you're burning the midnight oil a little too much. Get some rest, sweetheart and we'll talk again tonight."

"Sure thing," she said and was grateful he didn't throw another I love you in before he hung up.

*  *  *

A hot shower always helped put her to sleep, so after completing her nightly routine she did slip between cool sheets and was gone almost as soon as her head hit the pillow. The next thing she knew was when her cellphone woke her up late the next morning. Ritchie again. Sometimes he did tend to call a little too often, but that was okay. She'd forgive him, seeing as he had so few other shortcomings ... like practically none. She knew she was lucky to have him in her life.

Throwing back the covers she scolded herself for not bringing her cellphone to the bedroom before she went to bed, but managed to catch up with it before it went to message. It wasn't Ritchie, she could see just before she pressed TALK it was her sister, Ginger.

"Hi, Sis!" she chirped, or tried to, seeing as how her voice was still foggy with sleep.

"Were you planning on sleeping the day away, Naomi? It's almost noon time."

"You're kidding! I worked late again last night. I didn't even drop into bed until after three and then I absolutely died. What are you up to?"

"What am I up to? I'm sitting in a restaurant waiting for you. We were doing lunch at 11:30, remember? I'm not in the office today, but I do have an interview at one o'clock. That's why we decided to make it early."

"Oh my gosh! Oh no! I'm so sorry! It won't take me but a few minutes to throw something on and get over there. You're at Gerry's, right?"

"That's right, home of the best meat loaf in town."

"Can you wait?"

"As it turns out my one o'clock has cancelled so we don't have to rush but come right along. I'd like to order before the meat loaf is all gone. This place is starting to fill up fast."

"I'm there in under fifteen minutes, I promise. You're in jeans?"

"Yes, nothing fancy. Just grab something and get over here."

Naomi hurried in the door to Gerry's in just over twenty minutes and saw Ginger waving to her from the back of the room. Once their orders were taken, meatloaf of course which was the big draw every Thursday, they settled in for a little sister talk.

"So how are you feeling?" Naomi asked her. "Are you still having that awful morning sickness?"

"I am, but hopefully for not much longer. I feel sorry for Shane, having to listen to me in the bathroom every morning. The poor guy has a weak stomach and he has to get out of earshot or he starts gagging too."

"So how is the proud papa to be? Getting really excited about the baby?"

"We've got a long way to go yet, I'm only in my second trimester ... but yes, he's so excited. He's already picking out paint for the nursery and we don't even know if it's going to be a boy or a girl. My OBGYN wants to wait until I'm at least fourteen weeks so we can be sure of the sex. I can hardly wait, but like I say, Shane is off the charts excited."

"Is he hoping for a boy?"

"It really doesn't matter to him, he'll be happy either way."

"I'll bet you've already started picking out names too."

"We've been talking about it. If it's a boy we like George. That would be our number one pick. And if it's a girl I was thinking of having Heather in there somewhere, after Mum."

"Good solid Anglo Saxon names. What does Gram think of them? I can't imagine she hasn't been giving you suggestions."

"She has, but only as second names. She likes George, and of course, Heather."

Their meals arrived, the plates with their usual generous helping: a thick slice of meat loaf, a side of fries and two vegetables with coleslaw. Both women dug in and

106

conversation fell by the wayside as they satisfied their appetites with some of Gerry's home cooking, the ex-navy cook famous for his outstanding culinary skills.

Most of what was on Ginger's plate had disappeared by the time she sat back and dabbed her mouth with a napkin. "He's generous isn't he? Here I am three months pregnant and he managed to fill me up."

"Any chance you could be having more than one?" Naomi managed between forkfuls of meatloaf. "Multiples run in our family and you could get to use both George and Heather, and maybe one more if you got the same surprise Mum did when she was pregnant for us."

Ginger shook her head. "No, the doctor says there's only one."

"Even doctors can get surprised sometimes. How would you feel if you found out you were carrying more than one child? Would you freak out? Would Shane freak out?"

Ginger laughed. "It would definitely take some getting used to but no, I wouldn't mind if I was going to have multiples and I think Shane would feel the same way. It would blow our baby budget but so what? We could handle it."

Naomi looked at her sister's plate. "I'd say you're only carrying one baby."

"What makes you say that?"

"Because if you were carrying more than one you likely would have polished off that entire piece of meatloaf; not left anything behind."

"I might go back to it, so don't get excited. Have you been talking to Alexandra lately? The last time she called it was to say she'd gotten the part in Green Mountain, the miniseries, and it's a big part. Not the lead exactly, but a big supporting role and I'm thrilled for her. It'd be nice if she could come home for a visit. She hasn't been back to Franklin for a couple of years, but she doesn't feel she can take any time off right now where her career is so hot. I miss her."

"Me too! We had that Facetime visit a couple of months ago so I guess that's as close as we're going to get to her for a while. She is one busy lady."

"Personally I'd like to see her meet someone and settle down, have children, but that's the last thing she wants with the career she's chosen. I'll never get used to turning on the TV and seeing our sister smiling back at me. Remember when she used to be in those school plays? All she's ever wanted was to be a movie star, or a TV star, whatever, and she's making it happen. Mum would be so proud. She's actually done very well for herself in a relatively short time. Still, that old biological clock is ticking...."

Naomi swallowed another mouthful of meatloaf. "I wouldn't say meeting someone and settling down is the last thing she wants, but she feels she has to put her career first at the moment. I think she does want to do the whole married thing at some point, whenever that may be."

"And she'll wake up one day and realize she's too old to have children and she'll have regrets."

Naomi looked away.

"Sorry, Naomi, I know how you feel about that sort of thing. Let's just drop the subject, okay? Alexandra will make it all work in her own time. Now, I see you've finished everything on your plate, are you up for dessert? Maybe we could share a piece of Gerry's German chocolate cake, but it's a pretty big slice."

Naomi speared the last two peas on her plate before pushing it away. "Actually, I think I could eat a whole slice myself. It isn't that big."

"The servings here are huge, but sure, let's go all out and each get a slice. What we don't eat we can take home in a doggy bag. Shane likes chocolate cake, I could give it to him."

And so they ordered their desserts, Naomi deciding at the last moment to have a scoop of ice cream with hers. They arrived, drizzled with chocolate sauce and a dollop of whipped cream. Heads turned and nearby diners stared at the mega desserts being delivered to their table and the two slender women who had ordered them.

Halfway through, Ginger threw in the towel, or more to the point laid down her fork refusing to eat another bite. "I'll explode if I do," she explained to Naomi who was still ploughing through hers, full speed ahead.

Naomi paused long enough to toss a barb at her sister. "You're a disgrace to pregnant women everywhere," she teased. "Really, Ginger, finish the cake! Don't forget you're eating for two now. My niece or nephew, whoever is calling it home in there for nine months, would not want you to pass up this cake. It's delicious."

"A doggy bag it is for me," Ginger begged off. "I might be eating for two but I'm trying to keep my weight down. I don't want to be as big as a house by the time this baby is born, because what goes on now has to come off later. I wouldn't enjoy having to go on a major diet, not with the way I like to eat."

Naomi finished the cake then added double cream to her coffee, passing on the sugar.

"Gee, Naomi, are you sure you're not going to have a baby too? You tucked into all of this pretty good. You out-ate me and I'm three months pregnant for heaven's sake. If I didn't know any better I'd say you were eating for two, or three or whatever. Seriously, could you be pregnant?"

"Me? Pregnant? Hardly. You know how I feel about that. Ritchie and I aren't really serious, we never have been."

"You are sleeping together aren't you?"

"Well yes, but...."

"So? I ask you again, could you be pregnant? I know you like to eat, but I've never seen you go at food like this."

"Wouldn't that be something," laughed Naomi. "Now that would be the surprise of the century. No, sorry to disappoint you, but I'm just hungry. I didn't eat breakfast, so I am eating for two, two meals that is."

Ginger didn't look convinced. "Hmmm, now that you mention it, when we met for lunch a couple of weeks ago it seems to me you also ate everything on the menu. So again I ask you, could you be pregnant, Naomi?"

Naomi shook her head, amused. "There's no baby. There's only one pregnant lady here, and it's not me."

Ginger stirred her coffee. "I think Ritchie would make a good father; an excellent husband and he loves you, Naomi. If ever I saw a man crazy about a woman, it's him."

"Ginger don't even start matchmaking. I like my life just fine the way it is, okay?"

"But you have to agree that Ritchie is quite a catch."

"I do agree with that, you'll get no argument from me on that one."

"Soooo...."

"So, what?"

"So maybe give him a chance in the husband department. I'm here to tell you that married life is wonderful. I've never been happier. Shane and I were made for each other."

"And I couldn't be happier for you that you met your soul mate. I too once had a soul mate, but he went away. Remember?"

"Naomi, that was a long time ago. What's it been? Twelve years or so?"

"Exactly twelve years and I have never been able to think the same about another man. You can't even imagine how horrible it was for me when Hayden walked away. So I totally agree that Ritchie is a prize. Believe me, I do feel guilty I don't feel the same about him, I mean to the same extent, but I can't pretend. When Hayden and I broke up he took my heart with him."

Ginger reached over and laid her hand on top of her sister's. "Honey you have to try to move past that. He's married."

"I know. You don't have to rub it in."

"So you're going to pine away your whole life for the one who got away? You have to move on. I don't like seeing you stuck like this."

"I'm not stuck. Ritchie and I are fine just as we are. I don't hear him complaining, so why does everyone else?"

"Everyone else?"

"Well, okay, Gram. She thinks I'm wasting my life. But at least I've got someone in my life; Alexandra is married to her work with no man on the horizon at all so maybe Gram should focus on her and leave me alone. I'm doing okay."

"Okay, fair enough. We'll leave it alone and move on. So how is the computer programming business, as busy as ever?"

"I have three new clients and that puts me at my limit. I'm thinking now that maybe I shouldn't have advertised. I'm turning work away because I don't want to be inundated. I should have left well enough alone."

They finished their lunch on a high note, Naomi announcing to Ginger she and their grandmother were going to throw a baby shower for her when she got closer to her due date. Gram had wanted it to be a surprise but Naomi was all for letting Ginger in on the secret so that she could have some input as to where she'd like it to be held, who she wanted to invite, what she needed and so on.

Once she was back in her car and headed home she remembered what Ginger had said to her. "You couldn't be pregnant, could you?"

She'd laughed it off but now she gave it more serious thought and began to do the mental calculation. Had she missed a period? She'd been so busy she'd lost track, and she wracked her brain as to when her last period had been. Was it this past month or the month before? But she couldn't be pregnant, no way. Still, there was that night that she'd done an unexpected sleepover at Ritchie's, actually stayed the weekend and didn't have her pills with her. A couple of missed pills did not a baby make, but could it? She was notoriously bad with remembering to take medication when it was necessary to do so, although one would think that someone who was so detail-oriented wouldn't be forgetful when it came to something as simple as that. It was because she was so focused on her work that she did tend to forget personal things like dates, especially one very important one. Her mind was usually on her job.

Confound that Ginger for suggesting such a thing, because now she had succeeded in planting a seed of doubt in her mind. Okay, maybe she was a few days late. But then it struck her. She hadn't bought any tampons in a while. Her heart sank. She had to make a trip to the drugstore right away, like now, and pick up a home pregnancy test. In fact she'd pick up a couple, take it twice in case of a negative result. She didn't need the stress of thinking she might be pregnant if it weren't really true.

Her next stop was Forum's Pharmacy where she bought two tests. They were all the same weren't they? Pee on a stick and get it done. Okay. She was shaking when she opened the package and followed the instructions, then waited for the results, much faster now than they used to be she'd heard said. Negative. Whew! She then proceeded to take the second test. Positive! What! This was crazy. Well it had to be best two out of three, so pulling on her jacket again she headed back out into the fog and made another trip to Forum's Pharmacy and found the most expensive test in the display, paid for it, headed home and set up shop in the bathroom again.

The directions were the same, and her heart began to pound as she forced herself to read the results. Positive. She fought down panic. Could she really be going to have a baby?

# Chapter Six

Closing the lid Naomi sat down heavily on the flush, in a state of shock, the test still clutched painfully in her hand. POSITIVE. The sight of that result would be burned into her brain until the day she died.

Minutes later, when she had recovered her equilibrium, somewhat, she threw the wand into the wastepaper basket as though by doing so it wasn't real. It couldn't be real. Seconds later she foolishly fished it out and studied it again just in case she had misread the results. She hadn't. It was still positive. She threw it away again feeling as though she'd been shoved into the deep end of the pool and was unable to swim. As she continued to resurface she knew the first thing she had to do was contact her family doctor and get this whole thing straightened out because she'd obviously gotten hold of some faulty tests.

She called Dr. Sutton and luckily scored an appointment in two days time. She would have preferred to have it either confirmed or denied immediately, today, this minute, but she accepted the appointment knowing they would be the longest two days of her life. And they were, but finally here she was waiting under a pristine white sheet for the kindly old doctor she'd known since she was a child.

"Okay, Naomi, swing around and put your feet in the stirrups, dear, and I'll examine you. How late did you say you were?"

"I'm not exactly sure, a few weeks maybe. I'm afraid I haven't kept track as well as I should have. My periods have always been irregular," she explained, as if that would account for why she'd been caught unaware.

"That tells me you haven't been trying if you haven't been keeping track," he said, making conversation as he conducted the necessary examination before pulling the sheet down, removing his latex gloves and dropping them into the waste can.

"Well, dear, you're definitely pregnant. This is good news, right?"

Naomi felt close to tears but would certainly not share the maelstrom of thoughts racing through her mind at the moment. "It has come as a shock," she admitted. "I should have been paying more attention, or this would not have happened. I missed a couple of pills a couple of times, but...."

Dr. Sutton folded his arms, leaning back on his heels. "That can do it all right. I can see you need some time to become adjusted to the news. I'll ask Holly to make a referral appointment to an OBGYN for you and she'll give you a call when that's done. She'll also get you set up for an ultrasound."

She managed to keep her emotions in check until she finished at the doctor's office and again on the ride home. However once she was back in her apartment she let them come although when she finally gave them vent, there weren't that many after all. Not the deluge she'd expected.

Oh how she wished her best friend Solange were still alive at a time like this ... any time, she quickly amended. Dead a year now from cancer, she still mourned the woman who had been her best friend since the sixth grade. They'd shared everything, all of life's ups and downs, and she wanted with everything in her to have her to share this with. Get it cried out, hashed out. It was also at times like this that she missed her mother with a painful ache that would never go away.

She hadn't been best friends with either of her sisters, but since Solange's death, Ginger had stepped in to try and fill the void. And she had, as much as possible, although no one could ever take Solange's place. She'd been a true kindred spirit.

She looked at her watch. It was still only eleven o'clock in the morning and she was grateful Ginger was off work for the entire week, using up some of her banked vacation time before it expired. She couldn't remember if Shane was working nights or days, or was off, but she was sure Ginger would come right over if she asked her to. Of course she wouldn't tell her why over the phone, better to drop this particular bomb in person.

Shane answered and called for Ginger to come to the phone and she was breathless when she took the receiver.

"Is everything okay, Sis? You don't usually call me this time of day."

"Everything's fine," Naomi lied, then back came those tears she'd been playing hide and seek with since POSITIVE had been revealed on the test wand.

"Naomi, are you crying? What happened? Are you all right?"

She got her emotions under control. "There's no emergency, Ginger. I just need to talk to you is all. I don't suppose you could come over for a few minutes."

"Shane and I are going to go over to his father's for lunch. Can I drop over after I get back home?"

Naomi sniffed. "Sure! That'd be fine. Again, there's nothing wrong, it's just that...." and then the tears started up again.

"Okay, honey. Just give me a minute and I'll see if Shane minds if I don't go with him."

"No ... no ... no! I'm fine, so please don't cancel on my account. I don't mind waiting until you get back home. Really, it's not a matter of life or death I just need someone to talk to. Nothing more, okay?"

"If you're certain, because I'm sure that Shane...."

"I'm absolutely certain. Go and see what delightful dish Wes has created for you now. You said he loves to cook and the way he fusses over you now that you're carrying his grandchild, is adorable. Don't disappoint him on account of me. I'm having a bad day, that's all. Besides, I want to hear how Wes and Christina's wedding plans are coming along, whether they decided to get married here or go to some exotic island. You can tell me all about it when you get here, and don't rush either. Come over when you get back. I'll see you then."

"All right. Wes said we're eating at twelve so we'll likely only be there for a couple of hours. Shane works tonight so he'll need to get another few hours of sleep in."

\* \* \*

It was just after two-thirty when Naomi's doorbell rang and she leapt off the sofa where she'd been trying to get interested in a magazine and failing badly. She welcomed her sister inside with a hug, hoping Ginger didn't notice when she held on a little longer than she usually did. And darned if those tears didn't start up again now that she was about to spill the shocking news.

Ginger rubbed her sister's back soothingly before they separated and went to sit on the sofa.

Ginger passed Naomi a tissue from her purse once they were seated. "I've been thinking about you since you called."

"Leave it to me to ruin your lunch by calling up and blubbering. I feel better now though."

"Liar! And you didn't ruin my lunch, but naturally I'm concerned because it's not very often I see you cry. I think I can guess what's going on. You didn't see it coming?"

"See it coming! No, not at all."

"I know you tried, Naomi. It's always a shock when it happens, but everything will work out. It always does."

"I tried? What are you talking about?"

"Aren't you going to tell me that you and Ritchie broke up?"

"No, Ritchie and I didn't break up. We're still … together, whatever that means."

"What's got you so upset then?"

"I'm pregnant."

Ginger's eyes widened. "You're what!"

"You know, when you have a baby growing inside you that comes out in nine months, ready or not? Pregnant!"

"How can that be?"

"Well … Ritchie and I were together…."

"I know how it came to be, smarty pants. I'm just surprised that it … happened. I take it by your reaction that it wasn't planned."

"Not planned at all. I was careless with my pills … missed a couple here and there but I never thought about it. I mean I'm thirty years old.... I can't believe I got caught."

"You say I like you're the only one involved here, isn't it that we got caught? Like it or not you're in this together, Naomi. Ritchie is the father. Have you told him yet?"

Naomi shook her head on a fresh wave of tears. This would of course bring her and Ritchie much closer together, and that was the last thing she wanted. She liked the distance she had managed to create between them.

"How long have you known?"

Naomi sniffed. "I called you as soon as I got home from the doctor's office."

"And you haven't called Ritchie yet? Why ever not? Are you afraid to tell him?"

Naomi looked away, her eyes filling again. "In a way, yes."

"Because you're afraid he'll leave you?"

"Just the opposite. I'm afraid he'll want more of me than I'm willing to give. I like my life the way it is. I don't want anything to change and it will. That's what's really upsetting me."

"Surely you're not saying...."

"That I want an abortion? No, that isn't what I'm saying at all. I want to raise the child on my own is what I'm saying."

"Naomi...."

"I know what you're thinking, poor Ritchie."

"That's precisely what I'm thinking. He loves you, Naomi. Don't you remember what I said to you at lunch a couple of days ago?"

"How could I forget? I always feel guilty because everyone thinks I should let Ritchie come closer."

"Especially now. I can't imagine he won't want to be part of this baby's life. How does he feel about children?"

"He loves them. He comes from a big family and he'll be over the moon when I tell him I'm pregnant. He'll be all nurturing and protective."

"Naomi! Those are wonderful things. Maybe if you weren't forever holding him at arm's length you could get to enjoy being pampered a little bit. You don't always have to be so strong you know. And believe me, you are going to need a whole lot of TLC before you're through with this pregnancy. I'm only in my second trimester and I love that Shane hovers over me, well most of the time. It makes me feel special and I think if you allow Ritchie to do that for you, it just might change your mind."

"What do you mean? Change my mind as to how I feel about him?"

"It might change your mind about a lot of things."

"I doubt it, but right now I'm dreading making that call. I'd ask you to do it for me if it wouldn't make me look like a totally insensitive jerk. But of course I'll do it, next week. I just need a little more time...."

"Naomi! That would definitely make you a totally insensitive jerk. Make the call. Today."

"He'd be at work."

"He'll take a break if you ask him to. Do you want to be alone or would you like me to stay until he gets here, because he'll come a-runnin' or I'm not a triplet. I know you're scared. I also know you'll do the right thing, but you are a world-class procrastinator which is maybe how you got in this fix in the first place. Forgetting to take your pills."

"Guilty as charged."

"This is what happens. Anyway, I'll stay if you want me to while you call him. Ask him to come over. Don't tell him over the phone, okay?"

"I'm not that insensitive!"

"Good. In fact I'm going to stay until you call, just to make sure you don't wait until later. There's never a better time than the present, and he deserves to know right away. Like now, if not sooner."

Naomi squared her shoulders. Of course Ginger was right, Ritchie did deserve to know immediately and to wait any longer would be completely unacceptable. She was going to have the child she'd always dreamed about, but the harsh reality was that it was by the wrong father. The hope she'd been holding all these years reared up to mock her. Twelve years had happened and Hayden Barlowe was never coming back. He was married, to someone else, and had been for a long time. He had not chosen her, Naomi, to be his wife. So why was she still carrying this ridiculous torch? The hard cold facts were that she was pregnant. She was going to be a mother and the father of her baby would now understandably expect much more from her. The unvarnished reality was she had to get on with her life.

"I agree," said Naomi softly and reached for her cellphone.

Quickly dialling Ritchie's number she held it together, successfully keeping any tell tale quaver from her voice as she asked him if he'd mind dropping over for a few minutes. She dabbed at her eyes as she finished the brief conversation and hung up.

"Is he coming?" asked Ginger, reaching out to hold her sister's hand.

"He said he's on his way. I know I sound like a cold-hearted bitch, Ginger, but I can only go by how I feel. Don't worry. I will do the right thing because I'll put the child first now. Whatever I am carrying, whether it's a boy or a girl, they will be the most important person in my life from now on. I'll figure the rest out as I go along."

"That's all any of us can do, Naomi. You're a very strong, loving woman. There's no doubt in my mind you'll do the right thing. And I understand by the way, how confusing it must be to discover you're pregnant and it's a surprise. But you are in a loving, committed relationship and I don't believe that child can do any better than

Ritchie Jamieson for a father. You have to agree with me on that one, Sis. He's true blue. Can I tell Shane about the baby? Or would you rather tell him yourself?"

"Just wait a tiny bit until Ritchie knows first, he should be here in about ten minutes."

Eight minutes later the doorbell rang, startling both women. "He must have driven a hundred miles an hour to get here," Naomi chuckled as she hopped to her feet to go and let him in, and Ginger said her good-byes to both as she slipped out the door past him.

"What's wrong, sweetheart?" Ritchie asked, and the worried look on his face touched her heart. "You've never asked me to come over in the middle of the day before. Your eyes look puffy. Have you been crying?"

Nothing got past Ritchie, especially when it came to anything to do with her. She forced a smile to her lips, if only to reassure him nothing terrible had happened or she was not in some kind of mortal danger.

"This is not bad news I have to give you, Ritchie, or at least I hope you don't take it as bad news. Let's just call it a surprise. I'm going to have a baby."

He gawked at her. His mouth fell open and she almost had to laugh at the shocked expression on his face. "How did that happen?" were the first words out of his mouth, the same thing Ginger had said and she laughed as she told him: "Do I actually have to explain that to you?"

She could see that he was struggling to recover his senses as he automatically reached to take her in his arms.

"No," he chuckled, obviously still knocked offside, "but I thought you were protected. If I had thought you weren't, I would have taken care of it."

"I take all the blame but I am definitely pregnant. Gee," she said when he continued to stare at her, "I kind of thought you'd be happy about it."

"I am! Of course I am. Did you just find this out?"

"I saw my doctor this morning and confirmed what I saw on the home pregnancy test. I didn't want to say anything until I knew for sure. I called Ginger first, it's a sister thing, and then I called you. So what do you say? You're going to be a father, Ritchie."

Tears started again and she could also hear him sniff. Then they were holding each other, neither one trying to hide the fact they were crying. Honestly, she knew she could find no better friend in the world than Ritchie Jamieson and that's what she was responding to at the moment. They were going to be parents together, could there be any better way for them to share that connection?

"That's it, I'm taking the rest of the day off," he said as he guided her to the sofa and pulled her into his arms. "It's late anyway and I couldn't concentrate if I did go back to

the job. I just want to sit here and hold you."
He placed a hand on her belly; she could feel
his warmth through her clothing.

"It's hard to believe that in about eight
months or so we'll be holding a little baby."

"Our little baby," he said thickly.

"Yes, our little baby."

"What do you want, Naomi, a boy or a
girl?"

"There is a chance we could have
multiples you know, Ritchie."

"Twins or triplets don't run in my family,
so you can't blame me if there's more than
one," he joked, now wearing a broad smile.

"They obviously run in mine but I
couldn't blame you anyway because it's the
mother who is responsible for multiples. It's
her who releases the eggs, how many, and
whether they twin or not, so you're officially
off the hook."

"Are you serious we could be having
multiples?"

"I would say no right off the top of my
head, but it's possible where I'm a triplet. We
won't know for sure until I have the
ultrasound, and my doctor's office will call
when I'm scheduled for that."

"Can I come with you for the
ultrasound?"

"Of course, silly, you're the father. You
have every right in the world to be involved
in all of this. I'll let you know every date and
you can go to the doctor's appointments with
me too if you want."

"I want to be there with you, Naomi, every step of the way."

"Great! So, again, how will you feel if it turns out I am having more than one baby?"

"You mean like triplets? I'm not even sure how that works."

"Study up on hyperovulation. Only Mother Nature knows for sure."

He scratched his head, obviously still trying to adjust to this unexpected news. "That's certainly something to think about ... more than one baby at a time."

"So if you want to run for the hills, do so now and I'll understand. No judgements, although you'd have to help me support the child ... or children."

He chuckled, pressing her even closer. "Not on your life. I'm not going to abandon you if that's what you mean. I'm in this for the long haul, sweetheart."

"That's good to know because you will always be this baby's father, no matter what. That is an inalienable fact, my friend."

Pulling gently out of the embrace he folded his arms and leaned his head back against the sofa cushion, still wearing the same broad smile. "I'm going to be a father. I'm going to have a son. I can't believe it!"

"Ahhh, or a daughter."

"Nah, it's going to be a son and I'm going to call him Ormond, Ormond Reginald Jamieson, after my father. And maybe we could add Jotham for my grandfather, all good solid Jamieson names."

"Your grandfather was Jotham Jamieson? I never heard that one. That was Joe's real name?"

"Umm hmm. I think that's what we'll call the baby."

Naomi sat up and looked at him, frowning, checking to see if he was kidding or not. "Ritchie, I think we'll decide on a name together. You also have to prepare yourself it could be a girl. Fifty-fifty chance, right?"

He shrugged. "If it is, you can name her. How's that? Or I could, either one."

Fine, she'd play along because she could see by the twinkle in his eye he was joshing her. She'd long since gotten used to his dry sense of humour. "And do we name her after the women in your family, Ritchie? Ethel after your mother? Dorinda after your grandmother? Mabel after your aunt who lives with your grandmother?"

"Sure, why not?"

"Can we agree to keep an open mind about names?" she asked, laughing. "Are you agreeable to that?"

"Sure," he replied, all smiles. "I was just coming up with a few suggestions. Nothing's carved in stone, honey. You'll have to forgive me, I'm so excited I'm going off in every direction ... and having a little fun with you."

Fine, she understood where he was coming from and cut him some slack. Maybe the mood did need lightening a little.

\* \* \*

Naomi too decided to take the night off, which was really no big deal because she was well ahead of schedule with her work. Doing so would not be at the expense of her clients. Besides, as welcome as the distraction might be, she likely wouldn't be able to concentrate anyway. So at Ritchie's invitation she agreed to spend the night at his home, a beautiful sprawling ranch house in the suburbs.

He was especially gentle with her, cooking a delicious steak dinner with all of the trimmings. Later he held her tenderly in bed while she drifted off to sleep. Ritchie was no Casanova and he'd never truly made her blood boil with passion, not like what she'd thought making love with Hayden would be like. She'd never gotten the opportunity given Hayden's defection, but Ritchie was a considerate lover who always put her first. Tonight he hadn't even kissed her, as though any carnal thoughts were off the table now that she was pregnant.

He was gone when she woke up the next morning at eight o'clock, her typical rise time since she usually worked nights. Ritchie on the other hand was up and gone before six o'clock. He kept a workshop in town close to his contract projects and did all of his cutting and fitting there so as not to clutter his backyard. Glancing over she saw a note on his pillow. "To the most beautiful woman in the world, and the mother of my baby." How thoughtful.

She felt her eyes water. Ritchie was a gem. True they'd never lived together but he seemed to have all the makings for a good roommate, although after her broken engagement she'd always preferred to be alone. How she must appear to other people, essentially wrapping herself in a cocoon and warning other men away. Ritchie had been the only one so far to be able to penetrate that thick wall, although he had never been successful in completely dismantling it.

She'd followed Ritchie over last night in her own vehicle so she could leave when she woke up. Preferring to shower and breakfast at home, she was soon on the road. She hadn't gone very far when the first wave of morning sickness struck, and she now realized the cause of the queasiness she'd been experiencing lately. She'd blamed it on a touch of the flu. Luckily she was on a side road with no houses in sight so she pulled over and dry heaved her way through the unpleasant experience. It was what Ginger was suffering through too, and while she hadn't envied her sister dealing with that, her empathy was now tenfold. The nausea finally passed and she continued on her way, hoping no one noticed she was still green around the gills when she walked up the hall to her apartment and hurried inside.

It wasn't long before she was feeling much better, however she attempted only a light breakfast before she hit the shower. She was dressing when the phone rang. Ritchie.

"Hi, honey, how are you feeling?" he asked, always cheerful.

"Better now," she admitted, telling him about her side of the road stop for morning sickness.

"Oh no! I probably shouldn't have left so early and I wouldn't have if I thought you needed me. I apologize for being so insensitive, Naomi."

She chuckled. "I would say that a man who left the kind of note you did on the pillow could hardly be called insensitive. Morning sickness is all part of the journey as they say. I'm not going to enjoy it, but neither am I going to complain if it means I'm going to have a beautiful little baby."

"You're amazing! I was thinking I'd drop over after work to see you. I'd say I'd bring a bottle of wine to celebrate, but I know that's off limits. What do you think, do you plan to be home?"

"Sure, come on over for a while. We could watch a movie or something."

"How about I bring supper so you don't have to cook?"

"Sounds good to me, but you don't have to feed me, Ritchie. I can cook you know, but sure, if you want to bring supper I'll always say yes."

"Chinese sound good?"

"The best. I'll see you when you get here."

"I was thinking around seven if that's okay. I have an errand to run after work that may take a while, but I'll be along."

At seven sharp her doorbell rang and she could smell the delicious aroma of Chinese take-out before she even opened the door. When she did, there stood a beaming Ritchie holding two large bags. She was so hungry at that point the man had no idea how lucky he was he didn't lose a hand as he passed her the bag containing her favourites. She carried it into the dining room where she'd prepared the table.

"Ahhh, beef and broccoli," she gushed when she opened the take-out container. "And chicken balls and garlic spareribs. Oh Ritchie! This is wonderful!"

She also knew she should slow down a tad or she'd end up as big as that house Ginger was trying to avoid becoming during her pregnancy. It was a comfort too, to know she and Ginger were both pregnant at the same time and made a mental note to call Alexandra first thing tomorrow and let her know she was going to be an aunt ... again.

The next half hour was spent devouring the feast and when their appetites were finally satiated, they sat back, cleaning their hands on the wet towels included with the meals.

"Look," said Naomi, "they even included fortune cookies, but there's only one. Hey, you got cheated. There should be two."

He shrugged good-naturedly. "You take it. They must have forgotten to put in the second one. It doesn't matter. You go ahead and open it. I know you like to read those things."

"Sure, okay. They taste good too, so I'll eat it after I open it." She took the cookie and broke it in half, holding up the tiny piece of paper so she could see what was written on it.

"What does it say?" he asked.

"Okay, it says Will You Marry ... Me? What...."

She turned to Ritchie. "What's this? Why would...."

But she got no further as he produced an exquisite diamond ring and sliding off the dining room chair, got down on one knee.

"It's just me trying to be original, sweetheart, because I love you so much. I believe the question has already been asked? What is your answer?"

This was the second earth-shifting shock in two days and she could only gape at him as he waited. He looked so hopeful, so loving with him down on the traditional one knee doing everything he could to make her happy and secure. To do what he believed would be right now that she was carrying his baby. However that was not something she had the slightest hesitation about, raising this child without benefit of marriage. It had never seemed like a good reason to get married if you were not in love.

"Well, Naomi? I'm asking you again on bended knee, will you marry me?"

Her heart twisted painfully in her chest as emotions continued to churn inside. The moment of truth was at hand.

"Yes," she whispered as tears filled her eyes. "I will marry you, Ritchie."

# Chapter Seven

Hayden was still kicking himself mentally a few weeks after that night in the barn with Mary Rae. He still couldn't believe he'd allowed it to happen. You couldn't leave the door open even the slightest bit with her because she'd get her toe in and shove it open. She was smart enough to know a weak moment when she saw one. If there wasn't one, she created it and took full advantage. But he was surprised he'd not seen hide nor hair or her since then.

She'd walked her horse home, the animal perfectly sound. He imagined she'd have wet feet too by the time she arrived because there was a heavy dew that morning and she hadn't worn boots. Oh well, those were the hazards when you went night stalking without the proper equipment he smiled to himself.

He and Walt were making good progress with the fencing, although they still had what seemed like a million miles to go. There were four pastures, all sizeable and all but the front pasture needed to be almost completely re-fenced, postholes dug, posts set, and wire strung. Fortunately the posthole digger worked fine off the old tractor, so he was spared the expense of renting the necessary equipment. He'd need a new tractor soon, but that was still a ways off because the fence posts alone had set him back a fair bit. The mill had made a timely delivery though and he was more than pleased with the product. True, he would have liked to install cedar posts, which would have been the more expensive option, but hemlock was fine. Like white cedar, hemlock was known for its longevity against rot. If he'd chosen fir or spruce those posts would have to be replaced a lot sooner. In any event there was no cheap way to go about this, because there was a lot of catching up to do. He continued to watch the market closely. The price of beef on the hoof was slowly but surely edging up. Walt was experienced in the cattle market too, so between the two of them they were waiting to make their move. When the time came he'd have a good payday and so would Walt.

Walt was off today. His wife had a doctor's appointment this morning so Hayden decided to take a couple of hours after breakfast and do something he'd been wanting to get to before tackling the job of digging holes and setting posts himself. Every post in the ground, whether done together with Walt or by himself, brought him one step closer to finally having all of the pastures in good shape.

Their first order of business had been to repair the damage done to the fence on the front pasture, the scene of the nighttime escape. Or more to the point, they'd been purposely turned loose. It had been abundantly apparent in the full light of day it was an intentional act, but thankfully he and Walt were able to determine all of the cattle were accounted for. That's where good herding and roping skills came into play, and he and Walt had both.

Stepping out into the June sunshine he felt invigorated, ready to get going. First letting the horses out for the day to graze in the lush green pasture, he then fired up the truck for the short drive to the cemetery. He wasn't much of a grave visitor when he came right down to it, but he felt drawn there as he covered the distance down the road to the tiny church that had served many generations of Bloomfield residents.

Emotion began to build within him as he parked the truck and found the weather beaten granite headstone where his grandmother, Martha Barlowe, had lain in rest for many years. And there was Gramp's name right beside hers. At least they were together again and he knew if nothing else made the old man happy, being with Martha would.

He stood there reading the names and the dates, his vision momentarily blurred as tears burned the backs of his eyes. He'd been nineteen when his grandmother had passed away from early-onset dementia.

"Hi, Gram," he said, glad that nobody was around to hear him talking to a monument. Of course she wasn't here, neither of them were. Martha Barlowe had gone on to someplace much better; he wasn't so sure about his grandfather.

"I miss you," he told her, focusing on her half of the plot.

It bothered him how bare the grave looked with no flowers, real or otherwise, and he made a mental note to correct that as soon as possible. Maybe he could plant a small rosebush or something similar to what was on some of the other graves. The way it was now, it would appear as though no one cared about Martha Barlowe's final resting place; that she'd been forgotten. Before turning to go he glanced back again at his grandfather's name etched on the stone and unbidden, happy memories came to mind. There had been that terrible final parting, but he had to admit there'd been good times too. He was after all the only father he'd ever known. Maybe that's why it hurt so bad that he'd turned on him, cast him out without a second thought. Anger slowly began to build inside him again. Bad idea to come here. Time to go.

Something caught his eye across the narrow lane that split the cemetery into two equal halves. Mrs. Short. Great! She had been his teacher all through elementary school and the worst gossip who ever set foot in any county. He raised a hand in greeting as he made for his truck but he hadn't counted on her speed, which was impressive at her age.

"I heard you were back, Hayden!" she announced as she hurried up to where he'd stopped beside a leaning tombstone. "This is a surprise! I always wondered how you were doing, but of course your grandfather was never one to talk much."

His grandfather had not been able to stand Nolana Short either, and he had to grudgingly acknowledge they had at least that much in common.

Hayden began to inch toward his truck, still bent on escape, although he had to be polite despite how he felt about her. She had been a tyrant in the classroom, priding herself on having zero tolerance for nonsense. It seemed she was always strapping him or telling him he wouldn't amount to a hill of beans with his attitude. Come to think of it he and a lot of the other boys had given her a run for her money, but she'd singled him out more than once for extra punishment. Yet here she was now, chasing him down like he was her long lost friend.

"Nice to see you, Mrs. Short," he lied, still moving slowly toward his truck, "but I really have to be on my way. Got a lot of work waiting for me."

"Hold up now, young fellow! I like to stay in touch with my former students and you're the one I've seen the least of over the past few years. Why did you decide to come back? I heard you left the old place on bad terms."

He could feel his jaw clenching. "I decided to come back, bring Summer Vale back up to par."

"It certainly could use some work," she said in her usual flinty tone. "You said a mouthful there. You were married when you left...."

"I was," he acknowledged reasonably, his hand now on the truck's door handle.

"It's a shame that didn't work out. She comes from a good family. It would have been nice to see the two of you settle down and make a go of it. There's entirely too much divorce today. Annie Winters and I were talking about that very thing at the post office yesterday. Couples throw in the towel much too soon. Marriage is hard work. Myself, I would see it through to the bitter end. As you know my Marvin was killed not long after we were married, but it's still something I feel strongly about. I was here putting flowers on his grave."

Hayden sighed, only realizing he was gripping the door handle when his knuckles began to protest. He loved small communities. There was a closeness one didn't feel in bigger centres, but sometimes people were too close. They felt they had a right to meddle in everyone's business.

He shrugged as he pulled open the truck door. "Sometimes things don't work out. Now I must be going," and without waiting for her response slid behind the wheel and gunned the old motor to life. "Have a good day," he called out through the open window as he quickly reversed. She looked perturbed because she hadn't gotten any real information out of him. Coming up empty-handed in her news gathering would annoy her, and he wondered how long it would be before she turned up at his door with something home baked and wanting to chat.

The last thing he wanted to talk about was the past because that's what he was trying his best to forget. He didn't want to hash up all the bad stuff again, but it seemed that was all some people wanted to talk about. However there was one part of it he was most anxious to revisit. Naomi Martel. But he just wasn't ready to contact her yet. He'd give it another couple of weeks he told himself and he might swallow his pride enough to make that call. Until then, he kept busy.

One of the most difficult things he'd done, now that he was living in his grandparent's ranch house, was seeing his old room again. It looked exactly the way he'd left it, a lot of stuff he hadn't bothered to take down from when he was growing up. He'd laughed when he'd seen the posters of pretty young singers and movie stars whose careers had fizzled out years ago. There were also his 4-H awards, and pinned on the wall right beside his bed was a picture of Naomi. If Mary Rae had ever seen that she would have torn it to shreds, but fortunately he'd never brought her to Summer Vale.

He'd also found the love letters Naomi had written to him during their time together, tucked away in the drawer of his nightstand. On a whim he'd pulled one from the pack and read it. She'd written it maybe a couple of months after they'd met:

"My dearest Hayden: I love you. I could say it a thousand times, write it among the stars or shout it from a dozen rooftops and it wouldn't be enough. And when you told me you loved me too, I was the happiest girl in all of New Brunswick. I always dreamed my prince charming would come along. The first time I saw you, I knew he had. You are so tall, dark and handsome, Hayden, and I am so thankful every day that you love me and only me. We are going to have a perfect life together. Love and kisses, Naomi."

She'd had stars in her eyes for sure and he had loved her, still did, but she'd just hung on so damned tight he'd felt as though he couldn't breathe. He guessed she'd known right away he was the one. He'd thought so too at the time. He sighed. Maybe it was best to file all of that away and think about it another time.

When he pulled back into the yard Walt was there, climbing out of his truck.

"What's going on?" Hayden asked him. "I thought Alice had a doctor's appointment this morning."

Walt's smile would rival the early morning sunshine that made the dew sparkle on the grass like a million gemstones. "It got cancelled because the doctor is tied up at the hospital." He glanced at the tractor. "So, should we get back at this before it gets too warm? I hear it's supposed to be hot today."

"Absolutely," Hayden agreed, climbing quickly out of the truck. "I ordered another truckload of fence posts. We should have enough to finish the back pasture though and it'd be great if we could get that done today. I'd like to put the horses out there instead of in with the cattle. There's babies in that herd and sometimes Champion isn't too fond of the little ones. I don't want to lose any of them."

"Sounds good. Say, Hayden, I have a question I have to ask you. First I want to say I was close to your grandfather, I respected the man. I called him a friend and I still miss him. I didn't always agree with how he went about some things, but I only offered my opinion if he asked for it and he rarely did. But that's okay, I wasn't hired to give my opinions, was I?"

Hayden looked at him sharply. Where was this coming from ... now? "No, I guess not."

Walt looked uncomfortable but determined to get something off his mind. "But there is something I want to say."

"About my grandfather, or me?"

"About both of you."

"Walt...."

Walt was uncharacteristically insistent. "Hayden, I want to get this said. One thing I didn't agree with of course was what he did to you. That was wrong and a terrible thing to have happen. He was hurt when you married into the Sutherlyn's. He saw it as a betrayal."

He really didn't want to get into this, not now. "I know how he saw it, but it wasn't like that at all. If he'd given me a chance we might have been able to talk things out, but no. He wasn't interested in talking."

"You marrying into that family was like waving a red flag in front of a bull. He couldn't see past the name and ... well ... we all know how it went down. But I want you to know he missed you. I caught him crying one day when he didn't know I was around. Of course I never let on, but I know he was crying for you ... what he had done. You see, Hayden, your grandfather had a lot of pride...."

Hayden laughed harshly. "That I know, but I didn't betray him, Walt. Mary Rae and I decided to get married. I didn't feel like at twenty-three I needed to ask his permission. I wasn't a child. As it turns out it was a mistake, I can see that now. I should have stuck with the girl I had before Mary Rae and I got together. I bungled the whole thing, badly, and believe me I've paid for it."

"What was that girl's name in Franklin you were going out with?"

"Naomi Martel."

"Right! Naomi! Why don't you look her up again? Or is she married?"

"From what I hear she's not married, although you can't tell nowadays just because someone's not wearing a ring."

"So you've seen her?"

"My mother saw a picture of her online. She thinks I should try to contact her. Get in her life again, but that would be pretty high-handed ... asking to be with her after I dropped her like a hot potato. I can't imagine she'd give me the time of day and I couldn't say as I'd blame her. Besides, someone who looked like her wouldn't stay single long. She was probably snapped up a long time ago, ring or no ring now. She still goes by the same last name though, but again, today, women keep their name."

Walt folded his arms, as though getting down to brass tacks. "I agree with your mother, Hayden."

Hayden laughed again. "So I've got two matchmakers to contend with now?"

"I'm not matchmaking ... I'm just sayin'."

Hayden wasn't fooled. "You're just sayin' because you've heard that Mary Rae has been coming around here some."

"Could be."

"Word travels fast in Bloomfield."

Walt grinned. "It sure does. But anyway, take some friendly advice from a much older man. Go after the first one again."

Hayden smiled. "I'm thinking I might check that out one of these days. But I'd have to do some mighty hard swallowing. I've heard that pride has a tendency to stick on the way down. She'd probably have a few choice words for me."

"You won't know until you try, Hayden. Now, there's something else that I'd like to get said."

Hayden put his hands on his hips. "Are we going to get any work done today or are we going to stand here and talk?" he asked good-naturedly.

Walt was not to be denied. "Since I wasn't even supposed to be here this morning, I'd say if you got any work out of me at all you're ahead of the game."

"Right on. Fire away. What's on your mind?"

Walt reached into his pocket and took out his tobacco pouch. He carefully filled a paper with makings then rolled it with the finesse of a fine craftsman, pinching the ends and licking the narrow glue strip before lighting it. He might get half a dozen puffs off it at most, but he seemed to enjoy the process and he was never in a hurry. Walt Brisen took his good-old time with most things, but he was a hard worker and what you'd call a sure shot. Every move he made was with great intention and he wasted no effort on close calls. When he did something he knew how to do it before he started, and he got it done efficiently. His grandfather had loved the man, was grateful to have found such a valued and trusted employee, and now Hayden felt the same way. He was glad Walt was giving him as much time as he was, considering he'd told him he was looking to retire. When things started to pick up around here he'd have to do some more hiring, but the chances of finding another Walt, at any age, were slim at best.

Now puffing happily on his homespun cigarette, Walt paused, a thoughtful look on his sun-punished face. "You know, Hayden, I hadn't been working for your grandfather too long, you were just a little fellah, when Wilbur Sutherlyn came to my house one night and asked me to go to work for him. Offered to double my salary if I said yes. Of course I said no. I was happy right where I was. True, your grandfather couldn't afford to match that offer, I knew he couldn't, but there was no way I was leaving the Summer Vale Ranch to go and work at the Triple S."

"I never knew that."

"Neither did your grandfather. I didn't see the need to tell him either, there were enough problems without adding any more to the list."

"Why do you figure he approached you?"

"It wasn't because I set the world on fire, but he knew Duke valued me and he wanted to take that away. He probably wouldn't have kept me on staff long if I'd said yes, but I had no desire to go in the first place. It was not a hard decision to make."

"My grandfather might have liked to know you'd chosen him over Wilbur Sutherlyn."

"And it might have lit another fuse too, made your grandfather angry that Sutherlyn would try such a thing. Try to steal me right out from under his nose like that."

"We had quite a few hired hands in the early days."

"I know, but as the years went on they all kind of got whittled down to just me. You might say the Summer Vale Ranch was my career, and I have no intention of leaving. I like it here. It's like a second home to me and it always will be. Or I should say I hope it always will be."

"Of course, Walt. I want you to think of this as your second home. Like my grandfather said, you'll always be welcome at my door. You just remember that. Nothing has changed as far as I'm concerned, and it never will."

"Now that's the other thing I wanted to say."

Hayden laughed, leaning against the truck and folding his arms. "You're full of chat today, Walt. What else do you want to tell me?"

"Just that, and I won't spend five minutes on a Sutherlyn payroll, no matter how big the salary."

Hayden looked at him, perplexed. "What was that all about? I thought you turned that offer down years ago and besides, Wilbur Sutherlyn is long gone."

"But that son of his is still alive and running his mouth. Alice heard at the supermarket today, from Bugs Clark that Brian Sutherlyn is suing you for ownership of this place."

Hayden swore under his breath. "Don't listen to that foolishness. He was over here shooting off his mouth the day I got back. I found him right in the barn trying to saddle up a horse if you can believe it. Said he was buying Summer Vale, but he hasn't got a leg to stand on, Walt, and he knows it, otherwise I would have been served by now. If it's one thing a Sutherlyn doesn't wait on, it's getting someone served that they're suing. They're very litigious and they live to make trouble for people. He's full of hot air, just like his father. I guarantee you this place will never be his."

"I kinda wondered why you were fencing ground that you didn't own."

"I own it, Walt, I thought you understood that already. I can show you the deed if it would put your mind at ease. I had it in my pocket before I ever got on that plane in British Columbia to come home."

151

"Your grandfather left it to you after all? That's good."

"No, he left it to my mother and she sold it to me, for one dollar; just enough to make it legal. It was all taken care of out west. They couriered the papers to my mother, she signed as the grantor, had them couriered back to the lawyer and he registered the new deed. So no worries, my friend, you are standing on Barlowe land and you always will be."

Walt's eyes got misty, there was no mistaking it no matter how much he tried to blink it away. Foregoing the last puff on his cigarette he tossed away the tiny stub and stepping forward, embraced Hayden. That concluded with manly slaps on the back, but Walt's step was definitely lighter than when he first arrived likely thinking he might never be back.

"Come on, young fellah," he grinned, "we can't stand around all day talking. We've got fence posts to set."

Hayden laughed. "Right you are, let's get going," he said pulling off his T-shirt in favour of the heat, opting to go shirtless.

The pair worked until lunchtime whereupon Walt would not take no for an answer when he invited Hayden to come home with him for lunch. And so after polishing off two steaming bowls of homemade vegetable soup and fresh pan rolls, they headed back to the fields and continued fencing until four.

"Another hundred feet and we'll be done," said Walt, pulling off his straw hat and wiping his forehead. "I'd say let's stay with it, but I promised Alice I'd be home early because I'm taking her out for supper. It's her birthday and she likes to go out to eat at a fancy restaurant."

"I would have wished her a happy birthday if I'd known."

"Her age is the best kept secret in Bloomfield. They'll only find out what it is when it's engraved on her headstone, so she likes to keep her birthdays just between her and I and of course the kids. I imagine she'll have plenty of well wishes before the day is out."

"I've had enough for one day anyway," Hayden said, reaching into the truck cab to get his T-shirt and mopping his face with it. "I can't remember when it's been so hot in June. If this keeps up we're going to have one dry summer and that won't be good for the wells around here. I checked beef prices last night online, and they're steady. Could be I'll be selling soon, and I do hope it is soon because I need the payday."

"I'd say give it another week maybe and see what happens. They could still go up a bit more, but if they level off, sell quick because we don't want prices to start dropping on us. In the meantime we'll keep an eye on it."

Hayden was looking forward to a nice cool shower when he got back to the house, maybe pop a TV dinner in the microwave seeing as how his kitchen skills left much to be desired. And maybe before he did any of that he'd stretch out in the porch swing and have a snooze. That corner of the veranda caught a nice afternoon breeze. He remembered that as a kid when the nights got too hot upstairs and there was no air conditioning. He's sneak down to the veranda and go to sleep in the swing, although he'd be mighty chilly come morning.

Driving along the road through the upper field leading to the house he remembered the many times he'd made this trip, either on foot, on horseback, or in this very truck. Even though he'd only been ten or twelve at the time, his grandfather had let him take the controls because he'd wanted to learn how to drive. When he was sixteen he'd used this same truck to get his license. He'd even been allowed to take it to a dance or two, and out on dates.

He looked around as he drove. The view would never get old and now that he was back, he wondered how he had ever managed to make peace with staying away for so long. Knowing he was no longer welcome here had stuck in his gut like a saddle bur, although his grandfather might have relented if he'd known Mary Rae was out of the picture. Be that as it may, he had his pride and was not about to come back and ask for a second chance. No, someone either took him as he was, faults and all, or leave him alone. Duke had told him to get gone, and so he'd stayed gone.

He pulled up in front of the house, dust swirling around his truck tires as he ground to a halt in the yard. Yep, it appeared as though this was going to be a hot, dry summer, the yard already dusty in June. Getting out of the truck he pulled off his straw Stetson and wiped his forehead with his upper arm before settling it back in place, his dusty jeans riding low on his hips as he started for the house. And then he smelled it. Food, and good food at that.

Saints be praised! One of his neighbours had dropped off another casserole. And that did smell like freshly baked bread. Great! Another batch of Minnie Warden's biscuits or maybe it would be rolls this time. Awesome! He knew whatever it was, it wasn't going to last long considering how hungry he was right now. His stomach growled as he took the back steps two at a time, the screen door squawking in protest as he pulled it open. And there on the counter sat covered dishes, several of them. He had no idea who he had to thank for this feast, only that he would do so profusely after he was finished emptying them.

He was starting to lift covers for a peek at the tempting food within when he realized he wasn't alone. Wheeling around, there stood Mary Rae in shorts and a tank top, and what he recognized as his grandmother's floral apron tied around her slim waist.

"Welcome home, honey," she said crossing to where he stood, stunned, pecking his cheek with a chaste kiss. "I figured you'd be hungry when you finished in the fields so I whipped up some of your favourites and brought them over with me." She pointed at the containers, then looked back at him, her eyes wandering over his bare upper torso. "They'll keep the heat for a while yet, so you go and get washed up. On second thought maybe you'd like me to join you in the shower. Doesn't that sound like fun? Just like old times. Come to think of it, I'm pretty sticky myself in this heat so why don't we get cooled off together?"

"Mary Rae, come on. You can't just come in here like this," although he didn't feel much like scolding her or for that matter asking her to leave if it meant she was going to take all of this delicious-smelling food with her.

"Why not? The door was open and after all, we're neighbours. I thought you could use a nice home-cooked meal."

"I do appreciate the gesture, but...."

"But what? We have to start getting back into the swing of things if we're going to be a family again."

"We're going to be a family?"

"Yes, you and me and the baby will make three."

# Chapter Eight

Naomi woke up an hour or so after Ritchie left for work the next morning. It had seemed only right to invite him to spend the night, seeing as how they'd just gotten engaged ... and he had spent all that money on a ring. That was uppermost in her thoughts of course. So the first thing she did was take a better look at it and the trembling hand wearing it, as her state of panic inched up another notch. Had she actually said yes to Ritchie's proposal of marriage? Unbelievable. She had to talk to Ginger, even though it was still early. Before she could put that plan into action, her cellphone rang. Talk about the telepathy of multiples. The triplets had been aware of that from a very early age.

"So?" Ginger asked as soon as Naomi answered. "What did he say when you told him about the baby?"

Where to start? "He was happy as I figured he would be. He's already picking out names and they're awful, but he was only pulling my leg. Seriously, he's getting right into this."

"He was surprised though."

"Surprised! I guess he was surprised, just as shocked as I was. He's actually more than ready to be a father."

"And how about Mamma Bear?"

"I'm getting there. Don't get me wrong, I'm thrilled to be pregnant, it's just getting my head around everything it involves ... everything that's going to change. That's the big thing. And speaking of that, there's something else I have to tell you."

"I'm all ears! Dish!"

"I'm getting married."

"To whom?"

"To whom? To Ritchie of course, he proposed last night and I said yes."

"Okay, who are you and what have you done with my sister who has been keeping Ritchie Jamieson at arm's length for five years because she didn't believe he was the one. I want your name."

"Very funny. I haven't changed the way I feel about Ritchie. You can't just snap your fingers and make that happen. That's only in the movies."

"But you said yes when he proposed."

"I did, and I've got a rock the size of a pea on my left hand should I forget I did that."

"So my next question is why are you wearing an engagement ring, agreeing to marry a man you say you don't love?"

"I never said I didn't love him. We're the best of friends."

"The best of friends is important too of course, but are you in love with the man?"

"Not in the traditional sense, no, but isn't love overrated? How many couples do you know who are madly in love, get married and are divorced within five years? Maybe friends have a better chance of making it work in the long run."

"Naomi, I agree with you up to a point. I'm madly in love with Shane and he feels the same way about me, and yes, we're also friends. One goes with the other, but friendship without love in a marriage is more like ... roommates. Why did you accept his ring if you're not in love with him? And don't give me all this friendship stuff because I won't believe you. I think you're just trying to convince yourself."

"Did anyone ever tell you you're starting to sound like Gram?"

Ginger laughed. "Seriously, why did you accept the ring?"

"Are you busy this morning?"

"No, not really, why? I was going to catch up on some research for a story I'm working on. I try to stay quiet while Shane is sleeping. His shift ran over by a couple of hours because they had a hostage situation last night, but thankfully it ended relatively quickly ... and peacefully."

"Can you put the research on hold for a little while longer maybe? It sounds like the perfect time to come over and see the ring. You have to do it right away though because Ritchie plans to drop in at noontime to see how I'm feeling."

"Give me a half hour because I'm not showered yet, but I'll be right along."

Naomi had no more than hung up when the nausea struck and she spent the next few minutes in the bathroom retching before she felt like taking a shower. She had just finished drying her hair when the doorbell rang and she hurried to let her sister in.

"Okay, let me see it," said Ginger.

Naomi held out her left hand, fingers extended and flattened for the best view.

"Whoa, that's some ring!" Ginger exclaimed. "I hope it's insured. I'm going to get in the contracting business if he could afford that rock. Really, Sis, it's a gorgeous ring. Beautiful setting."

"I'll tell him you like it, at least one of us does."

"Naomi! What don't you like about the ring?"

Naomi shrugged, close to tears. "I don't know, the fact that it's on my finger. Let's start there," she said as tears actually welled in her eyes, one breaking free and rolling down her cheek.

"Naomi, come here," Ginger told her soothingly, putting her arms around her sister. That's when the dam really burst as Naomi deteriorated into a full-on ugly cry, sobbing in Ginger's arms.

Ginger waited until the worst of the storm was over and then directed her sister to the sofa, leaving her only for a minute while she fetched a box of tissues from the bathroom. Hurrying back she passed a handful to Naomi who immediately put them to good use.

Ginger waited until Naomi stopping crying altogether before she spoke, catching the few remaining tears with the pads of her thumbs and pushing them away. "Feel better now?" she asked her sister. "I expect that's been building since you came home from the doctor's office. A lot has changed for you, very quickly, and it's got to be scary."

"Try terrifying."

"All right, terrifying. I agree. It would be. It's true your life has changed, Naomi, but not in a bad way. Maybe you and Ritchie can make this thing work. Maybe you can fall in love with him. That's what I meant when I said give it a chance," but Naomi was already shaking her head.

"Well why on earth did you say yes to him then?"

"What choice did I have? I'm trying to think about the baby instead of myself."

"But, honey, you can't marry a man you don't love, or don't think you'll ever love, not even for your child. That would be a really bad idea. If it didn't work out it would probably be your child who would pay the price knowing their parents didn't love each other. It's hard enough to make a marriage work when you're in love. The rough spots will come, and a baby will make a lot of demands on both of you."

"People can grow to love each other...." Naomi insisted, still sniffing.

"Naomi, it's already been five years...."

Naomi put her head in her hands again. "What a mess. I can't help but remember when Hayden gave me my diamond, how over the moon I was. It's not the same at all with this one. I feel ... nothing because he's not the right one. I know you don't want to hear this, again, but the man I'll always love, left me."

"Hayden Barlowe."

"Yes, Hayden Barlowe. Now that was real love, Ginger, because I still feel the same about him today as I did all those years ago." She held up her hand in a STOP gesture. "And before you say it, I know he married someone else. I'm just being honest is all. Maybe someday I'll meet someone who makes me feel the way I did with him, although I doubt it."

"How do you expect to meet the right man if the space beside you is already filled? Ritchie's in it. And now, here you are expecting Ritchie's baby, but it doesn't have to be all doom and gloom. You're the baby's parents and you can both help raise the child, but I think you'd be making a huge mistake if you went ahead and married him with what you've just told me. Let me ask you this, if you could undo the last few hours ... say go back to when he was proposing, on one knee I assume...."

"You assume correctly."

162

"Okay, down on one knee, how do you think you'd feel right now if you had said no to his marriage proposal? Come on, say the first word that pops into your head."

"Relief."

"There you go, you just answered your own question. You can't marry him because it wouldn't be fair to either one of you. He deserves someone who'll feel the same way about him. Getting married to give the child a name almost never works because it's forced. Case in point, Mum and Dad. Need I say more?"

"But you didn't see the look on his face when he asked me, it broke my heart. If I had said no it would have really hurt him ... and he has been so good to me."

"So you said yes because you felt sorry for him?"

"All right, I admit it, but I also felt like I have to do it for the sake of the baby."

"Listen to me! Those are the wrong reasons, Naomi, and you'll live to regret your decision. You mark my words."

"Okay, now you're really channelling, Gram. I guess the apple doesn't fall far from the tree, because I see her in me too. Not that I have any intention of calling her about this, but what do you think she would say? She's from a different generation."

"I think she'd say exactly the same thing. She's told me more than once how much in love she was with Gramp when they got married; that he swept her clean off her feet."

"Like Hayden did to me," Naomi said wistfully.

"Okay, just like that. I guess not all stories have a happy ending, but I also remember Gram telling me one time she had another beau before she met Gramp. It was eerily close to the way you feel about Ritchie. But she refused to settle and I think you should too."

"But she didn't have a baby on the way."

"No, she didn't, but she still would have married the wrong man if she had gone through with it and not been available when Gramp finally came along."

"Great, now you're really cheering me up because I think if Mr. Right was going to come into my life, he would have arrived by now. Like I said I'm thirty years old and it looks very much as though he didn't show up on time. I'm expecting another man's baby."

"Remember that Gram wasn't a young girl when she met Gramp. But anyway, you know what you have to do, right?"

"What's that?"

"Give back the ring."

"That would break his heart. Wouldn't I be doing the same thing to him that Hayden to me?"

"If you didn't, you'd be doing him a disservice."

"I don't think Ritchie would agree. He said he loves me enough for both of us and is willing to go ahead with the wedding, even though I've told him many times that I'm not head over heels in love with him."

"He's okay with it now but give him a few years living with a distant wife and see how he feels. I think he puts up a big front, but inside he's hurting. You accepting his ring has given him false hope if you can't see yourself ever changing your mind. When is the wedding by the way?"

"We haven't set a date, but in the next two or three weeks I'd say. It would be just us going to the clerk's office and getting it done. Nothing lavish like you guys had."

"I'd hardly call a backyard wedding lavish."

"It was nice though, beautiful. Honestly, Ginger? I want what you and Shane have but I don't see it ever happening now. My chance came and passed me by. I'll just marry Ritchie if he'll have me and be done with it."

"Now isn't that romantic! Be still my heart."

"We all can't have a fairy tale ending. My prince got away. Remember? There aren't that many princes around, I've found. See, you're going home to a prince, Ginger, while I'm waiting for Ritchie to come over. You're right. He's not my prince and he never will be which is sad."

\* \* \*

As she expected, Ritchie called her at lunchtime to ask how she was feeling and told her he would come by after work with more take-out so she wouldn't have to cook. She forced herself to sound more cheerful than she felt, not at all like a woman who'd gotten engaged a few short hours ago. She hoped he didn't notice her lack of enthusiasm, but then again he'd likely assume she didn't feel well because of the baby. She was the same person she was two days ago before she found out she was pregnant. Now that they knew about the baby, in his eyes her health had somehow taken a nosedive and he had to keep an eye on her. There was also something different about him; he was not quite so easy going.

She hoped he wasn't bringing Chinese food again. She was not in the mood for any more surprises although she loved the proposal in the fortune cookie. He scored big points for that. Too bad it was a wasted effort. She was the wrong woman for him. Ginger agreed and no matter how she tried to defend her position to her sister, she hadn't bought any of it.

She dreaded hearing the doorbell ring when she knew it would be Ritchie because the ante had been upped considerably and he would now expect more. It was inevitable, as though he'd finally conquered her and brought her around to his way of thinking. In effect he had.

When it did finally ring she pasted a smile on her face and answered the door after taking a deep calming breath. As soon as she saw him she knew her gut feeling was right, there had been a shift in him. It was plain as day right now in his demeanour.

"I got Italian this time," he announced holding up the bag. "From Franconnelli's. Remember we went there with Shane and Ginger one time and we really liked it? They also do take-out so, presto, here we are. And I bought lots, so let's dig in."

It was delicious, just as good at home as it had been when served by one of the colourful, mustachioed waiters. She and Ritchie tucked into it as though they hadn't seen food in a month. Her appetite was definitely on the rise, and Ritchie, not a small man, had always enjoyed generous helpings although he kept himself trim through hard work. He was the type who never sat still for a moment, always on the go with one project or another.

"I'll feel like going to bed after I eat all this," she smiled before lifting another forkful of Linguini Alfredo with chicken."

"I think that's a very good idea, sweetheart," he said. "I want you to stay well rested from now on."

"I do stay rested," she quickly assured him, "but I've got to go back to work tonight because I have to keep pace with my contracts. Since I've taken on new clients I have to work a little harder."

"What about the baby?"

She looked at him, perplexed. "What about the baby? It's a little too small to work yet, but once it's born I'll get him or her set up with their own computer."

"Not funny."

She chuckled. "Not hilarious, no, but I thought it was kind of funny. Surely you're not saying I can't work because I'm pregnant."

Laying down his fork he wiped his mouth with the large white paper napkin. "I'm saying working until one or two o'clock in the morning is not healthy for you. You have to remember you're carrying our child now."

"Believe me, Ritchie, I haven't forgotten I'm pregnant. Even if it did slip my mind, my morning sickness serves as a good reminder."

"Seriously, Naomi, I make enough money for both of us. I can provide for both you and the baby just fine. There's no need for you to work anymore. I'd be looking for a way to get out of those contracts if I were you. Besides, my mother never worked and we always made out okay. I want the same thing for our child, a mother who is devoted to her family, not trying to make another buck."

She stopped eating to stare at him, her fork halfway to her mouth before she laid it back on the plate. "I have no intention of leaving my work, Ritchie. I enjoy what I do and I have a very successful little company; some very impressive clients. So no, I won't be looking for ways to get out of any of my contracts. Not now, not ever."

"You would actually put our child at risk?"

She stared at him even harder. "At risk for what? I've got the best job in the world right now because I don't have to leave the house and I can work right up to just before I go into the delivery room if I want to, and then again right after the baby's born. I'm not looking to make any professional changes, just so you know. I can give our baby all the attention it needs. My mother worked and she was very devoted to her family."

"All right then, what about the radiation?"

Her eyes bugged out, but to her credit she didn't laugh out loud. "From a computer? Are you serious right now? I know you're not IT savvy, but I am, and honey, there's no radiation. You have absolutely nothing to worry about. But if it will make you feel any better I'll do some research on it and if it recommends that I wear ... protective gear ... then I will not hesitate to do so. There, problem solved."

"I still think you should at least reduce your hours. You're going to need lots of rest now that you're pregnant."

She reached over and patted his hand. "And I will get plenty of sleep. Ritchie, I'm not going to do anything to endanger this baby I'm carrying. Just relax. I've got it covered."

He continued to eat but was uncharacteristically silent for the rest of the meal. What was up now?

"Ritchie," she said after they had cleaned up and were relaxing on the sofa. "You seem upset. What's on your mind?"

He shrugged. "There's an edge to you tonight, Naomi. I thought newly engaged couples were supposed to be happy."

She couldn't lie outright to his face. "It's just that you don't need to pick at me about the baby. I'm a grown woman, not a child. Believe me, this baby is my number one priority. Everything is going to be okay, you'll see."

"Your number one priority?"

"Yes, my number one priority as it should be your number one priority."

"I fit in there somewhere too I hope."

That false smile again. "Of course."

"There is another little detail that we need to take care of too, without delay."

"Oh?" she asked, knowing darned well what he was getting at but not wanting to have that conversation, although she knew she couldn't put it off. The nuptials. "What's that?"

"We have to get married. I booked off tomorrow so if you're free in the morning, put on your best dress and we'll go and get it done."

He sounded like she had earlier when she was talking to Ginger. "Get it done? What, like a root canal? Should I pay the water bill while we're there?"

He laughed. "Sorry, I didn't mean it like that. It's just that I'm not one for big ceremonies so I'd choose that route no matter what the circumstances were. So what do you say?"

"I say wait because we're not in that big of a hurry. I'd like to have Ginger and Shane with us when we do that, at least make something more out of it than a trip downtown."

What was wrong with him tonight? He wasn't behaving like himself at all. If she didn't know any better she'd think he was the reluctant party in all of this. Maybe he'd had a chance to think things over and changed his mind. He wouldn't be the first to do that.

"Whatever you want, honey," he said, "just let me know what you decide. So since I have tomorrow off, we could maybe start moving some of your stuff over to my place. I've already drawn up a few plans to add a piece onto the house. I have two bedrooms but I hate to be crowded so we'll have to get an expansion done right away. It'll come in handy anyway when we start filling up those rooms. How many children do you think we should have? As you know I come from a big family by today's standards, seven children, so I think if we get serious about this we could have that many or more. I'm set pretty well financially now, getting big bucks for my work. You say you want to stay working, so we'd be all right. Naomi? What's wrong, honey, you've just gone pale. Are you feeling faint? Here, lie your head back against the cushions and I'll get you a glass of water."

He was back in a moment with a glass of ice water, which he insisted she sip. Duty bound, she did just that.

"Do you think that's too many children, Naomi? We don't have to have seven. That was just a thought since I remember how much fun it was to grow up in a house with all those brothers and sisters. You know each one of my brothers and sisters have big families and I'm way behind. We have a lot of catching up to do," he laughed, tickling her, but number one, she wasn't ticklish, and two, under the circumstances the last thing she wanted was to be tickled ... by him.

It upset her to even think about leaving this beautiful apartment. She loved it here! She'd had her name on a waiting list for three years and she wasn't inclined to give it up. She'd heard once that life is all about sacrifices for the one you love, so why was she unwilling to make even one? The ring suddenly weighed heavily on her finger and she knew in that moment she could not marry Ritchie. All that stood between her and a good night's sleep was to tell him so. But she couldn't do it tonight, not when he was all carried away talking about their future; a future it seemed he wanted to be in one hundred percent control of. There was no way she could ever sign on for that, no matter what the circumstances.

But then she thought, what if I am having multiples? It would be a mighty long road if she had to deal with it all on her own. She quickly reminded herself that even though she could not go through with marrying Ritchie, he would be the children's father and would have to share equal responsibility. She knew he would do that because he was the soul of responsibility.

The rest of the evening passed pleasantly enough, that is if she didn't think about having to tell him she couldn't marry him. It would be the shortest engagement on record too if she did the right thing and told him right away, but she knew she couldn't. She thought of when Hayden told her he didn't want to go through with the wedding; rotten she'd felt being on the receiving end of that decision. Now she would have to do the same thing to someone else. Why had she taken the confounded ring in the first place? Said yes? She recalled how he'd leapt to his feet from the kneeling position and gathered her into an enthusiastic hug, but then again he was a man in love. What a shame she couldn't love him back.

She did manage to convince him she had to work that evening. She'd had to insist upon it and held out successfully over his protests. He'd eventually given in and gone home, reluctantly, calling her twice before he went to bed just to see how things were going. She'd known instinctively getting this close to Ritchie would be a bad idea, the way he was smothering her now was proof of that. He had it in him to be possessive, but it got turned up a few notches when she'd accepted his ring. It was like she was his property now, and moving ahead he would make all decisions accordingly.

A half hour after she got up the next morning her cellphone rang. She considered not answering it if it was Ritchie asking for an update as to how she was feeling. She could see it was Ginger, as she poked TALK and carried the phone into the living room so she could sit comfortably on the sofa while she talked.

"Soooo ... are you still planning to marry him?"

Naomi took a long pull on her peppermint tea before setting the cup on the coffee table, swallowing and answering her sister. "No, I'm not."

"Thank heavens!" Ginger shrieked, then lowered her voice. "Sorry, Naomi, I know how difficult this whole thing is for you but I think you made the right decision. The old adage, marry in haste repent in leisure has some truth to it."

"Who told you that, Gram?"

"No, I heard it one time and it sounded too sensible not to be true. Did you tell him?"

"Not yet. I just put him off. It's going to be really hard to do that so I'll give it a few days and then I'll try to let him down gently. I don't think he'll take it well though. He's already starting to drive me crazy worrying about how I'm feeling."

"I think they're all like that. Shane drives me a little nuts too some days worrying about me. It's like he wants to wrap me up in cotton wool to keep me safe. They wouldn't act like that if they didn't love you though."

"Spare me then because I'm already tired of it. Ritchie takes it too far. He told me last night he wants us to have seven kids. Imagine!"

"If you're carrying multiples, you might get a good start on that number."

"Very funny. And he says I have to start packing to move to his house."

"Most married couples do live together, Naomi."

"I'm glad I'm not getting married then ... to him. Funny, if I had married Hayden I would have had twelve children if he'd wanted that many."

"That's the difference between love and ... not love.... So what do you have planned for today?"

"How about two pregnant ladies going for a walk in the nature park? It's such a beautiful day. I'd leave my cellphone home to avoid the hourly check-ins, but he'd have the National Guard out looking for me if I did that. Sorry, I don't want to sound mean because I'm not trying to put Ritchie down, it's just that he does tend to hold on a little too tight. I was able to manage that all right until I got this rock." She held up her finger and considered slipping it off, but no, she would wait and give it back at the right time.

Later as they sat on a bench in the park, resting and sipping water after finishing the main trail in the park, Ginger looked around at the ocean that sparkled iridescently under a cloudless sky. "What a gorgeous day and look at that water. It looks like it's made of diamonds."

"Can we not talk about diamonds, please?"

"I see you wore yours today ... Mrs. Jamieson."

"Not funny."

"Sorry, just kidding." Ginger smiled. "I do feel sorry for Ritchie, but I am glad you made the decision you did. If you felt the way you should, you would have married him years ago. So, did you call Alexandra yet and tell her your baby news?"

"I sure did and actually managed to get hold of her on the first try. She was just leaving to go for a costume fitting. She was thrilled about the baby, but I didn't go into the whole engagement thing. We can have that conversation another time. She said she might be coming home.... Ginger...."

Ginger set down her water bottle, instantly alert given Naomi's tone of voice. "What's wrong?"

"Nothing's wrong, but I think Dr. Sutton was wrong. I don't think I'm pregnant at all.

I just started my period. I was late is all, and boy am I starting. It's a good job I wore dark shorts because...."

"Naomi, you're having a miscarriage. Are you in pain?"

"Cramping is all ... and gee are they starting to kick in, I...."

"Okay, you sit there and I'll bring my car over and pick you up. I've got a big plastic shopping bag in the back. We'll put that on the seat under you. Just give me a few seconds to get my vehicle and then I'll take you up to the hospital."

"I don't think I need to go to the hospital, do I?"

"I think we should, look at the blood you've lost already."

Naomi looked down and saw the stain on the wooden bench. It was one of life's embarrassing moments for sure.

It was all over in the next few hours, all except for the tears and they didn't seem like they were ever going to stop. Mercifully though it had been very early in her pregnancy, although she would grieve this child. Ritchie wept openly as he held her hand and in that moment she understood the connection between them was stronger than she'd believed it to be. Still, they would only ever be friends, and Ritchie seemed to understand that when she slipped off the ring.

"I know this is the worst possible timing," she told him through tears, "but I have to be honest with you, Ritchie. I should never have agreed to marry you, because my heart would not be in it and it wouldn't be fair to you. I care for you enough to say this and believe me it's breaking my heart to do so. We almost shared one of the most beautiful experiences two people can possibly share, and we'll always have that even if it was for only a few days."

His hand shook as he took the ring from her and shoved it in his pocket. "I do love you, Naomi. I will always love you, but I'm not stupid. I could see it in your eyes the other night when I proposed, you felt sorry for me. That's the only reason you said yes and that was quite a blow to my ego, I have to say. I don't know that my feelings for you will ever change, but I'm not about to start begging. I want the real thing and I think five years is long enough to wait for you to feel the same way about me. It's become very obvious I'm not going to find what I'm looking for with you."

"Ritchie....," she sobbed.

"Don't," he said, wiping ineffectually at his tears. "It's over, just leave me some dignity."

He stepped away from the bed, the look on his face tearing at her heart. Never had she cared more for him than at this moment, but she knew if given another chance she would do things no differently. All break-ups were painful, some more than most.

"I'm sorry," she whispered, "I truly am and I wish for you all the happiness in the world. You deserve it."

His face crumbled again not even trying to hide his emotions as he turned to go, then looked back one last time. "Good-bye, Naomi."

# Chapter Nine

"You and me and the baby will make three! What baby!"

"The baby you and I made in the haymow over a month ago," she winked. "I'm pregnant, Hayden, and if there's anything to you at all you can understand why we have to get back together. We never should have gotten a divorce. I can see that now, but under the circumstances we have to get married before people get wind of this and start to talk."

He had to laugh at that one. "And since when did you worry what other people said about you?"

"Not me, us."

"Okay, us. What happened to that free spirit of yours?"

"I still have my free spirit, but things are different now and I have to think about the baby. Your baby, which means you have to step up too." She leaned against the counter, watching him with a coy smile. "Maybe this is a wake-up call for both of us, but it's going to happen. We're going to be parents you and I, so we have to do the right thing."

"The right thing?"

"You don't want your child to end up like ... you are, do you?"

His eyes narrowed. "And just what's that supposed to mean? You know something, Mary Rae? You and your family are the only ones who seem worried about that. My mother didn't violate the Geneva Convention. She had a baby, me, and was smart enough not to tether herself to a loser. She was strong enough to raise me on her own ... well, with the help of my grandparents. I am loved and accepted, so end of story. I would advise you not to bring that subject up again. If you're trying to get on my good side, you're going about it the whole wrong way. You Sutherlyns think you're better than everybody."

"Are you done? I'm sorry if I touched a nerve, sweetheart...."

"Do not call me sweetheart."

"What would you like me to say then?"

"How about good-bye? How about I don't feel welcome here so I guess I'll leave and not come back?"

"How about you not be so rude? In less than nine months you and I are going to be parents, and we have to deal with that. Make plans."

He felt a slow burn that started in his toes and quickly worked its way north. The last thing he wanted to do after a day in the hot sun was ... this. "You set the whole thing up, didn't you? You were trying to get pregnant, that's why you came over here and manoeuvred me into that haymow."

"I don't seem to remember you putting up much of a fight."

"Whatever. Come on, let's get in the truck."

Her eyes widened in surprise. "Get in the truck! I've got a whole supper cooked for us."

"It can wait."

"For what pray tell? It's ready to be eaten now."

"You and I are going to drive into Hampton where you will buy a home pregnancy test, the most expensive one they have. Then we'll come back here while you do the necessary procedure, and I'll be in the bathroom with you to see the results. If it comes up positive, then I'll believe you're pregnant. Until then, I'm not buying it. So get your purse if you want to take it with you and let's go. I'll pay for the test, I don't mind."

"That's pretty highhanded, don't you think? Besides, I've already taken the test and it did come up positive, so save your expensive fuel on a wasted trip. I'm way ahead of you, cowboy. And I don't need your help. This isn't my first rodeo. I know how it's done. I don't need you violating my privacy."

"First of all you weren't shy in the haymow, so that argument doesn't hold any water with me, and how do I know you're not lying about having already taken the test? I wasn't born yesterday, Mary Rae. So come on, we're driving into Hampton."

"No, I'm not driving all the way down there, that's crazy. Besides, I'm hungry. I worked hard putting this meal together and I want us to eat while it's still reasonably fresh. It's the least you can do."

"I said come on. We're going to get that test and you're going to do it. I'm going to see firsthand that it comes up negative. Am I right?"

She was flushed, and not from the heat of the kitchen. "No, you're wrong."

He started for the door. "Let's go, I haven't got all night. I'm hungry too and unlike you, tired from a hard day's work and in no mood for your games. Take that apron off and let's get on the road."

She flounced away, folding her arms. "Oh all right, I'm not pregnant. I've got better things to do than have a kid."

"That's what I thought," he said tossing the truck keys back onto the counter.

"You know what your problem is, Hayden? You can't take a joke. I was only having a little fun with you."

"Fun? I can tell you one thing, you weren't expecting me to call your bluff, were you? Apologize."

He couldn't help but think how this sounded like a re-run from their marriage, not about her pretending to be pregnant, but saying one cockamamie thing after another. How many times had he told her to apologize and she always did, begrudgingly? And then it would happen all over again. He'd thought at the time she was just seeking attention, but it got old real fast and set the tone for most of their marriage. He'd guessed at the time, still did, that was how she got things to go her way with her father. She had been daddy's little girl and she'd played it to the hilt, although she too had fallen out of favour when she'd married a Barlowe. However, unlike his grandfather, Wilbur Sutherlyn got over his disappointment fast enough and forgave her. He wouldn't have anything to do with Hayden though. His son-in-law was not welcome on the Triple S Ranch, y6as if he'd ever be interested in going back there anyway.

"Okay, I'm sorry, Hayden. Satisfied? Now that I think about it, it wasn't very funny at all but I got you going, didn't I? So no, I'm not pregnant. But if I were interested in having a baby it would have to be yours because I still love you. Maybe I realized it a little too late, but that's how I feel."

"Whatever, but don't try to play tricks on me, Mary Rae. I didn't like them when we were married and I have even less patience for them now, understood?"

She flushed again; actually looked embarrassed. It wasn't often that Mary Rae was called on her behaviour and she seemed uncharacteristically contrite now. He guessed she was serious about rekindling their relationship, getting remarried. When

Mary Rae wanted something, watch out. So he had that to look forward to. He could only imagine the fiasco with Gil Furlong, a relationship that had gone south in record time. The rodeo cowboy was famous for riding some of the rankest livestock on the circuit, but he'd bet he preferred those to what Mary Rae had probably put him through. There was never a dull moment when she was around. And now he and his ex-wife were living just a few acres apart again, and she seemed to think she still had what he was looking for.

"I understand, Hayden, and again, I'm sorry. Maybe it was wishful thinking. Friends?"

"Friends. Now just to be clear, that does not mean friends with benefits, okay? It's strictly platonic from here on out. No exceptions."

"Hayden, I've always been honest with you, right?"

"You can stand there and say that after that stunt you just pulled? Mary Rae!"

To her credit she did redden. "Okay, that prank notwithstanding...."

"Prank? How long would you have played that out if I'd believed you? No, you haven't always been honest with me, not by a long shot."

"All right then," she said as though struggling to hold onto her patience, which he had always known to be in short supply. "I said I apologize. But believe me when I tell you I think it would be good for us to get back together." She held out her hand. "See? I've put my wedding rings back on, so I don't know what I have to say or what I have to do, but I will make you understand eventually. You said you loved me when we got married. They say love doesn't die it just goes to a quieter place. I believe that's true."

He sighed, leaning his butt against the counter. Damn! "I did tell you that, of course I did. I married you, but it turned out to not be the kind of love that stands the test of time, Mary Rae."

"Admit it, you still love me."

He ran his hand over his face tiredly. After an exhausting day in the fields he did not want to go twelve rounds with his ex-wife. Men were notorious for not wanting to talk about their feelings. He knew that and he was every bit as bad as the worst of them; present situation included. He had to say something to make this stop, make it go away so he could get on with what he had planned for the evening, which was nothing. Filling his belly with whatever he could find and stretching out on that porch swing in a cool breeze. Instead he was standing in a hot kitchen arguing with Mary Rae and he knew from experience she could keep this up all night. No, he had signed off on all of this and there was no way in God's green and fertile earth he wanted any more of it.

She was a beautiful woman, that was for sure, but she would try the patience of a saint. Well, he was no saint and he was also on the impatient side himself, so bad match from the beginning. It had just taken them a while to figure all of that out, once the glow went off of the fantastic sex.

"Mary Rae, what can I say to make you understand I don't want to do this ... have this discussion with you; listen to you trying to make me have this discussion with you. I have no interest in having that happen."

"I want you to admit you still love me."

He groaned. He was about to walk out that door, get in the truck and drive to ... somewhere, anywhere but here. She had to be one of the most frustrating women he'd ever met.

"Come on, cowboy, admit it."

"Mary Rae, I don't hate you, I...."

"I knew it! You still love me! Told ya!"

"Telling someone you don't hate them is not the same as telling them you still love them, far from it."

"Well isn't hate the opposite of love. If you don't hate me that means you must love me. Admit it, Hayden, I got you."

He struggled to hold onto what was left of his patience. "The opposite of love is not hate, it's indifference and that's what I am where you're concerned. Indifferent. I wish you well, but there's never going to be a you and me again. Come on, we tried it. It didn't work. We got married too fast, we should have waited and if we had, we never would have done it."

"I suppose you would have gone back and married that little mouse in Franklin, Naomi."

"I doubt she'd have me after what I did to her, and I wouldn't blame her."

"I won you fair and square is what happened. Maybe we did marry too quickly, but I think we would have done it eventually because we were good together. And so, if we were good together once, we can be again. Your love for me isn't dead, it's just .... sleeping. But I'm not going to badger you about it."

"Eureka!"

"Stop being a wise guy, you know what I mean."

"I think I do, and you're scary when you get that look in your eye. Seriously, both parties have to be agreeable, interested, before they can try to make a relationship work and I'll say this as plainly as I can. I am not interested, Mary Rae. Stop beating a dead horse. It's not going to happen."

She covered her ears. "Not listening! It'll happen because I'll make it happen, but don't worry. We won't talk about it anymore tonight. I'm tired of talking about it right now anyway."

"Thank you!"

"Now, since at the moment we're only platonic friends and I know how you like to eat, I really did outdo myself with all of this," she said as she waved her hand over the containers waiting patiently on the counter and would likely have to be reheated in the microwave. "So the very least you can do is have the decency to eat it. If you want to take a shower, make it a fast one. I'll have everything on the table when you come down."

He nodded. He'd agree to almost anything because he was so hungry, but there was no way he was going to strip off and get in the shower because he didn't trust her to get in there with him. That was not going to happen. One pregnancy scare was enough. He had no protection in the house and the last thing he wanted to do was make a baby with Mary Rae Sutherlyn, because thankfully she'd never given up her maiden name. Her father threatened her if she did take Hayden's name, he would see she was disinherited, and ... well, money talks. He'd been more than a little upset about her not taking the Barlowe name at the time, but it had turned out to be one of those blessings in disguise.

"Okay, we'll eat," he agreed, "I'm starved."

"Oooh, you're all sweaty, Hayden. Go shower."

"I'll shower after I eat, but I will go up and grab a T-shirt."

She looked him up and down. "Don't do it on my account. I kind of like the way you look right now. Sexy!"

"Whatever," he mumbled as he took the stairs two at a time, grabbed a T-shirt out of the laundry he hadn't had a chance to fold, and hurried back downstairs.

"Still sexy," she told him when he walked back into the kitchen, "although you know I prefer you half-naked. But you're cute in a T-shirt too."

He ignored her. "Now you say you cooked up a feast, so let's eat. I'd say we could move one of those smaller tables out onto the veranda and eat out there because it's too hot in here. Can we do that?"

"Have you got two small tables?"

"I'm sure I can find another one."

"Good, we'll put the food on one and our plates on the other and that way save steps running back and forth from the kitchen to the veranda."

And so the meal ensemble was arranged and to her credit Mary Rae's supper was delicious. She'd prepared Salisbury steak, buttered vegetables and homemade rolls. He hadn't realized just how ravenous he was until he began to eat and then it was damn the torpedoes and full speed ahead. And for dessert she'd made an apple pie, which was still warm thank you very much. Retrieving the carton of vanilla ice cream from the fridge, she added two generous helpings to his slice. It disappeared in record time and she'd even thought to bring a thermos of tea, steeped to perfection. When he was finished he pushed himself away from the table, satisfied, and moved to the porch swing. He didn't stretch out on it as he'd been planning to do, instead politely leaving room for her to sit. After a meal like that she could have anything she wanted ... except him.

Never one to miss an opportunity, she claimed the spot beside him and got the swing in motion, creating a most welcome breeze.

"I'll clean up later," she told him, holding her face up to catch the cooler air. "Let's just sit here awhile and let our food digest."

"I'll clean up after you leave."

She turned to face him, her hands on her hips, which she accomplished prettily despite the fact she was sitting. "Oh so you eat my meal and then kick me out! Nice."

He groaned inwardly. He should never have accepted her hospitality, but then again that meal was worth the angst that was sure to follow. She'd want to stay the night. After all, didn't one good turn deserve another? Not in this case. There would be no sleepover.

"I'm hardly kicking you out, Mary Rae. I'm just saying I'll do the clean up. You went to all the trouble of preparing such a nice supper, the least I can do is take care of the mess."

"Oh," she said, pulling in her horns. "Okay, sounds like a plan. I never like to leave a messy kitchen behind before I go to bed. I hope you won't be mad, but I took the liberty of taking a peek through the house before you got home. Is the room at the end of the hall with the double bed and a picture of some girl pinned to the wall, yours? That would be Naomi I assume. Did I get the right one?"

Anger flashed through him. "You went through the house when I wasn't here? It was bad enough you made yourself at home in the kitchen. I thought you'd have better manners than to go snooping through all the rooms. I can't believe you!"

"Hey! Sorry! Don't get all mad. If you didn't want anyone looking through your house you should have locked your door. Geez, I didn't take anything."

He hadn't thought it was necessary to lock the door since he was still on the ranch; no one he knew of in this tiny close-knit community had ever locked their doors. He'd certainly do so from now on though. Her nosing around really ticked him off, and she announced it as though she had every right to do so.

He held onto his temper with an effort.

"First of all I don't want you going through my house."

She chuckled sarcastically. "Your house."

"Yes, my house. And you had no business going into my bedroom. That was way over the line, Mary Rae."

"You're just mad because I saw that picture. Tell me, did she give it to you recently or was it from before? She looks young, so I'm assuming it's the former because I tell you, if it's not, she's going to get a run for her money. I'm the one you married, not her. She had her chance and she didn't measure up, remember? There's no way I'm going to stand by and let her worm her way back in."

He stared at her in open-mouthed astonishment. "You're unbelievable ... off the charts unbelievable."

"So are you back together again with little miss goody two shoes?"

"Mary Rae, go home."

"Nope! I plan to stay the night," she said, reaching over and sliding her hand up under the faded blue T-shirt. "And don't tell me you don't think that's a good idea because I won't believe you. And by the way, I'm on the pill. I always have been so there's no worries. We can have the same kind of wild ride you used to like when we were together, and don't bother to say you don't miss that. You told me often enough I was getting it right and guess what, sweetie, I still can."

Pushing her hand away, he stood up. "Okay, we're not going to do this. You have to go."

Her face fell. "Hayden, please don't turn me away tonight. Even if you didn't care for me at all before, please care now. I'm lonely. I knock around alone in that big old house all day, and that's fine. That's my lifestyle and I enjoy it, but my nights are horrible. I long to be held by a man the way you used to hold me."

"So that's it. You can't find another man so I'll do."

"It's not like that at all. I still have deep feelings for you, and just so you know, my love has not gone to a quieter place. It's still right here waiting like it always was."

"Like it always was? Mary Rae, you ran around on me at the end. You were having an affair with that Gil Furlong and you were only too happy to agree to a divorce because you thought you could get him to marry you, only it didn't turn out that way. You found out in a hurry you couldn't control him any more than you could control me, didn't you? And now you're high and dry and you think you can get us going again."

"You're mean!"

"No, I'm honest and there's a difference."

"So I made some mistakes, but I'm a good person. I'm not the bitch you're trying to make me out to be."

"That's what you act like sometimes. You're so damned persistent! You. Never. Let. Go. Ever. Mary Rae, have some self-respect and stop begging to get back in. I can't think of any other way to say it than I'm not interested. Period."

"Can't we still be friends?"

He groaned, throwing his head back. If this were any other circumstance he'd think he was being pranked. See what Hayden does with an impossible woman, only this was no prank and he'd never in his life met anyone as unrelenting. Once her claws were sunk in it was impossible to get them out ... like now. It wouldn't matter what he said. She refused to hear him. How had he ever married her in the beginning? It was said love is blind, or in his case, lust was blind because he'd gone into the whole thing willingly. It was like a blood oath. He was in it for life, no matter what the paperwork said.

"Mary Rae, I'm tired. I want to go to bed."

"I can massage those aches and pains right out of those tired muscles. I'll have you purring in no time flat."

"I meant go to bed alone. No massage, just a nice hot shower and I'll be off to dreamland."

A massage would feel great though. He remembered how good she was when it came to relaxing stiff sore muscles and working out the stress. The problem was, she'd been the cause of his stress most of the time. Naomi came to mind and although they'd never been intimate, he couldn't help but imagine now how wonderful it would have been. Her personality was so different from Mary Rae's, night and day really. Naomi had a gentler, sweeter personality. Oh she could be feisty, but not like this. He wished he had it to do over again, but then life did not come with a rewind button. It was true she'd gotten carried away with the wedding plans, but he rightly blamed it on youth.

Mary Rae was giving him her most radiant smile. "The bed I saw was big enough for two."

"So?"

"So, why sleep alone if you don't have to? It doesn't make sense."

"I want to sleep alone."

"For the rest of your life?"

"If I have to, yes."

"A handsome guy like you? What a waste. Hayden, you're even more sexy than when we were together. I can barely keep my hands off you."

"Mary Rae, it's time for you to go. It's not cool to act like this, not cool at all. Why would you want to stay someplace where you're not wanted?"

"Because I know you're going to come to your senses one of these days and realize you've made a mistake."

"I came to my senses years ago, that's why I asked you for a divorce. I don't see that as a mistake. Now, I want you to walk out that door."

"Fine, I can see you're tired and in a bad mood so I will go but what about my dishes?"

"I'll wash them and pack them up for you and leave them on the veranda. You can pick them up tomorrow, or whenever you want."

"What about the leftovers?"

"What about them? If you want me to save them I'll put them in containers and leave them with the dishes."

"A lot of good they'd be after they sit in the hot sun all day. No, you can have them if you want to be like that. And when you eat them, think of the woman who loves you so much she slaved away for an entire afternoon. And remember while you're at it, your way of saying thank you was to tell me to go home after you'd eaten. That doesn't sound too nice, does it? But that's the way you're acting."

He rolled his eyes heavenward. "I'm not going one more round with you tonight. I want you to leave, but not without me saying thank you again and telling you how much I appreciate you cooking supper for ... us."

She stood to go, taking a tentative first step down the stairs before turning back toward him. "Bye for now, Hayden," she said with that Cheshire cat smile of hers.

Plunking back down on the swing he watched as she made her way to her car, putting as much sway into her strut as she could manage. She waved goodbye before accelerating to the main road, typically not checking for traffic before she hit the pavement. Her tires shrieked their disapproval as she took the turn a little too fast.

He breathed a deep, cleansing sigh of relief as he could see her taillights growing smaller in the distance then disappear over the hill. He thought of the supper again. Boy, that was some meal, but the asking price was more than he could afford. If she came armed with food again he would have no choice but to turn her away. He would take no pleasure in hurting her feelings, but she was the type of person who didn't insult easily and refused to take no for an answer.

He felt guilty as he scraped the leftovers into some of Gram's old plastic ware and set them in the fridge. The reality was if he didn't want her attention he shouldn't be taking her food and vowed again it would be the last time he did. He next scrubbed all of the metal containers she'd brought the food over in, found a large shopping bag and carefully piled everything inside and set them on the veranda for pick-up tomorrow.

And then just as he'd originally planned, he took a refreshing shower. Returning to the veranda he stretched out on the old swing, well as much as it would accommodate his height, and promptly fell asleep. Something woke him just after dark and he sat up quickly. And then he heard it again. It was his cellphone on the kitchen table and he hurried to answer it. He was more than pleased to hear his mother's voice.

"How's everything going, honey?" she asked, and in that moment he missed her with a fierce longing.

True she had travelled west to visit him at the dude ranch last year, but he'd like to see a lot more of her now that he was closer. They engaged in the usual idle chitchat that usually kicked off a conversation, and then she surprised him when she said: "I had a call from a certain young woman tonight."

His heartbeat quickened. "Naomi called you?"

"Naomi! No, not Naomi. Mary Rae called me earlier."

"Mary Rae! What on earth was she calling you about? And how did she get your number?"

Then he remembered. His mother's telephone number was on the wall by the old landline phone in the kitchen. That woman! She missed nothing!

"I'm not sure how she got my number, but she told me the two of you are considering reconciling. By the way she spoke it was probably going to happen."

He counted to ten mentally to keep from shouting. "I can't believe that! You're not pulling my leg? She actually said that?"

"Yes, dear, she actually said that. I'm not making it up. And there's something else. She also hinted she might be pregnant. Is there some kind of an announcement you'd like to make?"

He was breathing heavily now. "The whole thing is nothing but a load of hooey!"

Was that a sigh of relief he heard? "Okay, because I thought you were glad the two of you were divorced. You're a grown man and you can do as you like, it's just that it would be helpful to have a heads up as to the family dynamics, that's all. I wouldn't want to stick my foot in my mouth by accident if I came to visit."

"Believe me, Mum, if we did get back together I'd certainly let you know, but that's never going to happen. I divorced her for a reason and I have no intention of undoing that. I'm happy the way I am, but she keeps coming over and trying to change my mind. She's wasting her time though and that's all there is to it. And she's not pregnant, not by me anyway."

She laughed. "I'm relieved to hear that too, honey. Sooo ... I don't want to stick my nose in where it's not wanted, or play matchmaker as you put it, but I am curious. What did Naomi say when you called her."

There was a moment of hesitation. "She didn't say anything because I haven't called her."

"Yet."

"I don't know, Mum. It's been such a long time and besides, I'd probably get shot down in flames. I've got enough problems with Mary Rae, again. I don't need to go looking for grief from another woman. I should just leave well enough alone."

"Maybe it wouldn't be like that."

"And maybe it would. On the other hand maybe I should give her the satisfaction of telling me off, because she was so hurt way back when. All she did was cry. I betcha now she could give it to me pretty good."

"You've got big shoulders, Hayden. You can take it, but please make that call. If there's nothing there, there's nothing there. I don't believe you when you say you don't even want to try. Swallow that confounded pride of yours and check it out. If you want Mary Rae to back off, there's no better way than letting her see you've gotten on with your life."

"I wouldn't even know where to start looking for Naomi."

"How about the phone book? I found her number for you, got a pen handy?"

# Chapter Ten

He'd been only too happy to get Naomi's telephone number that night, but now three more weeks had passed and he still hadn't made the call. It had been an exceptionally busy time as the full heat of summer settled over the valley. Haymaking was in full swing in the surrounding countryside. He'd decided to go with round bales, their size meaning less work in the long run and Duke's old tractor was still serviceable enough that he'd easily be able to feed the herd. He certainly had enough land to make his own hay, but his grandfather's ancient baler was completely caput and he couldn't afford the price of an expensive round baler at the moment. It was the cheaper option to pay someone else to make it for him.

At the present time he had a lot less cattle to feed though because the price of beef topped out and he quickly sold off most of his herd. That had put some much-needed funds in the bank and paid Walt for his time. He'd add another bunch of feeders to the herd in a week or so.

The best thing about the past three weeks was there'd been no sign of Mary Rae. She'd come and picked up her containers from the veranda but hadn't left so much as a note. Still, he kept both the front and back doors securely locked. He wouldn't have put it past her to climb in a window, but she had apparently chosen not to go that route. Probably scared she'd break one of those long polished nails of hers. Whatever the reason, he was grateful she had gotten the message they were well and truly done. He thanked his lucky stars she'd decided to back off and not give him any further trouble.

It was a beautiful Saturday morning and he sat on the old swing with coffee in hand, feeling like a man who was finally coming into his own on the Summer Vale Ranch. He had for the most part laid all of his ghosts to rest concerning his untimely departure from the ranch, and was closer, as his mother had suggested, to forgiving the man who had hurt him so deeply. He was even making some headway on the necessary refurbishments in general, and every pasture was now securely fenced. He was immensely proud of that fact alone.

He checked his watch. Six o'clock. Time to get up and get going if he wanted to get anything done before it got too hot. He thought about his next project. He'd like to have fresh eggs, so planned to invest in a flock of laying hens. Buster Crandall from down the road had told him at the store the other day he might have a few he'd be willing to part with and that's all he'd need. That meant building a new chicken coop, seeing as how a good sneeze in the right direction would finish bringing the old one down.

He thought again about Naomi and knew he had to stop putting off calling her. It had been on his mind day and night since his mother had given him the number, and he was grateful she hadn't called for an update. She was likely giving him lots of space because she knew how he thought; he wouldn't make a move on this until he was good and ready. Now he was good and ready and would make that call tonight. No fail. At seven o'clock. That seemed like the right time because she'd likely be finished with supper by then. If she were going out for the evening, it would still be too early to leave. Yes, seven it was.

He had a plan too. If a man answered he'd say he had the wrong number, apologize, and hang up. But at least he'd have his answer. He'd once and for all come to terms with the fact she was out of his life for good, again, and move on, with anyone but Mary Rae.

The lumber for the coop had already been delivered, so quickly draining his cup he carried it inside, let the horses out for the day and then made for the dilapidated old hen house over in back of the first barn. By noon he had the other mess hauled to the burn pile and the new building framed up.

Walt and Alice had gone away for a couple of days to see their daughter in Fredericton, although Walt had tried to postpone the trip when he found out Hayden intended to build a new coop. He'd refused his friend's help, telling him to go and relax for a change. He was looking forward to tackling the project on his own.

He grabbed a quick lunch and went back to work a half hour later. By suppertime he had the whole thing boarded in. He'd put the window in tomorrow, as well as hang the door. He also needed to install the roosts and nest boxes, but that was minor. He'd be ready to get the chickens day after tomorrow, as well as stop by the feed store to stock up; accordingly, pick up some salt licks for the cattle while he was there.

And now here he was, showered, changed and sitting beside the old landline phone with Naomi's number in front of him. He'd decided to keep the landline hooked up in the interests of privacy, seeing as how anyone could listen in to his cellphone calls or even a cordless phone, on a scanner if they chose to. He felt like a teenager looking to make a date with a pretty girl and scared out of his wits to even pick up the receiver. Big, strong, tough Hayden Barlowe, as nervous as a schoolboy. Ridiculous, he told himself. Dial the damned number already. And so he did. She answered on the third ring and his mouth immediately turned to sawdust.

"Hello?" she said again. "Who's calling?"

"Naomi?" It made sense to make sure he had the right person before he made a fool of himself, although he certainly recognized the soft lilt of her voice. It felt like the first time he'd ever called to ask her out and cursed himself for a fool that he had ever walked away. He'd thought a million times about talking to her again, apologizing, again, and now that moment of reckoning was at hand.

"This is Naomi."

He cleared his throat, now as equally as dry as his mouth. "Hi, Naomi ... this is Hayden."

There was a prolonged silence on the other end of the line, but at least she hadn't hung up yet. There was still that chance though and he realized he was holding his breath. Still she said nothing, so he waited for what seemed like an interminable period of time before he spoke again.

"Naomi?"

"Is this really Hayden Barlowe?"

"Yes," he said, "it's me. How are you?"

"I'm fine, why are you calling me?"

His heart was thumping so hard he was sure she could hear it all the way down in Franklin. "I'm calling to say hello."

"Okay, you're married so why are you calling to say hello?"

"I'm not married anymore, haven't been for quite a few years."

"So why did you wait so long to get in touch with me?"

It sounded as though she was still interested, so at least that was encouraging. He plunged ahead, hoping she didn't hear the deep breath he took to calm himself. He hadn't realized how much was riding on this call, well he did, but it wasn't until she picked up the receiver that it suddenly became very real. If she'd hung up, he wasn't quite sure what he'd have done then. The disappointment would have been terrible because she was the only woman he was interested in having in his life now.

"It's been such a long time I figured you'd be married or something. Are you?"

"No, I came close not that long ago, but I knew I couldn't go through with it and broke it off. I guess you know what that feels like, breaking someone's heart."

He deserved that. He had done his best at the time to let her down gently, but there were no soft landings when it came to the heart. It was just a face full of pain. And now judging by what she'd just said that pain had never gone away. He sensed her anger too and figured she had plenty she still wanted to say to him. That was okay. Let her say it.

"I guess you're right about that," he said, choosing his words carefully. "It's not an easy thing to do, especially when you care about that person."

"Yes, care, I guess, but not enough to marry them. So why are you calling me now, Hayden?"

He released another pent-up breath. "Because I was hoping maybe I could see you, take you for coffee ... dinner ... a walk, I don't know. I'm not very good at this, Naomi. I rehearsed what I was going to say to you a thousand times, but now it sounds lame. The truth is I had to swallow my pride to even make this call, to tell you I made a mistake, married the wrong woman. You were right all along. You and I should have gotten married. As it turned out, Mary Rae was not the one for me."

"You don't have to say you're sorry, you said that the night you told me our relationship was not going to work out." She paused. "But I know I have to take a lot of the blame too. I held on too tight, I ... wouldn't have sex with you." She laughed bitterly. "I wouldn't even let you get close as I recall because it'd be too tempting.... Anyway...."

"Aww, Naomi, you were so young and there's nothing wrong with wanting to wait until your wedding night. I can understand all of that now, but to a young guy ... well, I made the wrong choice is all I can say and I'm sorry."

"You know something, Hayden? I've held on to the hope all these years you would come back. Isn't that dumb? It's not that I wished your marriage would fail, although.... What I'm trying to say is I never stopped loving you, even though you walked away and married someone else."

"I'll always feel bad about that."

"Don't. People do what they think is right at the time. Like I said, I just did the same thing myself; broke somebody's heart and it was really awful. I felt terrible about doing it, I always will, but it would have been wrong to go through with marrying him."

"I tried to make my marriage work, but I think she always knew I still had feelings for you."

"Things can be complicated sometimes."

"Very true. So ... do you think you'd like to see me?"

"You're saying you want us to try to pick up where we left off?"

He shook his head although he knew she couldn't see it. "No, too much time has passed and we'd have to get to know each other again. We have a lot to catch up on, like twelve years."

"Date for a while maybe?" she asked. "See how it goes? Is that what you're saying?"

"Sure, that sounds like how we should go about it. Maybe in time we can get to where we need to be in this. I'd like to take it slow."

"Absolutely, I couldn't agree with you more."

He smiled. "Are you available for dinner tomorrow night?"

"Sure!" she said without hesitation.

They both started laughing.

"So much for taking it slow," she said, still laughing, "but I do need time to think, Hayden. The last thing I ever expected was to hear your voice on the other end of the line."

"I won't try to pressure you into anything, Naomi."

"Nor me, you. I'm a grown woman now, not some teenager with stars in her eyes."

He couldn't seem to stop smiling. "I hope you don't mind if I still have some in mine. I'm holding your picture right now, the one you gave me to pin up beside my bed. I took it off the wall and brought it down with me."

There was silence on the other end of the line, quite a few seconds worth. "I don't know what to say. I'm surprised you still have it after all this time."

"You were so cute, so innocent."

"Heavy on the innocent."

"Well, what else would you expect at seventeen ... eighteen? I know you still have those big blue eyes, but is your hair still long?"

"As a matter of fact it is. Not down my back the way it once was, but long enough."

"I love long hair, and it looked so nice on you."

She laughed.

"What's so funny?"

"You might be interested to know after you and I broke up I went and had it cut in the teeniest, tiniest pixie cut they'd give me. It was barely peeking through my scalp."

"You did not! You cut off all that beautiful hair?"

"I did! Women do that sometimes, especially if the guy liked long hair. It's a revenge thing, but I was sorry I did it as soon as I looked in the mirror. I was horrified. My sister Ginger wears hers longer now too because her husband likes it that way."

He tried to picture Naomi in a short haircut, the one she'd just described, but couldn't. "I'm glad it's long again, but it really wouldn't matter much at the end of the day because you'd look pretty no matter how you wore your hair. You're beautiful, Naomi."

"Thank you, Hayden. I imagine you've changed quite a lot in twelve years too. Do you still have hair?"

He chuckled heartily. That was Naomi, straight to the point, but that was something he'd always loved about her. "Yep, still lots of hair but I'm in my thirties now so I can expect a few grey ones to start showing up anytime."

They chatted for another half hour before they finally said good-bye. Hayden felt as though he was about a foot off the floor when he finally hung up because he was so happy. He'd taken the chance and couldn't believe how fortunate he'd been with the pay-off. He only waited a couple of minutes before he called his mother and told her about their conversation; that they had a date scheduled for the following evening. Predictably, Peggy was delighted with his success and spared him the inevitable I told you so.

The next day drug by at a snail's pace despite the fact that he kept busy. He not only finished the chicken coop and fenced in a sizeable run but drove over to get the chickens and stocked up at the feed store ... all before noontime! The sky had been dark with clouds all day and finally burst in a series of heavy showers as the afternoon wore on. He'd hoped it would be a good evening and maybe they could sit out on Sailor Jack's open-air patio on the waterfront but given the bad turn in the weather it wasn't going to happen. That was the restaurant Naomi had chosen for their date, and since they both loved seafood it was a good fit.

He was combing his hair in the mirror after his shower, when he realized he should have taken the time for a haircut or at least a trim. He had never worn his hair short, always just about collar length, but over the past few weeks it might have inched down a tad more. Oh well, it was too late now so he'd just have to go with the way it was. He never worried much about appearances, but he'd bought a crisp white western shirt and polished his boots to a high sheen. Paired with his faded denims he thought he looked about as good as he was going to get. He considered new jeans, but that would look like he was trying too hard. He was trying, yes, but he didn't want to overdo it.

He'd even pulled the old truck into the garage where he washed and waxed it and had to say it looked very nice when he was finished. It had a little age on it, okay a lot of age, but there was no rust he could see, although the paint was a bit faded. He got the chrome to look some shiny though. He felt sixteen again and polishing up the truck for a Saturday night date. He would have liked to have a fancy convertible to impress the girls but he was just glad to have any wheels at all because at sixteen, not many farm boys did. The Sutherlyns would be the exception in the valley. Never any shortage of cash there and while Brian Sutherlyn was several years older than he was, he could never remember a time growing up that his neighbour wasn't tooling around in something expensive. The cars had always looked great, but nothing could be done about the idiot behind the wheel.

He left in plenty of time for Franklin because he didn't want to be late. He was relieved at least the rain had stopped, although the sun didn't bother to put in an appearance. In fact it was as foggy as pea soup by the time he got to the city. He worried more than a little about the hours that lie ahead. He didn't want to do anything this time around to mess up and he still had to pinch himself that he was going to have dinner with Naomi Martel. If anyone had told him two months ago he'd be back on the ranch, actually own it, and about to go out on a date with his former fiancé, he would have said they were crazy. Yet here he was in that exact circumstance. Life had a funny way of turning things upside down, and ironically the man who'd torn the rug out from under him twelve years ago had made all of this possible with his passing. Maybe in his own way he knew his dying could make everything right.

Maybe his grandfather had wanted to fix things before he died, remembering what Walt had told him about seeing the old man cry. He just hadn't been able to get past his pride. More's the pity. But tonight was not a time for feeling bad, it was for being happy. He was so excited to see Naomi again his stomach was crowded with butterflies that didn't seem to have any intention of settling down, no matter what he told them. So he'd just go with the flow and hope for the best. He had one more stop to make before reaching her apartment complex. He found what he was looking for, a nice big bouquet of daisies and he was smiling to himself as he had his purchase wrapped to go. Daisies were Naomi's favourite flower.

* * *

Naomi changed her mind at least a half dozen times about what to wear, finally deciding on a cute little red and gold paisley shift she'd picked up on a shopping trip to Bangor. It had been over a month now since the miscarriage and although she felt more like her old self, she had lost weight over the past weeks because of the stress she'd been under. She had not heard from Ritchie since that night, and hoped she wouldn't. She still felt bad about how things had ended between them but knew in her heart she'd done the right thing. If she were Mrs. Jamieson right now, she would not be in a good place.

She now had a better understanding about what Hayden had done all those years ago, and why. But she was being given a second chance with the love of her life. It didn't get any better than that.

* * *

There'd been quite a workload to get through last night because things had slipped a little during her slump, and it had required a gargantuan effort to concentrate on what she was doing. She'd had to take extra time to ensure her codes checked out before she signed off and correct any mistakes.

She'd had all day to sleep but had only managed to get a few hours because when she closed her eyes she was immediately transported back to the phone call that had turned her world upside down last night. In a million years she would not have expected Hayden to be on the other end of the line. What if she had married Ritchie, and then

Hayden called? It would have been a much worse mess and didn't bear thinking about. Could life really be that cruel?

She finished drying her hair, put in a few curls with the curling iron and nearly burned herself because she was all thumbs. She applied minimal make-up and stood back to consider her reflection. Would he think she'd aged too much? Maybe she wasn't in too bad shape, but she was hardly the doe-eyed, eighteen year-old he remembered. She knew what picture he was talking about that she'd given him. It had been taken on graduation night, so no, she didn't look the same.

Her doorbell rang just as she was fastening the little gold chain belt around her waist, and she was trembling as she hurried to the door and opened it. And there stood Hayden, carrying a bouquet of daisies. She gaped, she knew that's what she was doing but couldn't help it. If she thought he was handsome at twenty-three, he was drop dead gorgeous at thirty-five, yet in a typically understated way. He was not one to stand on ceremony, she remembered, but now he looked different. For one thing his shoulders looked wider, fuller. He had filled out more, was more muscled, his hair a tad overlong but it only made him look sexier. Could he be taller? No! Not possible, but he looked formidable standing there in his boots and hat and jeans and shirt, all of which he wore to perfection. A big man, holding a bouquet of daisies ... and there was a sadness in his

216

eyes. She could see it, although if she mentioned it he would likely deny it. Pretend that everything was fine.

It was as though there had been no intervening years, her heart as full of love for him now as it had ever been. Tears sprang to her eyes, and even though he was smiling that sexy, slow smile she remembered so well, were those tears in his eyes too? Yes! He felt the same way, and every fibre of her being sang a praise of gratitude.

"Can I come in?" he asked in that drawl that was his alone.

She took the daisies, hoping he didn't notice the tremble in her hand. "I'm sorry! Please come in. You come all this way and I leave you standing on the doorstop. Oh, Hayden, it's wonderful to see you again. It's just that you look ... different."

"Well I'm a full-grown man now, not a twenty-three year-old kid who thought he had the world by the tail and knew everything. And you, Naomi, you look even more beautiful than I remembered. You look like a little girl in that picture now that I see you in person."

"A little girl who was in love with getting married. When I look back I wasn't mature enough to take that step but I thought I knew everything there was to know about it at the time."

"I'm still so sorry about how that turned out, Naomi."

217

She waved it away. "I can see now I drove you into the arms of another woman. As they say timing is everything, and the time just wasn't right for us back then. It almost killed me to lose you, but look, now we've found our way back to each other. I can't believe you and I are going out on a date tonight. I'm not dreaming, am I?"

He chuckled and she remembered how much she loved it when he laughed. He didn't do it often enough. She'd chided him on more than one occasion for being too serious; tried to loosen him up. It also occurred to her it was a case of the pot calling the kettle black.

"No, you're not dreaming because if you are, I'm right in there with you."

She was smiling so hard it hurt, but it was a good kind of pain considering past challenges. "You can have a seat in the living room if you like," she told him, pointing the way, "and thank you for the flowers. That was very thoughtful of you."

He went into the living room and sat down. "This is a great place you have here. I think you've done very well for yourself by the looks of this," he told her as she lingered in the doorway as though reluctant to leave him even for a second. "I have to warn you I'm driving Gramp's old pick-up. I hope you don't mind. It'll take me a while to get on my feet now that I've taken over the ranch. That's where all my money's going at the moment. To get it up and running the way it used to be."

Mind! She'd share a skateboard as long as it was with Hayden. "Mind? Not at all, you know I don't care about things like that. Okay, I'll be right back, I don't want these to wilt," and she happily smelled the flowers as she headed for the kitchen to find a vase for the beautiful bouquet. She was back in the living room in minutes, setting the daisies on the coffee table.

He smiled as he looked at his watch. "I don't mean to rush you, but maybe we should get going. Our reservation is for six and it's nearly that now."

\* \* \*

Heads turned when they walked into Sailor Jack's, Naomi and her tall dark cowboy, but she was in a world of her own. Hayden had come back to her. She was actually with him, and he seemed just as pleased to be with her.

She was sure she'd eaten something from her plate of succulent seafood, she seemed to recall doing that, although for the most part they were content just to look into each other's eyes. And they talked, catching up on twelve years worth of living. She told him about Ritchie and the baby and he held her hand tightly as he saw her fight back tears. He comforted her, and that was the Hayden she remembered, so kind,

219

thoughtful and gentle. She listened too while he told her what had happened to him when he married Mary Rae, how his grandfather had turfed him off the ranch. Banished him from his life and the couple had gone to live in the west as far away from Summer Vale as he could get and still stay in the country.

That made her profoundly sad because she remembered Duke Barlowe as a kindly man and she'd thought highly of him as she had of Hayden's mother, Peggy. Everyone had been onboard as her and Hayden's wedding plans progressed ... Naomi happily keeping them in the loop. Then, well, things had spun out of control and Hayden had changed the course of both their lives. Nevertheless, with the grace of time they were together again.

They had both agreed to go slow this time around, but there was no mistaking they were still in love. That in itself was exciting, but she felt she needed time and space yet to heal from her recent ordeal and he agreed to give her that. When they kissed goodnight at her door later that evening it was clear the same fires of passion still burned brightly. She happily accepted when he invited her to the ranch on Saturday.

* * *

Hayden drove back to Bloomfield a happy man. He even found a good country station on the old radio and cranked the sound, lost in the moment. He felt as though a thousand pounds had been lifted from his shoulders and knew as he climbed into bed that sleep wouldn't be visiting him anytime soon. He was still pumped from his date. It was much too soon to start making plans for the future again, he wouldn't jinx things by getting into that right now, but he knew how he hoped they would go.

Later, in bed, the old grandfather clock in the living room downstairs bonged twelve times, proof that he'd been lying awake for an hour. He was not the least bit tired as his mind continued its exciting review of the evening.

He heard another sound above the musical bongs. Now what was that, someone at the door possibly? He focused his full attention on listening. No, there was no knock at the door and climbing out of bed he opened the curtains. His bedroom window overlooked the front yard, but there was nobody there. It must have been the wind. It could have come up some since he'd arrived back home although it didn't sound as though it was blowing.

Getting back in bed he settled down once again, his mind drifting back to Naomi of its own volition. He smiled, feeling exactly like that smitten young man of so many years ago. The truth was he was still smitten. He'd just been too pigheaded to do anything about it … before now.

He heard the sound again. No, it wasn't the door. He listened carefully. Someone was in the house!

# Chapter Eleven

Mary Rae! It had to be! But how did she get in?

Throwing back the covers he swung his feet to the floor, grabbed his jeans off the nearby chair and hauled them on, zipping them up as he padded quietly from his room into the hall where he stood and listened. Nothing. Maybe it had just been the wind, but his gut told him otherwise.

He crept silently down the stairs and as his fingers sought the light switch at the bottom, he was struck on the side of the head with a solid object. He stumbled backwards, momentarily stunned, but quickly righted himself. He found the switch, flooding the hallway with bright light. A table lamp was lying on the floor next to the stairs. Obviously that's what had been thrown at him. He stepped past it and into the living room just in time to see a pair of sneakered feet disappear out the living room window, the bottom sash thrown high. Whoever had been in the house was now gone, there was no point in giving chase. How far would he get in bare feet? Besides whoever had dived through that window, obviously leaving the way they'd come in, would have more than a few scratches from the thorns on the huge rose bush outside. Good! Let them leave a little skin behind!

Leaning out the window he looked out into the night and was about to turn away when he noticed the soles of another pair of sneakers just barely visible from behind the sofa. It looked like there had been two of them involved, the second burglar hiding behind furniture. He closed the window, locked it, then turned back into the room.

"Okay, you can come out now," Hayden announced.

There was no movement, whoever was in those sneakers obviously believed they were well hidden and likely planned to make good their escape after Hayden went back to bed.

"I told you to come out from behind the sofa," he said, standing astride as he waited for the thief to show himself.

At least he knew it wasn't Mary Rae, and that provided some measure of relief. The sneakers moved, started shimmying toward him and a moment later a teenage boy pushed himself all the way out and stood with his back to the wall, defiant.

"Come on, sit on the sofa" Hayden told him. "I want to talk to you."

The youth hesitated a moment, then moved to the sofa and sat down stiffly, tears in his eyes.

"What are you doing in my house?" he demanded of the kid.

The boy did not answer, his eyes locked on Hayden.

"How old are you?" Hayden asked him.

"Fifteen," said the boy, his lower lip visibly shaking.

"I asked you what you were doing in my house! What were you looking for?"

The boy's eyes darted about the room as though still considering flight. "You can't keep me here if I don't want to stay! It's against the law!"

"So is being in my house, now I asked you what you were doing in here. What were you trying to steal?"

"I want to go home."

"Okay, play it your way. I'm about to call the police and have them come out here. You can explain it all to them, but then of course they'll have to charge you."

"You're going to call the police anyway, so what's the difference?"

Hayden folded his arms but remained standing. "I want to know what you were looking for. Tell me! And what did your buddy get that he took out the window with him?"

"Nothing! He just got away is all."

"And left you here to take the fall. He's some buddy. Now answer my question."

"We didn't take anything, because we couldn't find...."

"Find what?" Hayden demanded when the youth fell silent. "What were you looking for?"

"Money! Okay?"

"Money! What makes you think I have any money in here?"

"You were working out west, weren't you? Everybody knows people go out there to work and end up getting rich. We figured you brought tons of money home with you."

Hayden had to laugh, which only made his prisoner angrier. "Money! You don't get rich working on a ranch, kid. So no, I didn't come home with big bucks. Even if I did what gives you the right to come in here and try to take it from me? Breaking and entering is against the law in case no one ever explained that to you."

"They can't do anything to you if you're under eighteen."

"Well aren't you the smart-ass! Who are you? Where do you live?"

The kid folded his arms and looked away. "None of your business."

Hayden watched the kid trying to be brave but it was obvious he was scared out of his wits. "I'm going to tell you something, buddy-boy, unless you want my next step to be toward the telephone to call the police, you'd better change your attitude, fast."

"You can't hold me here!" the kid shouted.

"I can until the police come and then you're all theirs. I don't have to see you again until we're in court. Now what's it going to be? Talk to me or talk to them? Your choice."

He was glad for the sake of the kid's good sense to see his words had their desired effect, as the boy's tears began to fall in earnest. It appeared he'd decided to give up any attempt at false bravado as he swiped at his eyes with both hands.

"It's not fair I have to go through this. It wasn't even my idea."

"What's your friend's name?"

The kid squared his shoulders, although he was still blubbering. "I'm not going to tell you. I'm not a rat."

"Okay, how old is he?"

"Seventeen."

Hayden took a step closer. "I asked you what your name is and I want you to tell me. Now!"

The boy pushed back against the sofa cushions as though to distance himself from the man who was now standing much closer. "Are you going to call the police?"

"That's up to you."

"If you don't, what are you going to do to me?"

"That depends."

"On what?" The boy was crying harder, his hands occupied trying to wipe the tears away but losing the battle as they continued to flow copiously.

"Again, on you."

"I don't know what you mean," he hiccupped.

"I think you do. I asked you what your name is."

"I don't have to tell you that. I know my rights."

Hayden shrugged. "Okay, have it your way," and turning to the phone sitting on the side table, picked up the receiver.

"Wait! Don't call! My name is Dana Warden."

Hayden hung up. "Dana! Any relation to Minnie and Purdy Warden?"

The boy went even paler when Hayden made the family connection, nodding miserably, hunched over, sobbing. "They're my grandparents," he managed.

Hayden ran a hand through his hair, tilting his head back and releasing a long sigh. A local boy. "So you're Dave and Lorna's son?"

The kid nodded again.

Hayden shook his head. He'd held this kid when he was a baby, had seen him when he was just a toddler a few months before his exodus from the ranch; now this. Little did he know the kid would grow up to do B&E's.

Exasperated, Hayden sat down on the matching ottoman, not taking his eyes off the blonde boy. He'd thought he'd looked slightly familiar and it sickened him to see what that cute curly-haired little boy had turned into. A thief. A punk. The tears were a hopeful sign the kid wasn't all that experienced yet. He was scared, yes, and he had good reason to be. It was definitely a matter for the police, but he couldn't very well turn in the son of childhood friends. And of course the boy had cooperated, so he would keep his word too. How ironic, Dana's grandparents had been the first at his door to welcome him back, and a few weeks later their grandson had come into his house through a window planning to steal from him.

Drawing another even breath he continued to study the boy. "What do you think I should do with you, Dana? I mean you and your buddy not only broke into my house, but your friend also tried to take me out with a lamp."

"We didn't break anything, just came in through an open window."

"Don't play dumb, okay? You're just lucky you got me when I was in a good mood. So I ask you again, what do you think I should do with you?"

Dana looked up, hopeful. "Let me go?"

"Wrong answer. Try again."

"You said you wouldn't call the police if I told you who I was and stuff."

"That's right, I did. I'll keep my word, but if you think that's the end of it, you're mistaken. Let me see if you can guess what's going to happen now?"

It seemed the boy was cried out, but it proved to be a temporary condition when he realized what Hayden meant. "You're going to take me home to my parents?"

"You're a smart boy. You see, Dana, there are consequences for our actions, and those will be yours."

"They'll kill me! If you try to take me I'll run."

"I'm way ahead of you, Dana. You and I are going to stay right here while I call your parents. Imagine what a bad mood they're going to be in when I wake them up at this hour, but that's what going to happen."

"Please don't do that."

"It's either them or the police; your choice, buddy. Tell me your home number."

"No."

"Okay, no problem. I happen to know the number for the police off the top of my head. Let me see, 9-1-1, but he'd only poked the nine when Dana hollered for him to stop, providing him with his home number and sure enough Dave answered. Hayden told him briefly what the problem was and then hung up. Mum and Dad were on their way and he wouldn't want to be Dana when they got here. They could work out from there who the other boy was. He had a good mind when he found out who it was, to press charges on him, given the lump on the side of his head. Really though, he'd suffered worse injuries handling livestock.

Minutes later headlights turned into the Summer Vale lane and headed for the house. To his credit, Dana remained seated on the sofa as instructed while Hayden went to let them in.

He was glad Dave and Lorna saved the lecture and inevitable fallout until they got back home. After they left he checked the house for anything that might be missing, but everything seemed to be intact. Since he'd been lying awake when they'd come into the house, he'd likely heard them arrive. It would have been a much different story had he been sleeping because they could have made a royal mess of the place before he woke up. Picking up the lamp he set it back in its place. He found some rubbing alcohol in the medicine cabinet and applied a liberal splash to the lump on his head, remembering that was his grandfather's sure fire remedy for just about anything.

Back in bed he recollected his thoughts that had been so rudely interrupted earlier. It was now past two o'clock and if he was going to be of any use in the morning, he had to get some sleep. Walt would be back and they were going to fix the door on the main barn, replacing a few boards as well as the hinges. The barns themselves were in great condition, although there were definite signs of wear and tear from harsh winters that stormed the valley for months every year. It was July now and since he'd closed the windows downstairs and locked them, should Dana's accomplice decide to make a return appearance, his room like an oven, even at two a.m. His own second-floor window was pushed up as far as it would go, but if there had been even the slightest breath of wind earlier, it had folded its tent over the past couple of hours and left town.

The last time he remembered looking at the clock was three-thirty, so when his alarm rang at four-thirty he turned it off in his sleep and rolled over. It was Walt knocking on the back door that woke him just after seven o'clock. Shaking the cobwebs from his head he hauled on his jeans and rushed down the stairs and into the kitchen to let him in.

"You have a long night?" Walt teased. "I know you had big date. Oh, sorry," he said grimacing as he glanced up, "is she still here?"

Hayden laughed. "Nah, come on in. I'm alone, and yes, I was up half the night because I had a couple of visitors just after midnight," and proceeded to tell Walt about finding the kids in his house and getting clocked with the lamp.

"Who was it?"

"I don't know who the kid was that got away, and the other I'm not going to say."

"Okay, I'll trust you on that. Did you turn him over to the police?"

"No, his parents."

Walt chuckled. "If it was me I think I'd rather get turned over to the police, they might go easier on me. Did they get anything?"

"Not that I can tell. They were looking for money."

"Here?"

Hayden laughed. "Yeah, how crazy is that? Nothing here of any value to get, anyway, but I guess I can't leave my windows open from now on or I might have some unwanted visitors. I think I'll go into town later today and invest in a couple of air conditioners. I've got no intention of roasting here all summer. I remember as a kid trying to sleep in this heat, especially when the weather turns really hot in August and the house is like an oven. You'd sweat just lying there. I'm going to put a unit downstairs somewhere and one up in my bedroom. Enough already."

"You're in luck because the hardware store has them on sale, I saw it in the flyer this morning. But I think we should go early and get them or else you're going to be disappointed. Go finish getting dressed and I'll run you over. They open at seven, so we can get them and be back here in no time."

There were three air conditioners left in the store when they arrived, Hayden bought two and Walt figured that since they were marked down he and Alice should have a new one. So they emptied the display. Hayden stopped for a breakfast sandwich at the service station, and before long they were back at the ranch. After installing the two units, they got started on the barn door repairs.

"Have a good time on your date?" Walt asked out of the blue.

"The best," Hayden smiled. "She's going to come up to the ranch on Saturday, so I've got a lot of sprucing up to do in the house before she gets here. The place isn't in too bad shape, but I've been so busy outdoors I've let the inside go."

Walt smiled, and Hayden supposed he was enjoying himself. He and Alice would remember Naomi, they'd been fond of her. Of course Naomi could get along with anybody, she was always so sweet to everyone. He hadn't scored a lot of points when he'd decided to marry Mary Rae instead of her. But that was ancient history now, and he looked forward to the day when he could leave all those regrets in the past because his present was so darned good. He was working on it and thanked his lucky stars Naomi still felt the same way about him. He'd seen it in her eyes the moment he looked at her, as though time were turned back and they were going out on their first date.

And that kiss! It held the promise of so much more, and he tried not to think about the more part because he had work he needed to get done. He was a little too old to be walking around like a lovesick fool. He'd thought about calling her tonight, but ultimately decided against it because he didn't want to pester her. No, they had a date for Saturday and he'd call her on Friday just to confirm everything was still a go. She'd explained to him she had a substantial workload with her job, and he didn't want to interrupt that. This time around they'd let things play out as they were meant to go, not try to force anything too soon.

Walt hammered in a few more nails. "You know, Alice probably wouldn't mind coming over with a mop and pail to help you out."

"I couldn't ask her to do that where she's so busy with the church and everything. I know they've got that big blueberry and pancake supper coming up. The last thing she'd need is me bugging her to clean my house."

Walt set down the hammer and waved the notion away. "She'd love to, I know she would."

"I'd pay her of course."

"I doubt she'd take the money but you can certainly offer it to her if she agrees to do it. And that reminds me, she asked me to invite you to supper. She's got a roast in the oven. She's also making bread and we're already picking vegetables in the garden because we had a good early planting this year. Interested?"

Hayden found he was salivating just listening to him. "Interested? Try to keep me away. You must have an air conditioner in the kitchen do you?"

"Oh yes." Walt grinned. "Got to keep the cook happy."

Just then a car horn honked out front, and Hayden left Walt to go and see who it was. He recognized Dave Warden's vehicle as he walked around the corner of the house. Dana was sitting with his father in the front seat. They both got out as Hayden walked up.

Dana walked over to Hayden and tentatively held out out his hand. "I want to apologize, Mr. Barlowe, for...."

Hayden shifted his hat, while shaking Dana's hand. "It's Hayden."

Dana looked nervous. "Hayden, I want to apologize for what I did last night. That was the first time I ever did anything like that and I never will again, I swear. I'm very sorry."

Hayden folded his arms loosely across his chest. "Apology accepted, Dana. It took a big man to come and face me and I appreciate it. What about your buddy? Who was he? Where is he, and is he planning to come back?"

Dana shook his head. "I swear I don't even know his name and he lives in Franklin so he probably went back there. He said he was going out with some girl from around here, but he didn't say who it was. We were talking at the store and he said he knew of a place where there might be some money, and it was here. I went along with him and I shouldn't have. I made a really bad mistake."

Whether the story was true or not, it was over as far as he was concerned ... unless there was a return visit. Then he might not be so nice. "Well if you happen to be talking to him again, tell him I've got a security camera in there now," he lied, "and I will call the police next time," and that was the truth.

Dana slid his hands into the pockets of his baggy short pants. "There won't be a next time for me. I don't want to go through that again, I was so scared. I swear we didn't take anything though because you came downstairs so fast."

"Dana has signed on to be a camp counsellor for the rest of the summer," said Dave, speaking up for the first time. "Apparently they're a little short-handed and needed another body. I want to thank you, Hayden, for not turning Dana over to the police. I won't forget this, buddy. You sure there's no damage to the house? You mentioned a lamp, was it broken? We'll come good for a new one."

Hayden smiled. "The lamp is intact, it's a heavy old thing that's been around forever and no, I don't see that anything was damaged. I think we're good here."

All three shook hands again before Dave and Dana climbed back into the vehicle and left, and Hayden headed back to the barn.

"Everything all right?" asked Walt.

Walt wasn't stupid. He could see whose vehicle was driving up the lane and why they'd come, but Hayden also knew that neither Walt nor Alice were gossips. It would go no further. He figured too that his friends would now lock their own doors and windows at night, and that's why Walt had decided to buy that extra air conditioner. One could never be too careful.

It took a little longer than expected to finish the door and Hayden was glad when it was finally done as they sat back inside the open barn door in the shade.

"Hayden, if you yawn one more time you're going to put me to sleep," Walt joked, in one of his rare talkative moods.

That was the thing about Walt, he was the type of man you might get a word or two out of, and then other times he was downright chatty. It didn't matter to Hayden, he enjoyed his company no matter what frame of mind he was in. He'd told Hayden when he's first come home that while he was planning to retire, he would help out now and then. But it was as though he'd abandoned that notion; here every day ready to go to work.

"Sorry about the yawns, but I am tired. I only got about three hours sleep last night."

"It's only early afternoon yet, so why don't you go stretch out for a couple of hours and then come on over for supper at five. And make it five sharp. You know Alice, if she puts the work into preparing a lovely meal the least she expects is for people to come to the table when she asks them to. I've gotten on her bad side a time or two by not doing that, but I think better of it now if that's all she asks of me. I'm happy to do it."

"You know that sounds like a darned good idea to go and take a nap. We turned the air conditioners on high, so the house ought to be nice and cool by now. I'm going to take you up on your suggestion. I can hardly keep my eyes open, but I'll be ready and at your place on time. You can count on it."

"Remember, we sit down at five."

"Got it, five. I'll be there before five. Don't want Alice mad at me. You don't happen to know what she's making for dessert do you?"

Walt smiled. "I saw her washing peaches, so I wouldn't be surprised if it's her peach cobbler."

Hayden groaned. "She's going to make me fat."

"Hardly! The way you're going at this place, you work off anything you eat in no time."

When Walt left, Hayden climbed the stairs, the house now blessedly cool, and stretched out on the bed he hadn't even bothered to make yet. He knew he wouldn't be long drifting off, but lying down in bed made him think of Naomi, no Freudian connection there. He smiled to himself, but he knew it would be a long two days until she came up to the ranch on Saturday. That's one thing he'd have to get straightened out with Alice tonight, find out if she was indeed available, or interested, in doing a little light housecleaning. Nothing too drastic, just take the top layer of dust off.

He thought about Naomi coming to the ranch and wondered if she'd be interested in spending the night. She'd said she wanted to take things slow, and he had agreed, but you never knew. But there was that business about the miscarriage, so he'd give her all the time she needed to heal from that experience, both physically and emotionally. It would be so hard to lose a child, at any stage.

He thought about her being in this bed with him because that's where they'd be when she was ready to do a sleepover. They'd have to get together at his place because he had no intention of leaving the ranch unattended while he spent the night elsewhere.

When he and Naomi did eventually make love, because now that they'd reconnected he couldn't imagine ever being apart again, it would be their first time ... a first time many years in the making but well worth the wait. It would be paradise to spend a night in her arms. The kiss they'd shared last night at her door told them everything they needed to know. If there was any doubt their feelings for one another had stood the test of time, that kiss had certainly erased it. They were as hot for each other as ever, and he groaned as he rolled onto his side. He'd have to stop thinking about her if he intended to get any sleep at all before he went over to Walt and Alice's place. And that was his last thought before the alarm clock jangled him awake and he jumped to a standing position, at a momentary loss as to what time it was, befuddled as to why it was so light outside if it was early in the morning. And then he came fully awake and realized he had less than a half hour to shower and shave, and be there by five o'clock, no scratch that, at least five to five. Those were Alice's rules, and he didn't blame her for a second for making them ... her kitchen, her meal, her rules.

The dinner was as good as he anticipated, the roast beef succulent, buttery soft and able to be cut with a fork. The vegetables, as Walt had promised, were fresh from the garden and sweet as he smothered them in butter. And the bread! Not much wonder she took ribbons for it. He'd never tasted any as good. That included his grandmother who was an outstanding cook and had won ribbons at the county exhibition for her white bread as well, but always second place to Alice. His grandmother never minded, she took the competition results with her usual good nature.

Alice had indeed made peach cobbler for dessert. Still warm and topped with fresh whipped cream, it was so good it was difficult to find words that did it justice. Heavenly came to mind, and once he'd scraped the dish clean, a cup of coffee with cream was the finishing touch to a meal that many only dreamed about.

Hayden knew it would be rude of him to loosen his belt at the table, although that would have brought him great relief. That's what he did as soon as he was in the truck and headed for home, grateful too that Alice had agreed to come first thing in the morning and give the house a quick going over as she put it. And no, she didn't want any money for her efforts. She treated him like he was her son, and truth be told, he'd always thought of her in a motherly way, in line behind Peggy and his grandmother of course. If it was one thing that Hayden had had plenty of while he was growing up, it was mothering. Maybe in some way they were trying to make up for the fact that his father had never been in his life, but really, how could you miss what you'd never had?

After supper he and Alice and Walt played a game of crokinole. Alice was such a sure shot she had handily taken on both he and Walt, winning by a wide margin. He couldn't help but think how great it would be to be part of a couple again. To visit other couples, like this, together, instead of flying solo as he had been these past seven years. And right now the only person he felt like being part of a couple with, was Naomi, but it was much too early to think about anything permanent. No more impetuous decisions. This time he would make sure the timing was right before he asked another woman to be his wife, if that time ever came.

It was just gathering dusk as he pulled into the yard and parked the truck beside the back door. He was part way up the stairs when he noticed the piece of white notepaper stuck in the door and his heart sank. This could not be good; he could feel it.

Removing the note he went inside and turned on the light, locking the door behind him. Unfolding it he read Mary Rae's handwriting: "I meant what I said, I still love you. I've been giving you plenty of space lately, but I'm never giving up on us, ever."

# Chapter Twelve

Naomi was in seventh heaven. There was simply no other way to describe it. If she kept this up though she'd be skin and bones because her appetite had fled when a flock of fluttering butterflies took up residence in her stomach. There was no more room for food. It was the right thing to do, him kissing her goodnight at the door instead of coming in and staying longer. She was comfortable with that decision and still felt the scorch of that kiss. She didn't want to move too quickly into another relationship but knew without a doubt if Hayden asked her to marry him tomorrow, she'd say yes before he got the words out of his mouth. Okay, so she was easy where Hayden was concerned. The truth was her feelings for him hadn't changed one bit if anything they were stronger if that was even possible.

She'd forced herself to work when she got back home. As impossible as it had seemed at first to get into full concentration mode, she had eventually accomplished the task. It provided the necessary distraction from her feelings. Nevertheless they were waiting for her when she climbed into bed just after two a.m., as she continued to process the hours she'd spent with Hayden. Thankfully sleep did eventually claim her and she was pleased to see it was nearly nine when she again opened her eyes. She'd needed those seven hours and given the cat and mouse game she often played with sleep, was grateful when she was able to string more than a few hours together at a time.

Forcing herself out of bed she showered and managed half a chocolate chip muffin and a cup of coffee before getting to what she knew she couldn't put off any longer. Call Ginger. She knew she was at work, but she couldn't contain herself another minute as she dialled her office number. Her sister answered with her usual efficiency.

"Hi, Sis, I apologize. I know you're at work and can't take personal calls but I have to talk to you. I mean I really need to talk to you."

Ginger sounded instantly alert. "Are you okay? What's wrong?"

"Nothing at all," Naomi was quick to assure her. "Things couldn't be better, but we do have to talk. I know it's last minute, but are you free for lunch by any chance?"

"No, unfortunately I'm not. Shane's picking me up and we're going out to that new restaurant across town he's been wanting us to try. It's supposed to be really good. You can come along if you want, I'm sure Shane won't mind if you join us."

"No, I'm not interested in being a third wheel, but thanks anyway. How about tonight, can you come over then? Or I can drive out to your place."

"Ahhh, Naomi, sorry. We've got friends coming over; we're going to barbecue. Again, you could...."

"No, thank you. That's all right, Ginger, I'll give you a call tomorrow and we can talk then."

There was a momentary pause. "Look, Naomi, it sounds like what you want to talk about is important. I work so much voluntary overtime for this place it isn't funny, and I'm alone here for the day. So let's talk for a few minutes. It'll be okay."

"You're sure...."

"I'm sure. What's on your mind?"

Try as she might Naomi couldn't keep the excitement out of her voice, in fact she felt as though she was going to fly right out of this chair if she didn't tell someone. "I went out on a date last night."

"What! Good for you. You ended up missing Ritchie after all? Sometimes it just takes being apart for a while to make you realize...."

"Not Ritchie, Ginger. Someone else."

"You met someone else? Wow! So spill the beans. I can tell by your voice you're pretty excited about this so I'm guessing everything went well. Is it someone I know by any chance?"

"You've met him, and you liked him."

"Oh? Now you've really got me curious. Come on, tell me who it is."

"Hayden Barlowe."

There was a pregnant pause on the other end of the line, a very pregnant pause ... like nine months worth. "Hayden Barlowe! After twelve years? You're joking, right?"

"No, Sis, I'm not joking at all. He called me and asked me out on a date. Says he thinks we should get to know one another again."

"Well he has a nerve."

Now it was Naomi's turn to be surprised because she assumed her sister would be as delighted by this turn of events as she was. "Ginger...."

"After what he did to you I'd tell him to take off, in no uncertain terms. Anyway, isn't he married to that little rich girl just down the road from where he lived? Isn't that what you told me?"

"He's been divorced now for a long time, something like seven years. And just because he didn't want to marry me doesn't mean he's terrible."

"You thought he was pretty terrible at the time as I recall."

"I did, I agree. I was angry and hurt, but I do remember he tried to let me down gently."

"That was a big help. *I'm sorry I can't marry you even though I asked you, because I met someone I like better* I can't believe you even gave him the time of day,

247

Naomi. You don't need him coming back into your life after all this time."

"That's exactly what I do need, Ginger. That all happened a long time ago, and he apologized again. He made a mistake and besides, I've come to realize during these past years that I was pushing him away back then by the way I was acting. Everything about the wedding had to be my way. At the time I thought it was because I loved him so much that I behaved like that, but I was immature and he said he felt trapped. Of course you're right. I was devastated when we broke up, but looking back now I think I was pretty easy to leave. I'd told him I was saving myself for my wedding night and I was so young and naïve I thought that meant we shouldn't even kiss, not the way he wanted to. I kept him at arm's length. Not much wonder someone else looked better. He probably thought he'd only get more of the same when we got married and he wanted out."

"You can't take all the blame, Naomi. You had only just turned eighteen."

"That's what I'm saying, I was too young and didn't see I was driving him away. Anyway, he said it took him a long while to get up the nerve to contact me again. He thought I'd tell him to go pound sand or something, but I didn't. It's like we've both been given a second chance and I'm not going to blow it again."

"Okay, I can see what you're saying. I never thought he was a bad guy, but I was really angry with him when he broke your heart. I'm your sister, Naomi, I don't look for your faults. You were this great catch and he walked away. But yes, that was twelve years ago and everyone deserves a second chance. He was a good-looking guy too. Does he still look the same, or have the years not been kind?"

"Let's just say the years have been exceedingly kind to Hayden. He was handsome before, but he's even better now, Ginger. Something like your oh-so-hot police officer husband is what I'm saying."

She'd been telling her sister the truth when she'd said she wanted what they had, her and Shane; both of them more in love with each other every day. Now they were expecting a baby and were ecstatic about it. It was hard not to envy them, but now maybe she had another chance at happiness. Time would tell.

Ginger laughed. "Wow! That is hot! You're over the moon, aren't you? I haven't heard you this happy in years. So do you think you guys can just pick up where you left off? It sounds like you want to."

"We both agreed we need time."

"Right, like an hour or so."

"That's probably closer to the truth," said Naomi, chuckling. "I'd marry him tomorrow if he asked me, but I would imagine he's not all that interested in getting remarried."

"You say he's been single for a while?"

"Seven years I think he said."

"So his marriage only lasted five years."

"He said he married the wrong woman, that's what he told me."

"At least he said it out loud. When are you seeing him again?"

"I'm going up to his ranch in Bloomfield on Saturday. I was only there a few times, but I remember how nice it was. His grandparents are dead now and he owns the place. It's called the Summer Vale Ranch. I can hardly wait."

"I'll bet! I'm so happy for you, Naomi. Of all the things I thought you were going to say to me, that wasn't one of them. That Hayden Barlowe would come back into your life after such a long time. I don't think you ever gave up on him, did you?"

"I knew I still felt the same way about him, but honestly, I never thought he'd come back. That much was a huge surprise. In a way I can't believe it's real, but it was Hayden sitting on this very sofa last night."

"Well kudos to you, kiddo for hanging in there. Now, I've got to get back to work. Why don't we do lunch tomorrow and you can gush some more? I'm fully prepared to listen to all the wonderful things you want to say about him."

Naomi chuckled happily. "You're on, and there will be plenty more gushing. You can count on it."

* * *

They met the next day at Gerry's and since it was Thursday, enjoyed the usual generous helping of meatloaf. Naomi now ate sparingly, while Ginger tackled her meal with enthusiasm, although neither ordered dessert.

"I've got something for you," said Ginger after they'd finished eating, her eyes sparkling as she took a small envelope from her purse and passed it to her sister.

Opening the envelope, Naomi pulled out a picture and hooted, because there she stood with Hayden just shortly after they'd started going out together. Her hair was in side ponytails and Hayden's face was shadowed more or less by his cowboy hat. Both wore huge smiles, their arms around each other, crisscrossed in back.

"Where did you get this?" Naomi wanted to know as she studied the snapshot with obvious affection.

"It was in a box of pictures I have at home. I came across it a while ago and I was going to ask you if you wanted it, but then everything started happening with Ritchie and I didn't bother. You know, things have a way of working out in the long run, don't they? If you had married Ritchie, and Hayden called...."

"I was thinking about that myself. I can't imagine how I would have handled that one!"

"That would have been worse almost than Hayden calling off the wedding. But like I say, it all worked out."

Naomi nodded as she continued to stare at the photograph, memories tumbling over each other demanding her attention, most of them good. "I remember the night you took this picture. It was when we all went over to Gram's for Thanksgiving dinner. Gram was really taken with Hayden, wasn't she?"

"And she wanted to tear him apart when the two of you broke up," Ginger reminded her. "You know how loyal Gram is. Nobody messes with her granddaughters."

"Of the three of us though, I think you and Gram are the closest," she told Ginger, "not that she doesn't love Alexandra and I too. She's been very good to us, especially when Mum died so young. That was terrible for Gram, losing her only child like that. It was awful for us, but I'm thinking perhaps doubly so for her. It was the only time we ever saw Gram cry."

"It was a dark time for our family. Okay, let's talk about happier things."

Naomi couldn't seem to stop looking at the picture, remembering how in love she and Hayden were, well at least she was. "So I can keep this picture?"

"Sure! Have you told Gram yet that you're going to be seeing Hayden again?"

"Ahhh, no. I was kind of going to wait a while before I did that. Gram can be very fierce. I remember how angry she was when I told her Hayden had called off the wedding. Do you suppose she won't forgive him?"

Ginger sipped her coffee before setting the cup back in its saucer. "She might not because she was furious at how things ended between you two. You never knew this, but she was all set to drive up to that ranch and let him have a piece of her mind. Alexandra and I managed to talk her out of it, but she was determined to go and have it out with him. I wouldn't have wanted to be in Hayden's shoes if she'd done that. My money would have been on Gram.

Naomi smiled pensively. "I was just thinking, I met Hayden only a year or so after Mum died. Maybe that's why I held onto him so tight; was so terrified to lose him, because I had just lost one of the most important people in my life. It's funny how when you step back far enough from something you can start to put it into perspective."

"And then he dumped you and you had to face that loss anyway."

Naomi toyed with her coffee cup. "That's what happened all right, but maybe the marriage wouldn't have worked if I was still in that bad place. And you can't expect someone to marry you if they don't feel like it's the right thing for them to do. They can't go ahead with it just to keep the other person happy, just like I couldn't do that with Ritchie. Sometimes the truth is the most painful thing we can endure. I was in denial for a long time and when the blinders came off I don't know who I blamed more, him or me. I just knew I still loved him, and he was gone. But ... he's back and we get to try again."

"If the two of you can work it out, that's all that matters. But you really should make that call to Gram and get what she has to say over with. She's always been in our corner and there are bound to be some bad feelings left about it. You know Gram, if she feels something, it goes miles deep and she feels duty bound to share it."

"But I will tell her in no uncertain terms I still love him."

"I think she's got that much figured out already, Naomi."

"And I won't let her trash him."

"She won't trash him, but you're not a teenager anymore. Stand your ground. Make her understand things have changed. Besides, she's nobody's fool. She'll see things for what they really are and make no mistake about it. If I were to give you any advice at all, not that you need it, it would be don't fight with her over it. If there's one thing none of us can do without, it's having Gram in our corner. I don't even want to think about a time when she won't be there for us anymore. It's too scary."

The lunch ended on a high note and both sisters hugged goodbye before going their separate ways. Ginger headed back to the office and Naomi set off to update her casual wardrobe with new jeans, a couple of pairs of summer shorts and a few tanks and T's. She didn't want her wardrobe to appear too contrived, like she'd overdone anything, but she did need to add a few things and get rid of the dated stuff. There was no way she wanted Hayden to think she was going to go into overdrive again and start orchestrating things. No, she'd learned her lesson, maybe going too far in the other direction now because she was trying so hard to be laidback. Let what might happen, happen. Yeah right, as she felt that old familiar urgency where Hayden was concerned. No, she'd found the necessary balance and she was comfortable with where she was in her life.

When she arrived back home she decided she did feel like talking and knew that Alexandra would like to know Hayden was back in the picture. She'd likely have something to say too because after all, her family had rallied around her and her broken heart. But, just like Ginger, Alexandra would come to understand Hayden coming back into her life was a good thing. They'd gone out on a beautiful date and wanted to continue seeing each other. The conversation would be the easy part, the trick was to try to catch her sister at home to have it. There wasn't much time these days for spur of the moment phone chats.

She dialled Alexandra's home number and was shocked when her sister answered.

"Alexandra! How are you? Do you have a moment to talk?"

"Hi, Sis. I've been wanting like crazy to talk to both you and Ginger, but it's been like a zoo up here. We're getting ready to start shooting, and that means I'm actually leaving in a few minutes for Ireland. I meant to call both you guys, and Gram too of course, and tell you, but everything has happened so fast. The actress originally cast for the lead, Meredith Halette, had to bow out because of illness and I'm her last-minute replacement. I've had practically no time to myself since I found out. I thought it was my driver calling me, telling me he was on the way over to pick me up."

"So you can't talk. I understand."

"I'm so sorry, when I get back I promise I will come down to New Brunswick and spend at least two weeks if not more and get caught up on everything. It's just that I've worked really hard to get to this stage of my career and now things are starting to happen. It's red hot at the moment, and my agent would crown me if he thought I was not prepared to take full advantage of it. Getting this plum role is a dream come true and it's going to open doors for me."

"I'm really happy for you, Sis. I've got something to tell you real quick and then I know I've got to let you go. I wanted to tell you that Ginger and I had lunch and she and the baby are doing fine; and oh yes, Hayden and I are seeing each other again."

"Hayden...."

"Hayden Barlowe."

"Not that gorgeous cowboy!"

"That gorgeous cowboy! The one I was going to marry ... and ... well ... didn't. Anyway, he's divorced now and back in the picture."

"Are you sure that's a good thing? I wouldn't want to see you go through that again. You were flattened."

"I know, it wasn't a good time, but he came back for me, Alexandra. We're both still very much in love."

"With each other?"

Naomi laughed. "Of course with each other, what do you think?"

"Well then I'm happy for you, Sis. I honestly am. Now, honey, I have to run but I will be in touch as soon as I possibly can and I love you all so much. We'll really catch up one day soon, I promise. Right now I've simply got to go. I can hear the beep on the line and that means my driver is probably downstairs waiting and calling me to see where in the heck I am because we're already late. Bye for now, sweetie!"

The click on the other end of the line meant the call was over. She missed Alexandra something terrible since she'd gone to live in Toronto but was of course ecstatic she was enjoying such a successful career. Her sister the star. She'd seen her picture on the nightly entertainment show a week or so ago, walking the red carpet. Naomi had been more than a little interested in the handsome man by Alexandra's side, but her sister had told them a long time ago she wasn't seeing anyone, didn't have time. When she needed someone on her arm for a public event, there was always rent-a-date. Maybe someday she'd want the real thing, but in the meantime she was living her dream.

Feeling completely at loose ends she flipped on the TV but found she was in no mood for a cooking show or anything else when she spun through fifty-six channels of so-called entertainment. Daytime television left her cold; she wasn't a big fan of the boob tube at any time, but today it bored her stiff. No, she was too restless to sit and watch anything, but what to do? She wouldn't start work until after supper and since it was only two-thirty, that left at least six or seven hours of thumb twiddling. Great! And then she had an idea. Why not get a manicure? A pedicure? A massage? Hot stones? The works? Alexandra had given her and Ginger each a generous gift certificate to one of the best spas in town and what better time to use it? She'd thought she'd save the gift for a time when she needed cheering up, although she hadn't used it yet. She'd thought it would be the perfect way to lift sagging spirits, but now could not think of a better way to celebrate her new and unexpected happiness.

Getting an appointment on the spur of the moment would be another thing altogether. However it seemed with the unexpected balmy weather, some people would prefer to be outside than lying in a spa, so there had indeed been cancellations. Fantastic! And so an hour later she was relaxing under the soothing touch of a talented masseuse. Then came the hot stones treatment during which she actually fell asleep. She finished the visit with both a pedicure and manicure, choosing a matching soft shell pink shade. She felt marvellous when she left the spa, and now wished she had something more exciting waiting for her than a night of computer coding. Nevertheless, that paid the rent and she loved what she did.

Before she got comfortable at the computer, she steamed a plate of vegetables, vowing to try to eat healthier and indeed eat when she didn't feel like doing so. Making herself a tray she settled down on the sofa in front of the television for the evening news, setting her tray beside the vase of daisies that Hayden had brought her. She wished she had a picture of him standing at her front door holding the flowers. It was something she'd never get out of her mind; a big, rugged cowboy carrying a bouquet of daisies. Sweet! She picked up the vase and bringing the flowers to her face, inhaled their fragrance. Not a heavily perfumed blossom, she still revelled in their fresh scent, and loved the simplicity of the flower itself.

She thought back to the picture Ginger had given her and the memories that snapshot brought back. She'd keep it in her purse and show it to Hayden on Saturday, or should she? Maybe not because it might stir up unpleasant thoughts for him and there was nothing to be accomplished by rehashing the past. No, she'd tuck it away and enjoy it herself. It didn't matter now anyway because she'd spent the evening with the real thing not quite twenty-four hours ago.

She knew she'd be nervous going to Summer Vale again because so much had changed over the years. It would be different with his grandfather gone. She hadn't seen that much of Peggy because she'd already married and moved away by the time she and Hayden started dating, but there were still bound to be ghosts. Would a lot of painful memories be stirred up? The old adage said better remember than see, but maybe that didn't really apply in this case. He said he'd only been back in New Brunswick for a few weeks, so he wouldn't have had a chance to change much about the old place. She still felt bad Hayden had gotten kicked off the ranch when he married Mary Rae Sutherlyn. She knew how much that must have hurt because all he ever talked about was his grandfather, and how close they were. There had been too much pain all the way around, now maybe there could be some happiness.

She wondered too if she should bring something with her when she went to Summer Vale on Saturday, but what would it be? A bottle of wine? No, that would imply she meant to be asked to stay for a meal when perhaps he just wanted to show her around, maybe visit for a few hours. He had asked her to come in the late morning so she likely would be staying for lunch, but would they want wine with lunch? Maybe she could bring some sort of lunch dish, but what? He probably didn't intend for her to provide the meal. A housewarming gift then? After all he'd told her he had only recently become the ranch's new owner. That was it, a housewarming gift, and she spent the next few minutes trying to come up with an idea for a masculine housewarming gift. Nothing came to mind right off, but she'd think of something by tomorrow. Should she have it wrapped? No, Hayden was not a formal guy and maybe her going there again might be awkward enough without her producing something glitzy and bowed. No, low key was best.

She'd look online for gift suggestions to fit the occasion and was sure she could come up with something that way, and nothing too expensive because it might look like she was once again trying too hard. She laid down her fork and flopped her head back against the sofa cushions. "Relax!" she told herself out loud, and hoped she would take heed. But this was Hayden and she just couldn't lose him again no matter how big she talked to her sisters. So much for being laidback she taunted herself.

When the phone rang she actually yelped in surprise, jolted out of her daydream. Hayden! She knew he'd call!

She quickly picked up the landline receiver. "Hi there," she said cheerfully.

"Naomi? I miss you like crazy. I wanted so badly to call before this, but...."

"Ritchie!"

Another telephone surprise, although she hadn't really expected her ex-boyfriend to call her again. She'd thought she'd been very clear about everything when they'd broken up over a month ago, and he'd certainly led her to believe he wouldn't be back. It had been terribly painful for both of them, and she'd felt sorry she had to do it. Nevertheless once the worst of it was over she did not regret her decision to end their relationship.

"Aren't you glad to hear from me, Naomi? Now that you've had some time to think about what you did?"

"Ritchie, I...."

"You don't have to say anything, just let me do the talking. I know you went through a difficult time losing the baby, we both did, but I would like to get back together again.

We don't have to rush into marriage because I think that's what spooked you. I don't mind going back to the way things were before, as long as I have you in my life. We can't just throw five years away, sweetheart. I've already returned the diamond ring and got my money back so we can pretend that never happened, okay? Please say you'll give me another chance. I love you."

"Ritchie, I don't want to get back together with you. I'm so sorry. It wasn't because I was in a bad place when I broke up with you, well I was of course, but that's not why I decided to do it. Please don't make me go through all that again."

It had been difficult enough to break up with him the first time, turning him down again would be awful. But hadn't she considered calling Hayden and asking him for another chance after they'd broken up? At that moment she couldn't think which was worse, being the dumper or the dumpee. Both were no fun. One thing she knew for sure, she had not made a mistake. She had no regrets whatsoever that she'd given Ritchie back his ring. She'd feel the same about that no matter how much time went by.

"Come on, Naomi, we made a baby together. People who don't love each other don't do that."

"Me getting pregnant was an accident pure and simple. I was careless and we got caught. It doesn't mean I wouldn't have loved that child with all my heart, I already do and I always will, but I'm not in love with you Ritchie and that will not change. I can't be anything but honest with you. To not be honest would be to disrespect you. I wish you all the happiness in the world and I say that from the bottom of my heart, but I have no desire to go back to what we had."

"Okay I hear you loud and clear as to what you don't want, Naomi. Now tell me what you do want, the type of relationship I mean and I'll go along with it. No pressure, I swear, I just want you in my life whatever way I can have you. Is that too much to ask?"

"Ritchie, please. It's over. I don't want us to get back together. Look, you're a great guy, it's just not there for me."

"Well it's there for me and I think it could be there for you again too if you'd just give it a chance. You went through a hard time. You're bound to feel mixed up for a while. Your emotions are all over the place, but you'll settle down. A few months from now you'll be your old self again."

"Ritchie! Listen to me! I'm not mixed up. I know exactly what I want in life. I never should have let it go on between us as long as I did. We just got comfortable, but there were always more feelings on your part than there were on mine. I'm sorry."

"Don't shut me out, Naomi. Please."

"Don't do this, Ritchie! It's over."

He paused for a moment, the increased tempo of his breathing telling her he was getting angry.

"It's over, huh? Just like that? Tell me, Naomi, did you know it was me calling when you answered the phone? Did you look at the caller ID?"

"No, I just answered, why?"

"Because you sounded like you were waiting for a call, and you obviously didn't expect it to be me."

She took a deep breath, wishing she were doing anything else, anything other than having this conversation. "I did think it was someone else calling. I have moved on with my life, Ritchie."

There, it was out.

"You've moved on after just five weeks? That means you have another man in your life. Was he waiting in the wings the whole time? Is that why you decided not to marry me? You were playing me for a fool all along."

She sighed. "It was not like that at all. What I told you that night, and again tonight, is the truth. I could have said the same thing to you four years ago, three years ago, two, and I should have."

"So you're going out with someone else?"

"Yes."

"Are you serious about him?"

"Yes, I am, Ritchie."

"Boy you never moved that fast with me."

"It's complicated."

"I'll just bet it is. I want to know what his name is because he and I are going to have a nice long talk. If you think I'm going to let you just waltz out of my life that easily, you've got another think coming."

# Chapter Thirteen

Hayden held Mary Rae's note in his hand. He didn't need to read it again, he was sure his blood pressure was already starting to spike from frustration. It was a good job he was healthy, that his blood pressure was fine, and he heretofore had no bad habits to speak of because she'd drive a man to drink. He had a good mind to drive over there right now and have it out with her, lay down the law once and for all. However he knew her well enough to know that's what she wanted. He would not lower himself to play this stupid game. Besides, he swore he wouldn't set a foot on that place and he had no intention of breaking that personal pledge.

He had to wonder for a moment if perhaps she might be sincere in her feelings for him; some people did come to their senses too late, but it didn't matter now. He didn't share those feelings, as he'd already explained to her umpteen dozen times. Maybe all she wanted to do was play dog in the manger. She might not want him back at all but didn't want anyone else to have him either. She liked to brag she had won him away from Naomi, although that wasn't the way he looked at it. Still, he knew how competitive Mary Rae was and if she thought she could throw a monkey wrench into a relationship he might have with someone else, especially Naomi, she'd not hesitate to do it. He knew he wasn't done with her yet, and the thought infuriated him. It seemed there was always a fly in the ointment. He was happy to be back at Summer Vale, but now she had inserted herself into the picture, uninvited, doing as much as she could to take the pleasure out of it for him. Or perhaps it was because she was so beautiful that she couldn't contemplate him, or any man, not wanting her. How much time had he wasted in his life trying to figure that woman out? Too much.

He doubled the note up and threw it in the stove, determined to put it out of his mind. If she showed her face again he'd make sure she understood this time he didn't want her coming around anymore. That included cooking, leaving notes, showing up practically naked ... anything, and he cursed himself for a fool yet again for that little rendezvous in the haymow. He'd known at the time it would come back to haunt him. She'd even tried the pregnancy angle, but he hadn't bitten and she'd backed off. You couldn't relax for a moment around her or she had you. That wildness he'd found so enticing as a young man now irritated him to no end.

* * *

He woke the next morning with renewed vigour to the sun ascending boldly over the horizon, heralding another sweltering day. He wasted no time hopping out of bed, grabbing a quick breakfast and heading for the barn to tend the horses and do the necessary shovelling. At least he had good pasture fences now so he could turn them out safely. That would make for peace of mind when he brought the next bunch of young cattle in to fatten up for sale next year. In the meantime, Champion and Aries would enjoy the lush grass of a huge pasture all to themselves and they ran and kicked up their heels like foals when he closed the gate behind them. He paused for a moment to watch them frolic. It seemed everyone and everything enjoyed a fresh new summer morning.

There was plenty to be done around the place before Naomi arrived tomorrow. By the time he got back up to the house there was Alice unloading her car with buckets, mops and cleaning supplies in hand and obviously ready to go to work.

"I wasn't sure what you had on hand," she announced cheerfully, "so I brought my own supply. I know what I like to work with anyway, so this way's the best."

"I can't tell you how much I appreciate your help, and I do want to pay you, Alice.

269

You've got your work cut out for you because I'm afraid I haven't given the house much attention in the last few weeks."

She held up a hand to forestall any additional explanation. Alice was a woman of action, and in minutes she'd carried her gear inside and was surveying the interior.

"This isn't as bad as you made it out to be, Hayden. I'll just go through the whole house and give it a once over because we only have today. I'll have this place shipshape in no time."

"That'd be great, and of course there's laundry to do, bedding, and I intend to take care of that myself. I'm a pretty good hand at running washers and dryers because I've been on my own for a long time. So if you want to have at the mopping and dusting, I'll get the first load of laundry going."

"That sounds like a good plan. I'll start in on the kitchen so as to stay out of your way and make the laundry room my last stop. Okay?"

"Perfect!"

By noontime both loads of laundry had been done, one still waiting to be dried. He'd used his time away from the laundry room to sweep the veranda and pull down any cobwebs from the corners and mow the lawn. In the meantime Alice had the downstairs sparkling. He'd never seen anyone work like she did. She was a human dynamo. If she could bottle that energy and sell it, she'd be a rich woman.

"I think we should stop for something to eat, Hayden," Alice told him in her usual efficient manner. "I brought sandwiches with me, they're in the fridge. So if you want to heat the kettle and make us a cup of tea, we'll have a little lunch. Walt's going to come back down too and we can all eat together. That all right by you?"

He spread his hands as if to say you're in charge. "Sounds great. I didn't see you bring anything in and put it in the fridge, but I am hungry and I know your sandwiches. They're always good."

"Oh and those double-fudge brownies you like. I made a pan of those last night too and brought a few along for your sweet tooth."

"Alice! You're too good to me!"

"Walt and I like them too so it looks like we're all in for a treat."

And lunch was a treat as they all sat on the veranda and ate sandwiches and dessert, then relaxed over tea. Within the half hour though they were up and at it again, Walt leaving to run an errand. By three o'clock the spruce up was finished. Hayden had the laundry all folded and put away. He remade his bed, wondering while he did so if Naomi would be sharing it with him tomorrow night. No, he told himself, I agreed to take things slow so I'll let her set the tone. Still though, he smiled to himself, he did stock up at the drugstore just in case.

Coming back downstairs he found Alice sitting on the veranda enjoying the cool breeze that made the colourful splash of perennials in the front flowerbed, dance to a lively tune. The wind chimes at the corner of the veranda provided the accompanying melody and he remembered giving those chimes to his grandmother when he was just a kid. His mother had provided the suggestion and he'd scored mega points with them. Gram had made him a batch of his favourite cookies because he'd spent most of his egg route money on that gift. He'd been pleased to do it because after his mother, the sun rose and set on his grandparents.

"Alice, you did an amazing job on the house, and in such a short time. You are a wonder worker for sure."

Up came her hand again in a good-natured attempt to silence him. It was obvious she was uncomfortable receiving compliments, but he was determined to give her one anyway.

"I just want to thank you for your help," he told the older woman. "I look forward to the day when I can return a few of these favours."

She smiled. "You being back home again is payment enough. Both Walt and I missed you something terrible when you were gone, especially the way you went. We were all just sick about it but didn't want to interfere in a family matter. I'll never forget either that you came to say good-bye that morning. We thought the world of your grandfather, Hayden, but he was a stubborn man and that stubbornness got in his way a lot of the time. But things have been made right, and the fact that you're back where you belong does both our hearts good."

"Well it's good to be back, I can say that now. I tried to shut this place out of my mind. I refused to think about it, but waking up every morning now in this old ranch house has made me a happy man again." He looked out over the fields that stretched all the way to the distant tree line skirting the Kennebecasis. The river was no more than a meandering strip of silver in this part of the valley before it regained its usual size and vigour a few miles away. "Is Walt coming to pick you up? If he's busy I can run you home so you don't have to wait. It's the very least I can do."

"Thanks but no, he should be right along." Sure enough, Walt's vehicle turned into the lane and rolled slowly toward the house. "There he is now. Hayden, would you run in and make sure I haven't left anything behind, like a mop or a cleaning cloth? I'd hate to get all the way home and be missing something and need to come back."

Hayden was on his feet. "Sure, I'll take a look around. Be right back," he said before disappearing into the house.

When he came back a few minutes later Walt was sitting on the swing with Alice, both smiling widely. He heard a whimper, cocking his head in the direction of the sound and Walt passed him a small black and white butterball that had been nestled down between them. It was a border collie pup and it yipped excitedly when he saw Hayden, his ears alert, his mouth now lolling open in a canine smile of greeting.

Hayden stared. "You got a dog!" he said crossing the distance to the swing in an instant, his hand stretched to pat the ball of fluff.

"No you've got a dog!" Alice and Walt said in unison, the two of them enjoying themselves immensely.

"I've got a dog! This is for me. That's a border collie, a cow dog."

"And you're a cattleman!" Walt pointed out happily, now balancing the pup on his knee.

"But I can't afford a border collie. I know those pups don't come cheap, and I can't accept such an expensive gift because...."

Walt was still smiling. "Do you want the dog or not? I figure with some of the shenanigans going on around here, you could use some help."

Hayden squatted down beside the pup who was eagerly licking his face with its soft pink tongue. "I'd love to have a dog; I'd love to have that dog, but like I said...."

"If you want the dog, he's yours. He's not a purebred border collie though. I know a guy in Hampton who raises purebred border collies and the husky next door got into the kennel somehow when one of his females were in heat. You can figure out the rest on your own. She had a littler of nine pups and he was looking for homes for them because he can't sell them. So if you want to give this little guy a home.... It looks to me like the two of you have already bonded. He hasn't stopped licking your face since you squatted down there. And don't worry about when you have to be away, like say in Franklin to see a certain young woman, Alice and I would love nothing better than to dog sit for you. So what do you say? Does this little guy get to stay or not?"

Hayden lifted the pup into his arms. "He sure does. I've been thinking of getting a pup for a while now, but I wanted a cow dog for obvious reasons and there's probably a decent chance that he'll be good at that."

Walt put his arm around Alice. "He's got the cow dog thing in him for sure. I watched him with the other pups, he was nipping at their heels just the way a border collie does. That's why I picked him. You've got yourself a cow dog, Hayden. I'd say by the look of it there's more border collie in him than there is husky. Now, what are you going to name him?"

The pup was squirming to get down so he set him on the floor. The little guy waddled out to the edge of the steps, looked around momentarily, then made his way back to Hayden and yipped, obviously wanting to be picked up again.

Hayden looked at Walt. "Would you like to name him?"

Walt shook his head. "That's probably a good job for you, Hayden. He's your dog."

Hayden was shaking his head too. "No, I want Alice to name him. What do you say, Alice?"

Alice looked surprised. "Me!"

Hayden continued to hold the pup in his arms. "Yes, you. What's a good name for roly poly here?"

She pursed her lips, deep in thought. "How about Dash? He's going to be doing plenty of running around, very shortly, so I think his name should be Dash. That's short and clear and the dog will understand you when you train him to start working."

Hayden fluffed the pup's thick coat. "Dash it is then."

Walt batted away a housefly that buzzed annoyingly in front of his face. "You know, Hayden, I think he's got enough border collie in him he'll be easy to train. I read that if you walk with that dog while he's still young enough and let him see the borders of your property, he will never go beyond them from that point forward."

Hayden nodded. "I heard that too." He turned his attention to the pup. "But I think I'll wait until you get a little steadier on your legs before I take you to boot camp, right, Dash?"

The pup yipped, right on cue and all three laughed. This dog, even though just eight weeks old, was smart enough all right.

Hayden passed the pup to Alice who immediately cuddled it as though it was a child then sat down himself in a nearby wicker chair. "I think Bondy's old leash should still be around here somewhere," he said. "I can use that until I get a new one. And I'll have to have him neutered and get his shots."

Walt reached over and patted the pup, now curled up on Alice's lap. "He's already been needled, and the neutering will be taken care of when he's six months old. I had to sign an agreement you'll bring him back for that, but I know you'll honour it. Ewart has to protect the reputation of his kennel. So you've got nothing to worry about. Everything's been taken care of."

Hayden was amazed. "Gee, it doesn't get any better than that, does it? I'm pretty lucky."

Walt nodded. "You are, but they're just glad to find good homes for the little guys. One female and eight males if you can believe it."

Hayden couldn't take his eyes off the pup. "Unbelievable. And I think by the look of his paws he's going to be big. But that's okay, isn't it, Dash?" he asked the pup as he reached forward and stroked his fluffy coat again, the animal glorying in so much attention.

After Walt and Alice left, Hayden settled down with the pup on the veranda, Dash fast asleep beside him on the swing. He remembered the dog he'd had growing up. Bondera, called Bondy for short, had been a mixed breed with one ear that stood up and one that flopped. He wouldn't have won any beauty contests, but he'd loved him dearly. When Bondy had died of old age, he'd refused to even consider getting a new pup. His grandfather had wisely left him alone to grieve and did not try to force another pet on him. Now, all these many years later, he was ready. He suddenly didn't feel so alone in the world. He had his mother of course and good friends; he'd reconnected with Naomi and had now been given this little sidekick. Things were definitely looking a lot more promising.

He spent the next hour or so fixing up a bed for Dash to use come nightfall. He figured he wouldn't have to worry much about alarm clocks for the next little while with Dash needing potty breaks through the night. He also expected to be stepping in puddles, in his nice clean house, but that all went with the territory. Next he found Bondy's leash hanging on a hook in the downstairs closet, and dog dishes in the cupboard under the sink. He'd use those until he could replace them with something in a little better condition.

Dash stayed right at his heels wherever he went, but the little guy tired quickly.

Hayden found him stretched out on the mat in front of the back door before it was time to go to bed and took him outside to see if he had to answer the call of nature. Dash didn't quite understand though, thinking it was playtime after that nice little nap. He did eventually pee although he was still much too young to lift his leg. Hayden then took him upstairs, stopping by the linen closet to grab some towels. He laid them strategically on the floor beside his bed, Dash's bed a few feet away.

It was still only nine o'clock, and he took a chance Naomi didn't plan to turn in early. He wanted to touch base with her about her trip to the ranch in the morning, that is if she still intended to come. He steeled himself as he punched in her number on his cell, preparing himself that she might have changed her mind after she'd had a chance to think things over.

She hadn't, and he could hear the excitement in her voice when she'd apparently seen that it was him calling. She answered with a warm hello.

"Just wanted to make sure we're still on for tomorrow," he said, making a mental note to get a landline in his bedroom in case his conversations with Naomi became ... intimate.

"Absolutely," she beamed, "I'm really looking forward to seeing the ranch again. I'm really looking forward to seeing you again."

"That makes two of us, Naomi. But something has come up on this end, I'm afraid."

"Really?" she asked, her tone now guarded. "Are you saying I shouldn't come?"

"Oh no, not that! For sure we're still on, but I got a call just a few minutes ago that means I have to go out in the morning, that's all. I'm looking to buy some feeders, young cattle to restock my herd, and I got a line on some good ones on a ranch up in Urney. The problem is the guy won't be available until about ten-thirty or so tomorrow morning, instead of nine as he'd originally said. Walt and I are going to take a drive up to check them out. That means I probably won't be home until almost lunchtime, maybe a little past that. What time were you planning to get here?"

"I was thinking I might arrive about ten or so, but I can wait and come later. That's no problem."

"You can stay with your original plan, I just don't want you to have to sit around and wait for me is all. I don't like to leave the house unlocked and I only have the one key. I'll get another one made the next time I'm in town, but unfortunately that won't be before tomorrow morning."

"I have an idea, Hayden. Is there still that walking trail down along the river, the one where we used to go on horseback?"

"Yeah, sure, it's still there and just as pretty. Why, do you want to saddle a horse and take a ride there by yourself? I put the horses out tonight because it's so warm and there'd be no bugs chasing them, but I can put them in the barn in the morning so you can take your pick and go for a ride. The tack room is just off to your right when you come in the door of the main barn. Help yourself."

"My goodness no, Hayden. I haven't been on a horse since I was last on your ranch, so that's not going to work. I do remember telling you I was going to take lessons and get more comfortable with horses, but I'm afraid I never did that."

"No worries, but if you haven't ridden since then it's not a good idea to go alone. Just wait and you and I can go together if you want to. Maybe tomorrow evening."

"That sounds wonderful," she gushed, "an evening horseback ride. Very romantic! No, I was thinking I could bring my sneakers and go for a walk along the river. I'd really enjoy that. A walk along the river and back should take about an hour or so and I could time it so as to be at the house by the time you get back. Do you still have that lovely old front porch swing? The one we used to cuddle on back in the day?"

He grinned, remembering those times very well, holding Naomi in the moonlight. "It's still here and it still works."

"I can hardly wait to get there. So how does that sound, me going for a walk along the river and then waiting for you on the veranda?"

He glanced over at Dash who was sound asleep. "I think it's a great idea. You always did like to get off by yourself and go for a walk."

"And I still do. Actually, I do a lot of walking, hiking too. I love to let nature swallow me up and that river trail on a beautiful summer morning would be perfect."

"All right then, it's a plan. I have a surprise to show you when you get here, one I think you're really going to love."

"Oh? Now you've got me curious. And you expect me to sleep...."

He sighed as naughty images began their seductive dance through his head. "Are you in bed right now?"

There was a pause. "I am. I'd just gotten into bed as a matter of fact when the phone rang. Are ... you in bed too by any chance?" she asked softly.

His voice was husky. "That's exactly where I am."

"Ohhh, Hayden. I wish...."

The sound of her voice and picturing where she was at the moment was having the predictable effect. His heartbeat slipped into second gear and steadily continued to climb.

"Maybe you should plan to stay the night tomorrow night."

There was an awkward silence on the other end of the line. Uh oh, he'd gone too far. He'd promised to give her lots of space and now here he was suggesting she go to bed with him. Maybe after what she'd been through, physically, she wasn't up for intimacy for a while. Nice move, Barlowe!

He was getting ready to apologize, when she laughed, sounding breathless as she did so. "Hayden, there's nothing I'd like better, trust me. It's not going to be possible though, not tomorrow night. I'm on my period so maybe we can take a rain check on that. Okay?"

"Absolutely," he breathed, relieved that it was just Mother Nature at work and he hadn't stuck his foot in his mouth after all. "We could just hold each other, but no problem, we've got all the time in the world to get to know each other again. There's no rush. Okay?"

"Okay. Thank you for understanding."

"There's no problem there, so I'm going to let you go and get some sleep because we've got a big day tomorrow. Enjoy your walk along the river, and I'll see you as soon as I get back. All right?"

After he hung up he lay there with a smile on his face. This certainly felt like forever this time around. Once again he couldn't believe his good fortune to find her unattached and willing to go out with him, after all these years. In some ways it felt like months rather than years, and in other ways it felt as though he'd been without her for a lifetime.

Trying to shut out any distracting thoughts, and he could certainly think of a few after the past few minutes, he tried to get to sleep. That might take a while though, considering his circuit board was all lit up at the moment. He shifted his thoughts to his cows and the new feeders he hoped he'd be buying tomorrow. That should help take his mind off her, because he didn't feel like getting up and taking a cold shower and probably waking the pup.

He wasn't sure when he'd drifted off, but something woke him from a sound sleep. What was going on now? There was never a dull moment around here, and then he remembered the puppy sleeping a few feet away. He turned on the bedside lamp and sure enough Dash was bedside the bed, mewling for his attention. It must have been him licking his hand that had woken him.

"Okay, buddy, let's go outside."

The pup seemed to know that his desire for the great outdoors was about to be realized and backed up to let Hayden get out of bed. Sitting up he grabbed his pants from the nearby chair and stood to haul them on, stepping onto a cold wet towel. Well, Dash hadn't awakened him soon enough, but he'd do better once he was trained. He'd put the towel in the washer downstairs and clean up any leftover liquids when he came back up. So with the pup at his heels he descended the stairs, got rid of the towel, pulled on his boots and took the puppy outside. Dash ... waddled to the perennial bed and proceeded to water it before padding back to his master.

Hayden scooped him up and started inside, but there was something else pulling at him. Something had woken him from a sound sleep and he didn't think it had been the puppy's wet tongue. No, that wasn't it. He'd thought long and hard about leaving the horses out for the night, having always stabled them before dark out of long-standing habit. However both Aries and Champion were in a secure pasture with no foul weather in the forecast, but with everything that had been going on around here, maybe he shouldn't have taken the chance.

It had been quiet for the past two or three weeks with no sign of Brian Sutherlyn and his threats. The fences had all been repaired or replaced. He'd even opted for metal ranch-style gates to replace the rickety wooden ones, so what could possibly be wrong? At a few hundred dollars a pop the metal gates had been an expensive proposition, but security in the long run had won out over cost. It was important everything be in topnotch condition because he was about to add a whole bunch of yearling feeders, so he'd be pasturing about a hundred head again. There was no room for error seeing as how a busy secondary road ran straight through the middle of his land, and because of that his property insurance was sky high.

Setting the pup down inside the house he grabbed a flashlight from the counter by the door then closed the door firmly behind him. As soon as he was on the other side of the door the pup began to make a fuss, yipping loudly. Could that be the sound he'd heard while he was still asleep? He struggled to pinpoint exactly what had wakened him as he walked down in back of the house and followed the path to the front pasture where he'd left Aries and Champion to spend the night grazing under a full moon. It was balmy, millions of stars twinkling overhead with not a hint of a breeze so he felt no chill as he continued on, still wearing only his jeans.

Somewhere in the distance a dog barked, probably a few ranches away, the sound carrying on the still night air. He glanced toward the river sparkling like gold dust in the eerie light cast by the moon. He didn't even need the flashlight, so he switched it off because he could easily find his way. He'd already decided when he got there to bring the horses in; always better in the long run, he now decided. He'd know where they were, tucked in their stalls all safe and sound. It could be too that he was just feeling paranoid because enough had happened since his return to make him suspicious of every sound. He'd get over that he guessed when things started to settle down a little bit.

He strode up to the pasture and couldn't believe his eyes when he saw the fastening chain undone, the wide gate itself swung all the way open. A rock was jammed in place to keep it from closing. He walked into the pasture, his gut tightening. Everything seemed quiet ... but where were the horses?

# Chapter Fourteen

Naomi had no sooner hung up the phone from speaking with Hayden than it rang again. She hoped it wasn't Ritchie. She wasn't up for that.

"Hi, Sis!" chirped Ginger when Naomi answered. "Hope I'm not interrupting your work but I have some news to give you."

"No, you're not interrupting me. I took the night off so I could be rested up because I'm going to Hayden's ranch tomorrow. I'm not used to going to bed this early so I'm having trouble falling asleep. Luckily I don't have to leave until nine or so in the morning. What's your news?"

"We found out the sex of our baby. It's a girl, and yes, there's only one. We're so excited! I would have called you before now but our appointment wasn't until four this afternoon and then we went out to dinner and stopped by to see Gram."

"A girl! Yea! Are you going to go with the name Heather?"

"That's my pick, but Shane may want to name her after his own mother. I'm sure Gram would be thrilled to have her name in there too. Sylvia is so pretty. I never thought it would be this hard to think of the right name. Once it's out there, it's out there forever or until the poor kid changes it if what we come up with is a dud."

"I'd be the worst person in the world to think of a good name. Remember that canary I had one time? I called it Trigger, so I'm not going to be any help. Was Shane disappointed at all that it isn't going to be a boy? Another little Shane?"

"He's fine either way because it could be a boy next time. We want to have all our children close together. I'm not necessarily looking forward to getting that done, but I'll be glad in the long run."

"Gee, just think, Ginger, if you end up having multiples you could have the rest of your family in one fell swoop. You could get all of the relatives names in there too. That would solve the problem right there."

"Let's just hold off on the multiples for now, okay?" Ginger laughed. "One at a time is just fine with me. There are only three bedrooms in this wonderful old house. We'd likely have to make some lifestyle changes if they started coming in bunches, but if I did end up expecting more than one we'd be just as happy. Whatever nature has in store for us. I guess we can't do anything about that anyway, can we?"

Naomi turned on her side, punching the pillow up under head. "Guess who I heard from yesterday?"

"Hayden I would say."

289

"No, Ritchie."

"Ritchie!"

"I was actually quite surprised he'd get in touch with me, but he called and wants us to get back together again. Give it another try. He was really insistent about it."

"You said no, right?"

"I said no. I felt terrible having to reject him all over again, but even if Hayden were not in the picture, the answer would still be the same. That chapter of my life is over. He was even unhappier when I said I had moved on and was seeing someone else. He wanted to know the guy's name, but of course I didn't tell him. He said he wanted to talk to him, about what I have no idea. Probably how terrible I am."

"How did the call end?"

"With him saying he was coming over to talk to me in person. Said he wanted me to tell him to his face it was over, which as you know I already did. I know he's hurting; I know the pain of being rejected like that. It's dreadful, but I'm not going to change my mind. At least when Hayden and I broke up I didn't call him and beg, although I felt like it. I've always been glad I didn't sacrifice my self-respect. What would it have accomplished anyway? If someone wants to go, they want to go and you're not going to talk them into coming back. Even if you managed to do it, the relationship still wouldn't work because the person was talked into it."

"I know about the talking into thing. I used to do that when I called someone for an interview. If they were reluctant I'd try to convince them it was a good idea to do the story, but it almost never worked out. They'd be the ones who stood me up every time. Now if someone says no, I ask what their concerns are and if after I address those concerns they're still undecided, I let them go. I tell them if they change their mind to let me know, and I've never had them call me back; not a single one."

"Are you still going to continue working two jobs after you have the baby? I don't see how you can."

"Something will have to give, that's true, but I'm not ready yet to walk away from my writing because I enjoy it too much. We'll work something out when the time comes. So about Ritchie, do you think you talked him into letting it go and moving on?"

"I don't think so. He was still angry when he hung up. He slammed the phone down. But he did say he was going to give me more time to come to my senses, or something to that effect. I'm thinking he'll probably accept it when he's had more time to think; calm down a little. I feel terrible about what he's going through."

"If he calls back again do you want me to ask Shane to go and have a talk with him? Tell him he can't be harassing you on the phone?"

"I don't want to do something like that, but if he starts calling me all the time maybe I'll take you up on that offer."

"Okay then. He's already had well over a month, but we'll see what happens. Just let us know. Now, I'm going to let you go so you can get some sleep for your big day at the ranch tomorrow. Sleep tight."

Naomi hung up, remembering exactly how Ritchie had acted on the phone. She hadn't told Ginger, but Ritchie had actually threatened her. But she didn't want Shane to get involved at this point because she could handle it herself. This was such an exciting time in their lives with a baby on the way. She didn't want to rain on their parade. Ritchie had told her if he ever caught her with her new boyfriend, she'd be sorry, and so would the new boyfriend. Now that was a direct threat. She hadn't given him any names of course, had never discussed Hayden with him at all during their time together. So Ritchie would have no idea who he was, or where he lived.

It was laughable to think of Ritchie doing any harm to Hayden, because if ever there was a man who could take care of himself it was Hayden Barlowe. Ritchie wouldn't stand a chance. But anyway, Ritchie will probably back off this whole caveman thing soon enough; get over her rejection. She really felt he would move on once he got some of it out of his system. By the way he'd let her have it on the phone tonight, he might have already accomplished that by the time he hung up. If she'd gone ahead with a quickie wedding because of her pregnancy, she'd be in divorce court now anyway.

At least Ritchie hadn't called her today, yet, so that was a good sign. Anyway if intervention became necessary, who better than Shane, a trained negotiator, to help her former boyfriend see the way things had to be?

So with that resolved, for the moment at least, her thoughts immediately went to another upsetting conversation. It was the one she'd had earlier today with her grandmother. She hadn't mentioned it to Ginger either because again it wouldn't be fair to get into all of that with them so happy about their latest baby news.

Naomi had waited until early afternoon to call Gram, knowing that's when she relaxed after eating her lunch. It felt as though it had only been a few minutes since they'd spoken, not hours. That's how it was after talking to Gram, her intense energy seemed to linger long after the words had been said. She went back over it in her mind where it was indelibly etched.

"Hi Gram," she'd said when her grandmother had answered with her usual brusque hello.

Her forthright, take no prisoners attitude didn't seem to bother Ginger any, but it never ceased to raise her hackles. It always felt as though she was spoiling for a good fight right out of the gate, as though even calling her was throwing down the gauntlet. But to her credit, Gram had been nothing but kind when she'd finally screwed up the courage and called to tell her she was pregnant. There had been absolutely no judgement, only concern for her wellbeing and she'd shifted into name suggestions early in that conversation. She also knew if she hadn't used any of those suggestions, her grandmother would not have been happy. And when she'd had to call her back and give her the unhappy news she'd suffered a miscarriage, Gram had been instantly sympathetic; had cried with her on the phone over the sad loss.

Gram liked Ritchie and so she'd been dragging her feet to tell her grandmother they'd parted and she'd been the one who initiated the break-up. Part of her felt she didn't owe her grandmother any explanations about what went on in her life. After all she was a grown woman, but she loved Gram and knew it was only fair to keep her in the loop. That they didn't necessarily get along was just a personality thing. So the purpose of this latest call had been to give her a two-pronged piece of news, and she swallowed her irritation at her grandmother's demand of "what's on your mind, Naomi," and dove in.

"First of all, Gram, how are you?" Now well into her nineties, that was a legitimate question, whether Grandmother Bridger considered to be so, or not. "Are you feeling okay?"

The reaction was immediate, and unfortunately predictable. "I'm just fine! Why would I be otherwise? All these people worrying about my health and I haven't got an ache nor a pain."

"That's good."

"Now why are you really calling me, Naomi? How are you feeling? Better I hope."

"I'm completely back to my old self, I've never felt better."

"I would imagine Ritchie is still feeling badly you lost the baby. When's the wedding? You said he gave you your diamond. What are you waiting for?"

She still regretted making that call. She'd felt it in her bones at the time it was a mistake to tell her grandmother about the engagement, but she'd done it during that tiny window when she thought she would actually go through with getting married for the sake of the baby. She'd been putting off telling her grandmother there would be no wedding.

She took a deep breath. "Ahhhh, about the wedding."

"What about it! Don't tell me you've changed your mind just because you had a miscarriage. Now is the perfect time to get it done before you discover you're pregnant again."

Naomi ground her teeth. "There isn't going to be a wedding, Gram. I've changed my mind."

There was an ominous silence. Visualizing the storm clouds she knew were gathering quickly, she waited for the sonic boom. She didn't have long to wait.

"I beg your pardon, Naomi? Did you actually just tell me you were not going to get married?"

"That's right. The wedding's off," she replied bravely.

"Don't tell me you let another one get away!"

Naomi's mouth dropped open, and she waited until she got control of her temper before she answered her grandmother. "It was me who changed my mind, Gram. I'm not in love with Ritchie, I never have been. I know I agreed to marry him, but it was for the sake of the baby. It wouldn't have been for the right reasons and you have always told me to be a hundred percent sure before I walk down the aisle."

Another pause. "I did say that, but why in creation did you allow that poor man to put his ring on your finger, then turn around and throw it back in his face? I can only imagine how hurt he must have been when you pulled the rug out from under him at the last moment. If you weren't going to have his baby, you didn't want him."

She had wanted to ask her grandmother whose side she was on, but wisely held her tongue as she took another deep breath. "You're right, Gram. He is taking it very hard."

"I don't blame him," she snapped. "Why did you do it?"

"Because I knew I couldn't go through with it. Ritchie and I were more like companions, and I never at any point led him on. He knew right up front I wasn't marriage minded and I wasn't looking for anything more than friendship."

"Apparently you were, Naomi. You let him get you pregnant. Not much wonder he thought he might have a future with you."

"Gram, please, this is hard enough."

"I should think so, you broke his heart. I'm very disappointed that a granddaughter of mine would treat someone in such a fashion. Didn't you think after five years he might get the idea he was more than just a passing fancy? In my day you would have been held to your promise and done the marrying."

Naomi was out of deep breaths; she'd hyperventilate if she took any more. "But wouldn't that have flown in the face of the advice you gave us girls about getting married? Gramp was not the first man in your life was he? You're a very beautiful woman, so I'm sure he wasn't."

"No of course not, but I never led a man on to think he might have a chance when he didn't. I'm simply not made that way."

"I know I shouldn't have continued on with Ritchie as long as I did," Naomi admitted miserably. "I guess I did know he was in love with me, but we got comfortable and I just let it happen. It's not that Ritchie doesn't have his very good points, but there's no spark there. Not like you said there was with you for Gramp. That's what I was holding out for."

"I know dear," she said, softening, "but I do feel heart sorry for Ritchie. He must be devastated."

"Well, he's not happy. I do feel terrible that things turned out the way they did. I acknowledge the fact that for him it's a double loss, but I have to be honest. I didn't plan to get pregnant, I was just ... careless, but that's what brought everything to a head. It is sad the way things turned out, but I'm not changing my mind. I'm surprised he hasn't contacted you already and asked you to talk to me about it."

"Would it have done any good?"

Naomi shook her head, although there was nobody there to see it. "No, it wouldn't. I'm sorry, Gram. I know you really liked him."

"I did, but it's not me making the decision of who I want to spend the rest of my life with, dear, it's you."

Finally, Gram was beginning to relent, but she knew when she told her about seeing Hayden the sparks were going to fly again. He'd hurt one of her granddaughters and it wasn't wise to be on the fighting side of Grandmother Bridger.

"There's something else, Gram. It's something I wanted to tell you about before you heard it from somebody else. I'm going out with Hayden Barlowe again. We've already had one date and I'm seeing him tomorrow."

Now there was some serious silence on the other end of the line. It was like waiting for a volcano to blow its top.

"Not the same Hayden Barlowe who practically stood you up at the altar I assume. Tell me there's another man by the same name."

"It's the same Hayden Barlowe, but before you get upset, Gram...."

"Before I get upset!" she exploded. "I'm already upset! Just hearing that man's name makes me upset. He left you high and dry, Naomi, and now you're letting him back into your life. I thought he was married. What happened to his wife?"

"They've been divorced now for seven years. He admits he made a mistake by marrying her and not me, because we both still love each other very much."

"He left you in the lurch, Naomi! You already had your dress! The bridesmaids had theirs!"

"Gram, I returned the dress for a full refund and I reimbursed the girls for their dresses."

"Umm, hmm, and what did you do about your broken heart? There was no way to fix that was there? He didn't think twice about ruining your life, did he? Running away with that floozy."

"It was an awful time for me, I agree, but I never stopped loving him. You used to like Hayden."

"Used to being the operative words here," came the harsh rejoinder. "If I could have gotten my hands on him when he ran out on you I would have torn him apart. The nerve of him doing that to a young bride."

"He was young too, only twenty-three."

"He was a grown man acting like a young pup. He was old enough to ask you to marry him, then dumps you and runs away with somebody else."

"That's ancient history now. He made a mistake."

"Not that ancient because I well remember the call you made to me, crying your eyes out. So what's he doing sniffing around you again?"

Naomi fought a headache that was beginning to throb in her temples. Going a couple of rounds with Grandmother Bridger was not only intimidating, it could be downright depressing but she knew she had to stand her ground. It was her life to live, not her grandmother's, although she could see where she was coming from. She'd be just as protective if it were her own daughter or granddaughter.

"Gram, we're still in love with each other."

"You said he got divorced seven years ago. If he's so much in love with you, where's he been? Was it because nobody else would have him?"

"You always thought Hayden was a great guy; handsome."

"He is handsome," she allowed, "too handsome for his own good. So can you answer my question? Where's he been for seven years? Why didn't he come back for you sooner if he was so besotted with you?"

"Because he only moved back to New Brunswick from British Columbia a few weeks ago."

"What, he couldn't have sent you airfare to where he was living out west? Is he cheap on top of everything else?"

"I guess he assumed I was married too after such a long time."

"Hmmph!" she sniffed. "Sounds fishy to me, but it's your life. Don't expect me to invite him over here."

"Now come on, Gram. People make mistakes. All we're doing is getting to know each other again, but we could tell right away that the old feelings are still there. I love him, Gram, and he loves me. I can see it in his eyes."

"I'd wait until I hear it from his lips if I were you." She sighed wearily, as though her vehemence had run out of steam. "Oh, Naomi, what am I going to do with you? You were always so headstrong and I suppose that will never change. Okay, if you two go out and decide you want to try again, I guess I can let bygones be bygones. Is he still as handsome as he once was?"

She was relieved her grandmother had finally thawed; sometimes it didn't happen. "Even more handsome, Gram."

Grandmother Bridger sniffed again. "That I'd like to see."

Naomi chuckled and sent up a silent prayer of gratitude when her grandmother chuckled too. "I guess you know your own mind, but you give him a message for me. He better know what he wants this time around because if he changes his mind and bows out again, I will find him and I can assure you, he won't be happy when I do. I won't put up with any more nonsense."

"Gram, I love you."

"Sure you do, honey, now that I've come around to your way of thinking. I'm sorry I was so tough on you. Naturally I don't expect you to marry someone you're not in love with, no matter how much I like him. You have to pick with your own heart, and it sounds as if you have. I want to see you happy, dear, like Ginger and Shane. Even if it was my job to choose a suitable husband for each of you girls, I couldn't have chosen any better than Shane Elliott. I felt the same way about Hayden, although I had grave reservations about how young you were at the time. I thought he would make an excellent husband and then he turned around and dropped you. It makes me very angry to think my judgement was so skewed. But, if I liked him once, I'm sure he can win me over again without too much effort. You can't beat those ranch boys, or cowboys I guess they call them.

"You see, Naomi, it almost killed me when I lost your mother at such a young age. It's no secret to you girls that your mother made the wrong choice when she married your father. He and I went more than a few rounds about the way he treated her. I don't want to see any of you girls hurt the way she was, and when she left us I made it my personal responsibility to look out for each of you. I don't take that responsibility lightly, as you might have already figured out. I'm not afraid to speak my mind to anyone, and since I've taken over as the Mamma Bear, I'll suffer no fools."

* * *

Naomi turned over onto her side again, back in the present but still deep in thought. Yes, it had been a lively conversation. That was to be expected with Grandmother Bridger, but one thing you could say about her was that she called a spade a spade. You always knew exactly where you stood. As difficult as it was at times to deal with her, Naomi much preferred direct people rather than game players who hid behind a sweet façade. They tended to agree with everything you said then attacked you behind your back when you weren't around to defend yourself.

How she would have loved to meet Grandfather Bridger. He must have been quite a man if he could stand toe to toe with his wife and come out of it intact. She knew that Gram had adored her husband and although he had passed away when she was still young and beautiful, she never seriously entertained other suitors and there had been several.

She and her sisters were fortunate to still have their grandmother with them, and that she was so vital and engaged. No one ever got anything over on her because Grandmother Bridger was a worthy opponent in any battle of wits. She dreaded the day they would lose her, although given her vitality they would probably not have to face that for some time to come.

* * *

This trying to get sleep early thing just wasn't working out, she decided. She had to get up for a while, maybe read a book or watch some television to stop her brain from racing with all these thoughts. So putting Ritchie from her mind, and her grandmother, the latter with love, she went into the living room and snapped on the television. Most of the shows on TV could be the cure for insomnia and it certainly seemed so tonight because she eventually fell into a sound sleep. She woke up around midnight, yawning as she turned off the television and headed for bed before she got too wide awake.

As she walked down the hall to her bedroom she nearly jumped out of her skin when the doorbell rang behind her. She slapped a hand over her mouth, stifling a yelp of surprise. It had to be Ritchie. There were no lights on in her apartment but there would be a light in the corridor to see who it was through the peephole. It was Ritchie. Damn!

Okay, enough was enough, and even though it was late she'd have to take Ginger up on her offer to have Shane come over and talk to him. That way there wouldn't be an official call to the police, during which Ritchie could end up arrested. She didn't want to see that for him. Maybe he was drinking, although he wasn't one to do much of that. And it would apparently do no good for her to try to talk to him, considering she hadn't seemed to be able to get through to him so far.

Sneaking back down the hall to the bedroom she dialled Ginger's number. It was Shane himself who answered. She felt terrible when she heard the sleep in his voice.

"Shane, this is Naomi. I'm very sorry to call you so late, but it's about Ritchie...."

"Ginger told me he was bothering you. Is he at your door by any chance? You should speak to your landlord about having secure entrances."

The doorbell rang again, on cue.

"I heard that," he said. "Don't answer the door, I'll be right over. Is it okay if we come in when I get there so I can talk to him without waking your neighbours?"

"Yes, of course," she said, tears pricking at the backs of her eyes. "I never thought he'd take things this far, but he's starting to scare me."

"Has he been yelling? Do you think he's drunk?"

"No, he hasn't said anything. I looked out the peephole."

"Is there any chance he could have a weapon? Did you see one?"

"Ritchie wouldn't know one end of a gun from the other, he hates them. His hands were on his hips, so I saw he wasn't holding anything."

"Okay, Naomi, don't try to talk to him. I'll be right along and I'll see if I can get this resolved. You can let us in, but I want you to go into another room while I talk to him, okay? If I need you I'll call you. Deal?"

She agreed, and in a surprisingly short time she could hear Shane's voice in the hallway. She ran to open the door, then left them alone as he'd told her to do.

She could hear them speaking, Ritchie's voice raised on occasion. It was nearly an hour later when Shane called for her and she met him in the living room.

"He's gone," Shane told her, "and he promises he won't come back. He knows he went way over the line by coming here, and he's sorry. I explained to him he was stalking you and he could be arrested and charged. That got his attention. He's pretty torn up, as you know, and it's going to take some time for him to get over it. I think you'll be okay now, but if you do see him now that I've warned him he has to stay away, let me know. Don't open your door unless you know who it is first, and for heaven's sake, get your landlord to install security locks at both your front and back entrances. With the money you pay for this place, people shouldn't be able to walk right in off the street. Anybody could be in these halls when you come home, day or night. Speak to him, okay?"

Naomi promised she would, with tears in her eyes. "I just feel so bad for him, Shane. I know how hard it is."

"I know you do, but you've told him it's over and not to come here anymore, correct?"

"I told him exactly that, several times. I guess he thought he could get me to change my mind."

"He knows now you mean it. If you've told him he can't be here, then he can't be here. I think he got the message this time, loud and clear."

She thanked him for coming over so quickly and taking care of the situation. "And by the way, congratulations, papa! A daughter!"

Shane's face shone in one of his rare full smiles, one that lit up the entire city of Franklin. "Thank you," he said quietly. "We're very happy. Now," he said starting for the door, "do me a favour? Call your sister and tell her you're all right and I'm on my way home."

After seeing Shane out she made that call to a very relieved Ginger. She then turned out the lights and despite the craziness of the past hour or so, managed to fall asleep again despite the butterflies still doing a mini tattoo in her stomach when she thought about seeing Hayden in the morning.

# Chapter Fifteen

Naomi didn't need an alarm to wake her the next morning as she bounced out of bed at eight o'clock, managed to eat a light breakfast and enjoy a refreshing shower. She chose a pair of olive green walking shorts and paired it with a soft pink tank, laced on her sneakers and was ready to hit the road. On second thought she threw a pair of jeans and a pullover into a bag just to have in case it cooled off before they went riding.

The drive up the highway was beautiful, the sun rising with great promise in a cloudless sky. She took the exit that would carry her through the quaint little village of Hampton and couldn't remember when she'd felt this happy. On second thought she could, it was twelve years ago. Bloomfield was only minutes away and although she hadn't been to the ranch for many years, she could find it in her sleep, so excited at the thought of seeing Hayden again.

She glanced at the housewarming gift she'd found in an antique shop downtown. She'd slipped it into an oversized shopping bag with the store logo on the front, finally deciding on a copper weathervane in an original rooster design. She was sure he'd love it. As she pulled into the yard she was relieved to see there was no such fixture on the house or either of the two front barns. She was all the more excited to give it to him now, delighted when she'd found something he didn't already have.

Parking beside the wild cherry tree that hadn't been there when she'd originally visited, she got out, stretched, and looked around remembering how much she loved this old place. She'd seen only a few cattle in the pastures, at least the ones handy to the road, and marvelled again at the sizeable acreage of the Summer Vale Ranch. Insects buzzed and birds sang in the lazy Saturday morning sunshine, the whole vibe of the place completely welcoming. She'd missed coming here, but now was a new day and she was going to enjoy every moment of it. She didn't trust herself to drill down too deeply on the future, although her mind couldn't help but stray in that direction now that Hayden was back in her life. She was determined to try to live in the moment, embrace the ride ... or in this case the beautiful walk along the river. She grabbed her bottle of water, locked the car with her purse in it, pocketed the keys and started off down the long path that led to the walking trail.

She realized when she was too far down to want to turn back that she'd forgotten her sunscreen and her cellphone. Talk about being preoccupied! Oh well, she could see there were plenty of shade trees lining the trail not far from the riverbank, so she shouldn't have to worry about too much sun. Besides, she wasn't light-skinned and had already acquired a deep tan, her skin naturally picking up colour even with the shortest of stays in the sun. As for the phone, she wouldn't be gone that long anyway. She was already thoroughly enjoying herself and was glad she'd worn her older sneakers instead of trying to find a better-looking pair in honour of the occasion. She was a no-frills kind of girl anyway, comfort ahead of style, so if her sneakers looked like they'd had better days, so be it. There was still plenty of walking in them yet.

It didn't take long to get to the river, the walking trail a shared space by mutual agreement of ranchers in the valley. She stopped and looked in either direction, green pastureland stretching as far as she could see; those using the trail unimpeded by livestock fences. She hadn't gone very far when she caught sight of a very shy songbird. It was actually quite common in New Brunswick although not often seen, the American Restart. It was a mature male, glossy black, with distinctive bright orange patches on its sides, wings and tail. She stood and watched the elusive little bird and as if knowing it was under surveillance, quickly flitted away.

She turned and started on her away again. This would not be the soul-pounding walk for exercise she did on the nature trail at home, often with her sister, Ginger. This morning she was content to meander along, like the river, in no particular hurry to get anywhere ... just enjoy the journey.

Up ahead, a few hundred metres away, sat an old hay barn she remembered from earlier visits. She was surprised to see it still standing after all this time, utilized when there was a surplus of hay brought in from the fields. The narrow cracks between the boards allowed plenty of daylight to sneak in.

She'd only gone a relatively short distance when she heard hoof beats pounding up the trail behind her. Her pulse quickened. Hayden! He must have come home early and ridden down to see her. How perfect was that! The only way a beautiful day like this could get any better was getting to be with Hayden sooner, rather than later.

The hoof beats were getting louder as it neared the turn, the horse coming fast. Smiling she stepped off the trail to allow it to pass, knowing Hayden would rein in as soon as he spied her up ahead. But when the horse came into view it was not Hayden in the saddle, but rather a woman, her long red hair flowing behind her. It occurred to Naomi it was much too warm to be running the animal that hard, but the rider seemed bent on getting to wherever she was going as quickly as possible.

And then the large horse veered off the trail right in her direction, so she started to run to increase the distance between them. But she was essentially hemmed in by fences on one side and the tree-lined river on the other for another few feet until she could reach the open hayfields, a major portion of which had been reduced to stubble following the second cut of the summer. Machinery droned as it went about it's work not far away, although she doubted they'd be able to see the drama being played out down here by the river. She was an accomplished runner, but she knew she could never stay ahead of the horse. She sprinted with renewed vigour anyway rather than stand there and be run over. Her chest heaving she slowed; the rider with plenty of room now to go past her, but she saw to her horror that the horse stayed close behind her.

Digging deeply she ran as fast as she could. She made it to the hay barn, lifted the long wooden latch, tore the nearest door open and went to her knees on the earthen floor inside. At least now she'd be out of the way. Whoever was determined to hog the trail could continue on their way. But then the hoof beats stopped, the horse blowing hard.

Regaining her feet, Naomi watched the woman dismount, riding crop in hand and start for the barn. If she was about to get a blast for being on the trail, she was more than ready to defend herself. But then again

313

perhaps in the intervening years it had become a riding trail exclusively, where people trained for timed events. If Hayden had known about that he should have told her, not agree it was a great place for a morning stroll. She might have easily been trampled.

Naomi stood in the open doorway, hands on hips. Before she could utter a word, the other woman went on the attack.

"When you hear a rider coming on horseback, you're supposed to get out of the way. You always give way to the larger vehicle, in this case a horse. Everyone knows that."

"I thought it was the other way around, but anyway, I did do that. I thought it was someone I knew, someone who was coming to meet me. You could have called out, or stopped, moved around me when I got to the field where there was more room. You kept on full speed ahead leaving me nowhere to go. You deliberately tried to run me down!"

The redhead scoffed. "I did no such thing, it's easy to see you're not used to horses. Is your name Naomi Martel by any chance?"

Naomi was surprised. "Yes, that's my name. Why?"

"What are you doing up here, on this property?"

Naomi was taken aback at the nerve of this woman. "I was invited onto this property

314

if you must know, and how do you know who I am?"

The other woman still held the riding crop, folding it back under one arm in military fashion. This woman was aggressive, it seeped out of her pores as she said with a sneer: "I've seen your picture. It was taken a long time ago, but it was you all right."

Now Naomi was completely at a loss. Where would this woman have ever seen a younger picture of her? On the internet? No, that was a recent shot, but who knew? It didn't really matter in the long run anyway. She didn't even care. She just wanted this rude woman to leave.

"Great, you recognize me from somewhere. Now if you don't mind, I'd like to continue my walk. I imagine you want to be on your way too. You seemed in quite a hurry to get somewhere."

"I'll go on my way when I'm darned good and ready, in the meantime I've got a very important message for you."

Naomi stared at her. "You have a message for me?"

"I most certainly do. Stay away from my husband. Consider this your first and final warning."

Naomi felt the ground shift under her feet, or was it the sudden weakness in her legs? There had to be some terrible misunderstanding. She wasn't hanging out with anyone's husband.

"Your husband?" she asked stupidly.

"Oh come on, don't tell me you've never seen my picture on social media or a picture of my husband and I together because I won't believe you. Don't play stupid with me."

"I'm not on social media. Am I supposed to know you ... or your husband? What's your husband's name?"

"Hayden Barlowe as if you didn't know. I'm his wife, Mary Rae Barlowe."

Naomi felt the breath woosh out of her, although she tried not to show it. Hayden was still married. No, it couldn't be.

"The Hayden Barlowe I know is divorced and has been for seven years."

Mary Rae took a step closer. "I'm here to tell you we're not divorced, no matter what he says. We are apart at the present time, but still very much married I can assure you. We separated a few months ago. It was just before we returned to New Brunswick, but we're going to work it out. Marriage is a sacred thing and you'll rue the day you got in the middle of mine."

"I don't believe you and Hayden are still married!"

"I'm here to tell you you'd better believe it because if you're messing with my husband, lady, you're messing with me. I won't put up with it. That's why we're apart in the first place. He ran around on me, but we're trying to get past that. Obviously he's had another weak moment or you wouldn't be skulking around here. I can promise you one thing, I'm not going to let anyone or anything stand in the way of us getting back together."

"Hayden wouldn't lie to me," Naomi threw back at her. "The Hayden I know isn't like that. I think you're the one who's lying."

"Hayden isn't like that! Ha! I'd think you above anyone would know he is. Didn't he dump you to be with me? I'm sure you remember that fun time in your life. Let me tell you something else, I got him back before and I'll get him back again."

"Get him back ... before?"

Mary Rae laughed cruelly. "Yes, get him back. We weren't married at the time, but he was sleeping with me while he was going out with you. He let you have your little fantasy about the two of you getting married until I put my foot down. You aren't so foolish as to think he wasn't with me back then are you? He was, trust me. He couldn't get enough of me."

Naomi felt her stomach churn. In fact it felt as though she was about to lose her breakfast. She noticed the wedding rings on the woman's left hand, but she swallowed hard and took a deep breath. This couldn't be happening. She had walked into a hornet's nest! Hayden was still married. He wasn't divorced at all, and worse, he'd been seeing this woman all those years ago while she, naïve Naomi, was busily planning their dream wedding. Saving herself for their wedding night. She'd felt like a fool then. What she felt like now she couldn't find a word for.

"If Hayden loves you so much why is he running around all the time?" Naomi asked, barely keeping her tears at bay.

"He has a wandering eye, always has had so I have to ride herd on him every now and then, run off the riffraff who think they have a chance with him. I'll tell you one thing though, Hayden and I might have our troubles like every other couple, but we're still hot in the bedroom. He can't keep his hands off me whenever we're together. We like to spice it up, like not that long ago in the haymow! Wow! I get hot just thinking about that night. I might even be pregnant, I'm not sure yet. I'd like to know for certain before I make any announcements and believe me that will bring him running back. We'd love to have a child and we might just have accomplished it this time."

Naomi felt as though she'd stepped off the edge of the cliff, in free fall, without the blessed oblivion at the end to take away the pain. She was sure it would bend her double if she gave into it.

"I've heard just about enough," said Naomi, starting out around Mary Rae in an attempt to get away from here to.

"Excuse me, but did I say I was done with you? You go when I say you go, now get back inside."

Pushing the door shut, it connected with Naomi and sent her sprawling backwards onto the barn floor still scattered with the remnants of old hay bales. Before she had a chance to regain her feet Mary Rae dropped the latch into place, effectively imprisoning her.

Naomi pulled herself up onto a broken bale of hay in the corner and tried to keep her world from spinning off its axis. Hayden was married, but if that was so, why had he invited her up to this ranch? And then she remembered. Mary Rae had grown up on the next ranch over, so she was obviously staying at home while she and Hayden were separated. That worked out well for Hayden, but why would he ask her to come here and put her in that awful woman's line of fire?

What Mary Rae said had to be true because there were things she'd only know about if Hayden had told her. What reason would she have to lie? If he was in such a difficult position with his ex-wife as he called her, why hadn't he said something about it? Told her if she happened to run into her, not to pay attention to anything she said. He hadn't done that, so there must be an element of truth in all of this. Element! The woman said they weren't divorced at all and she was still wearing her wedding rings. She'd seen that much with her own eyes. She'd also said they were still sleeping together; that she'd been sleeping with

319

Hayden while he was engaged to Naomi twelve years ago.

The tears did come now and she let them flow, glad she had somewhere to hide away until she got them shed. But then it occurred to her, she might still have time to get back to the house and leave before Hayden returned. Her face wet, she quickly got to her feet and hurried to open the door. It wouldn't budge. Peering through the boards she could see the latch was in place. That's exactly what his wife had done. No matter how much she rattled it or kicked at it, the old latch held tight.

Swiping at her eyes and warning the rest of her tears to remain unshed, she waited a few minutes until she'd calmed down. If someone did come to her rescue, the last thing she wanted them to see was her teary-eyed. No, she would look like a woman in control. So when she felt a little more self-possessed, she understood her best option was to be heard, because who would see her way down here? There were men working nearby, so she began to yell at the top of her lungs and did so until her throat felt hoarse, but no one heard. The men bailing hay couldn't hear her above the roar of machinery, but wouldn't they be putting hay in this barn at some point? Fine, that probably wouldn't be too long so she'd get out then. However she could see through the crack they were also wrapping it, which told her the bales would be left outside. That's why they were protecting it from the weather. She realized with a dead feeling in the pit of her stomach no one would be coming to the barn today, or tonight, to put hay away. Maybe they left it wrapped in the fields all year, who would know!

It was warm in the barn but at least she had a full bottle of water so she wouldn't get dehydrated, but she hadn't expected to be holed up here until God knew when. Of course, she reasoned, it was as good a place as any to have a broken heart. Why are these things happening to me, she asked no one in particular. I'm a good person, I try to treat people with respect. There was no answer, other than to remind herself she was not a very good judge of character. Maybe it came down to believing Hayden over that creature he was married to. However if they were legally divorced, why was she wearing her wedding rings and warning other women away from him? She had trusted Hayden again with her heart. Grandmother Bridger was beginning to look smarter by the minute; he wouldn't have fooled her for a second.

* * *

Hayden and Walt finished early in Urney and Hayden was anxious to get back to the ranch where he knew Naomi would be waiting. He headed straight back to

Bloomfield. Dash was nestled between the two men, fast asleep.

"He sure had a good time with that dog of Vaughan's, didn't he?" asked Walt.

"It was hard to tell which one was more rambunctious, that German shepherd pup or the collie mix, I'd say it was dead even myself and it wore them both out." Hayden reached down and fluffed Dash's coat, but the pup never stirred. "I can hardly wait for Naomi to meet him. She loves animals and my bet is they take to each other right away."

Walt shot him a sideways glance before returning his gaze out the passenger window. "Seems to me you're looking to pick up where you left off with Naomi. You fixin' to marry her?"

Hayden chuckled and shook his head, but he knew he wasn't fooling his friend. "We'll see what happens, but yeah I am serious about her; very serious. Those old feelings came right back."

"Sounds to me like they never really went away."

Hayden grinned. "They probably didn't. Anyway I'm hoping she'll come up here often and I want her to like my dog; get along with him."

"As I remember Naomi, she'd get along with just about anybody or anything. Nice girl, she was, and I'm betting she hasn't changed all that much."

"She hasn't," Hayden said, lost for a moment in his daydream of her.

Hayden dropped Walt off at home before driving back to Summer Vale, and sure enough, there was a car in the yard. It had to be Naomi and his heart gave a lift. Parking the truck he set Dash on the ground, and the pup immediately made a small puddle. He was training fast. He'd even licked his hand when he needed to go out in the middle of the night. It sucked to climb out of a nice comfy bed, but he was impressed with the pup's progress in the potty training department.

The pup was at his feet as Hayden looked toward the river but didn't see any sign of Naomi. Well, she'd be along. He didn't want to interrupt her walk just because he had gotten back early. She'd be along soon, so he and Dash went up onto the veranda to wait. Soon Hayden felt himself drifting off, and so settling back gave in to sleep.

It was over an hour later when he finally woke up, instantly alert when he remembered Naomi was here. Great, he must have been passed out sound asleep when she'd come back and knowing her, she wouldn't want to disturb him. She must have gone into the house where it was cooler with the air conditioner at full blast.

But there was no Naomi. He called her name several times, both inside the house, around the yard and down in the barn, but there was no sign of her. Gee, she should have been back by now. What would have gone wrong walking on a trail along the river? She wasn't a child, she wouldn't take dangerous chances with anything, but then again what dangers were down there? The river was relatively shallow and the trail was well back of the tree line so it wasn't like she could fall in or anything. If he had her cell number he could call and see what was keeping her; make sure she was all right. She'd probably ended up going further than she intended because the trail actually went all the way down to Hampton. That would be quite a hike on foot. He knew she was in good shape. She'd mentioned she did a lot of walking and hiking, running, so that was it. She'd decided to take the longer route, possibly thinking he might run a bit late and she'd be back any moment.

He wouldn't push the panic button just yet. He didn't want her to think she couldn't take care of herself. After all, it was just a little walk along the river. She wasn't hiking through a jungle. What could possibly happen?

By two o'clock he knew he'd waited long enough. There was no way she'd be this late. It wouldn't be like her to worry other people needlessly, and he was getting worried. She'd probably left earlier than ten this morning, so even if she did walk all the way into Hampton, she'd be back by now. Something was wrong. He was going to go down there and check things out, but not on foot. He'd saddle Aries and walk the trail with the horse. That way if she'd hurt her foot or twisted an ankle she could ride back to the ranch with him. He'd had a scare last night when he'd discovered the pasture gate propped wide open but had found both horses standing at the far end of the pasture, unharmed and apparently not interested in leaving. Thank God, but someone had opened that gate. Nevertheless that was a problem to be solved at another time, right now he wanted to know what had become of Naomi.

* * *

Naomi heard the sound of hoof beats on the trail, a few metres away. Great, the witch was coming back. She hid behind some broken bales at the back. Let her think she'd found a way out somehow, and when she came closer she'd push the bales on her and get away. Two could play this game, because if she thought she was going to keep her in this hay barn for any length of time, she had another think coming.

She heard the hoof beats stop, the horse moving around on the soft dirt, but she didn't dare move from her hiding place because when she came inside she wanted to be ready for her. And then the hoof beats started to drum away. She was leaving. Good! No, not good! How was she supposed to get out of here? This old barn might appear to be rickety, but it was actually sound. It didn't give an inch when she kicked at what she thought might be boards weakened by age and weather. They'd held tight. She was still a prisoner.

* * *

Hayden did ride all the way to Hampton and back, and there was no sign of Naomi. Where in the heck had she gone? He'd even thought she might have gone into the old hay barn not far from the river, maybe to rest, but he could see from where he stood on the trail the door was latched from the outside; nobody in there. He was beginning to get worried now. It had been over five hours. He'd ask Walt to come and help him look, but he and Alice had gone to Franklin to shop and planned to stay for dinner and a movie. Besides, where could she be? There was either the river, the pasture or the open fields. He'd been able to see in the sparse tree line that she wasn't sitting there in the shade, which might also have been a possibility because the temperature had climbed to a sweltering thirty degrees Celsius. His horse was sweating from the hot two-hour ride.

This wasn't at all how he thought the day would go, Naomi going for a nice little walk by the river and not coming back. He was at a loss. Should he call the police?

* * *

Naomi had had enough. She wanted out of this barn, now! Examining the bottom boards more closely she found one that seemed to have fared a little worse than the others in terms of remaining sturdy through winter snow and ice, spring floods, and punishing summer heat. And upon closer inspection the board next to it wasn't any better. Perfect. Lying on her back she kicked for all she was worth until she heard the board crack, then splinter. Good, one down, another one to go and then she'd be able to squeeze through the opening. While she didn't necessarily want to damage the building, it was likely Hayden's, and at the moment she felt like tearing the entire thing apart with her bare hands. He deserved no less.

In minutes the second board broke off, and she managed to wiggle through the opening and taste fresh air again. She was so angry at this point that if Hayden's wife came at her again she would fight back. She might have been cast unwittingly as the other woman, but she wasn't a nervous, stupid little eighteen year-old anymore ... Hayden Barlowe!

\* \* \*

Hayden was just coming up from the barn where he'd cooled Aries down, and also put Champion inside out of the sun. At least the horseflies wouldn't bother them in there.

He'd already decided to take his truck to look for Naomi, although the multi-use trail was much too narrow for the vehicle. There weren't supposed to be any motorized vehicles on the trail, but he couldn't wait another minute. Something had definitely happened. And then he spied her coming up the path toward the top of the field leading to the front yard. By the way she was marching along, he was relieved to see she hadn't hurt herself, but she was walking much too quickly in this heat. The closer she got the more he could see how angry she was, no make that furious. What was going on? He couldn't imagine why she was in such a poor mood, but he had no doubt that Dash could make her smile because he was a ten plus on the adorable metre.

Naomi stomped into the yard, going straight to her vehicle, and that puzzled him. Had she expected him to walk down and meet her? They hadn't agreed on that, but if he'd thought that's what she wanted he would definitely have done so. But he had gone on horseback and there'd been no sign of her.

He covered the distance from the veranda to her car where she now had the door open, flinging her water bottle onto the passenger seat where it bounced off onto the floor with a metallic thump. She then retrieved her purse from the trunk.

"Naomi, honey, what's wrong? You look upset."

"I look upset do I? Well maybe that's because I am upset. Very upset!"

He blinked, feeling the full force of her wrath. "What happened, Naomi? What's wrong?"

She wheeled on him. "What's wrong? You have the unmitigated gall to stand there, looking so innocent, and ask me what's wrong? Well I'll tell you what's wrong, mister. I never want to see you again in my life, so step back from my car if you don't want to get run over."

# Chapter Sixteen

"Naomi, what in hell is going on? Are you crazy?"

"Am I crazy?" she fumed. "I suppose you could say I am, taking another chance on you, you are two-timing liar! You were lying the first time and you're lying again, only I have to say it's a lot worse this time. I can guarantee you one thing, it's the last time. You're no good, Hayden Barlowe! No good, and I never should have fallen for your lies!"

He got a death grip on the driver's door of her car and wouldn't let go, her furious attempts to snatch it out of his hands, futile. "Let go of my door or my next call is going to be to 9-1-1 and if you think I'm kidding then think again. You can't hold me here against my will, although you and that wife of yours have got that down to a science! You make a very good pair now that I come to think about it."

He held fast to the door, so she grabbed her purse and started digging for her cellphone.

"Me and that wife of mine? Come again?"

"You heard me, now are you going to let go of this door or do I make that call?" Holding the phone up triumphantly now that she'd found it, her finger was poised over the keypad. "I'm serious! I will call, Hayden! So if you want to make a fool of yourself, just keep hanging on."

"You call all the 9-1-1's you want, I'm not letting go of this door until you answer my question. What wife of mine! The last time I checked I didn't have a wife."

Her beautiful blue eyes had turned to ice. "Really!"

"Really! I've been divorced for seven years. Seven years and a few months if you want to get technical."

"You've been divorced for seven years, is that still your story?"

"Would you like to see the divorce papers? It'll take me a few minutes to find them because all of that stuff is in the attic. If you can settle down long enough for me to look, I can show them to you."

For the life of him he couldn't remember where he'd put them, probably in one of the dozen or so boxes of his stuff stored in the attic. He hadn't looked at what was among his papers in years. He'd just cleaned out his desk drawer at the dude ranch and thrown everything into a box. He hadn't exactly had a long time to pack because everything had happened so quickly after his mother's phone call, and him being so anxious to get back to New Brunswick.

Was that hope that flickered in her eyes? "Certainly. I'll give you five minutes to show me you're actually divorced ... from Mary Rae Sutherlyn. The clock is ticking, Mr. Barlowe."

He sighed, but wisely held onto the door because he knew if he let go, she would be down that road and out of his life for good. "As I just told you, Miss Martel, I can't put my hand on them right at the moment, but...."

"Just as I thought. You're lying aren't you? There was never any divorce, was there? How could you do it, Hayden? How could you lie to me all those years ago? Why are you lying to me now? Doesn't it mean anything that I trusted you?"

He just about started blubbering himself when he saw her bottom lip tremble and those big blue eyes fill with tears. He had no doubt that Mary Rae figured into all of this somehow, he just had to get close enough to Naomi now to calm her down and get the whole story. When she covered her face with her hands, he made his move, putting his arms securely around her. He expected a struggle when he did so, although he hadn't expected her to be quite so strong. Still, he held on and after a few moments she sagged against him as she dissolved into tears.

"Naomi, I'm not married, sweetheart. Who told you I was?"

"Your wife!" she managed between sobs. "I trusted you, Hayden. I gave you another chance, and you let me down. You cheated on me while we were engaged, and now you're trying to cheat on your wife, with me. You're despicable!" she wept against his shirt as she struggled again, but he would not let her go.

"Naomi, I never cheated on you when we were engaged, not once. What I told you when we broke up was the truth. I honestly didn't think it was going to work out between us and I've already told you the reasons why. I did meet the woman I married before we broke up, but I swear before God I did not sleep with her until it was over between you and me. I couldn't have lived with myself if I had done that to you. Mary Rae and I were married for about five years, just like I told you, but we did get divorced about seven years ago. I am not legally married to that woman anymore."

"But you're still sleeping with her, even though we've started seeing each other again, isn't that the truth?"

He sighed deeply. Would he ever be out from under the curse of Mary Rae? He also knew he owed Naomi the hard truth if they were ever going to have a chance this time, and he desperately wanted that to happen.

"Yes, we did sleep together a few weeks ago. It's a long story, but I didn't plan for it to happen ... but it did and I take full responsibility for it. That took place quite a while before I ever contacted you, Naomi. I am through with Mary Rae. I wish her well, but I have no interest in getting back together with her. I hadn't seen her in years, but as soon as I moved back home, there she was chasing after me ... just like before."

Naomi sniffed, no longer struggling in his arms. "She said she might be pregnant."

"That is nothing but a lie. She brought supper over here one night and was waiting for me when I got home. After that I started locking the doors. Anyway, she told me at that time she thought she was pregnant, but admitted after I pressed her about it that it wasn't true. Mary Rae is one of those people who will say anything to get what she wants. She's got it in her head that she wants her and I to get back together and she's trying to make it happen. She's been driving me crazy with that foolishness. She went through the house that night before I came home; that's when she found the picture of you I had up on my wall from when we were first going together. Now you're on her radar too I suppose. I'm guessing you ran into her while you were down on the trail."

"I did, and she not only said you two were still married, but she's wearing her wedding rings. Why would she do that if you were divorced like you keep telling me?"

"She can wear them whenever she wants to as far as I'm concerned because they don't mean anything anymore. Look, Naomi, I asked Mary Rae for a divorce because I no longer wanted to be married to the woman, and I still feel the same way. Marrying her was a mistake; it would be a bigger mistake to go back with her and I'm not about to make it. It's you I want, Naomi, it's been you I wanted all along. I was just too stupid to realize it at the time. When Mary Rae gets hold of a man she twists and turns him all up inside until he doesn't know left from right, and at the time I took that for being in love. The crazy wild ride she took me on was nothing but that, a crazy wild ride. Her behaviour when we were together was terrible, and I stood it as long as I could before I eventually wanted out. There wasn't anything of any substance left anyway, no deep love, not like there was with you."

"Well if you loved me so much, why wait seven years?"

"I already explained that to you. I certainly did think about getting in touch with you, but I let my pride get in the way of calling you and eating humble pie. I told myself you were probably happily married with kids by then and would laugh in my face. I figured I already burned that bridge and there'd be no going back. Thank heavens for my mother. I guess she knows how hard headed the Barlowe men can be. So do you still feel the same way about me, Naomi? Do you love me?"

She looked up at him through tear-swollen eyes. "You know I do, Hayden. I have never stopped loving you. What about you? Do you love me?"

He stroked her hair. "And you know I do, love you with all my heart. You, and only you."

They kissed then, hungrily, and it was Naomi who broke it off first, breathless, laying her head against his shoulder. "But what about Mary Rae?"

"What about her? She doesn't matter. All we need to think about are you and I and what we have together. Nothing else matters."

"I can see what you're saying about her because she was very forceful with me, Hayden. She's scary."

He held her back at arms length to see her face. "What did she do?"

Naomi recounted what had happened on the trail, how the other woman had tried to run her down on horseback; locked her in the hay barn and left her there.

Hayden's eyes narrowed as he listened, his jaw tightening until it felt as though it was going to shatter into a million pieces. "Okay, I'm going to settle this once and for all. You stand right there, honey. She called me on my cell so I have her number, and she's about to get an earful. I would suggest you listen, and that should take care of any lingering doubts you still might have about me and my ex-wife."

After finding Mary Rae's number he made the call and anyone standing within ten feet could hear the woman on the other end. Mary Rae had a loud speaking voice, that in itself a complete contrast to Naomi's softer, more sultry tone.

"Mary Rae? This is Hayden."

"Hi, baby. I'm really glad you called."

"Is that right?" he asked stiffly. "I guarantee you won't be by the time I'm finished. What in the hell did you think you were doing trying to run Naomi down with your horse, locking her in that hay barn?"

"I was just having some fun. Those city girls could use a little loosening up. Besides, she has no business being up here trying to come between you and me. You married me, Hayden, not her. Remember? She should stay in Franklin where she belongs. Little mouse."

"Let me tell you something, Mary Rae, and this is for the very last time, so listen up. There is no more you and me and there hasn't been for a very long time. There never should have been. I'm not trying to be cruel here, but marrying you was the worst thing I could have done. But be that as it may, it's over. Done. Finished! We are divorced and it's going to stay that way whether you like it or not. You need to get that through your head."

"If you hate me so bad, why did you sleep with me?"

"That was a mistake too. That never should have happened and it probably wouldn't have if you hadn't kept pestering me until you got what you wanted."

"So now it's my fault."

"No, I take the blame because I should have been onto your game, showing up over here practically naked and coming onto me like you did."

"What if I'm pregnant? Did you ever think of that? I certainly could be because you didn't use any protection."

"You're not pregnant and you know you're not. You even said so to me the night you came over here and brought all that cooking with you. So are you pregnant or not? Tell me right now once and for all or I call a lawyer and have you compelled to provide evidence you're carrying my child. And if you should happen to be pregnant, whether it's even mine or not. Am I making myself crystal clear?"

"No, I'm not pregnant. I already told you I'm on the pill. There, satisfied?"

"Very! I can assure you one thing, it will never happen again no matter how hard you try!"

"Never say never, baby."

"I am saying never right now and you'd better hear me when I say it. We're divorced. It's over. Now have the good sense to stay home where you belong instead of over here trying to get at me. If you ever come near me or Naomi again, either on this property or anywhere else or come here to leave one of your stupid notes, I will have a restraining order taken out on you and prosecute when you violate it. Do you understand what I'm saying to you?"

"You're bluffing! Even you wouldn't do something as despicable as that."

"It's not despicable, and yes I would; in a heartbeat. So don't push me. Tell me you understand."

"Understand what?"

"Don't play dumb, Mary Rae, because I know you're not. Tell me you understand what I'm saying to you; that I don't want you near either Naomi or myself ever again. I don't want you here and I don't want you to call, for any reason, ever again. Stay away! Am I getting through to you? If I am, I want to hear you say you understand. I'm not going to play games with you. I've had enough."

"I understand, okay?"

"Great, now lose my number. I never want to see or hear from you again. Good-bye."

Before she could respond he ended the call and slipped his cellphone back in his shirt pocket.

"Now do you believe me?" he asked Naomi.

She nodded.

Cupping the back of her head he urged her closer for another kiss, this one of the territorial kind. An, I love you and I mean it kiss that left them both breathless when it was finally finished.

"I believe you, Hayden, and I'm sorry for the things I said a few minutes ago. I thought...."

"Shhh, it's over now. I'd be madder than a wet hen too if I was locked in that barn for hours in this heat, nearly run down by a horse and lied to like that. I don't blame you for being angry, but I've never seen that side of you before. You've got a temper!" he said as he dried the rest of her tears with the pads of his thumbs. "I was beginning to get frantic wondering where you were. I was down there on horseback looking for you, but you're back now and I still have that surprise for you. It's waiting in the house. Come on in and get cooled off. You look like you could use a nice cold drink of lemonade because the water in that bottle of yours must be as warm as soup by now."

They made their way into the house, hand-in-hand, but the tell tale yipping as they neared the back door gave the surprise away. Naomi turned to him with wide eyes. "A puppy?" she asked as though daring to hope it was really true.

"A puppy," he smiled, and opening the door, Dash ... well ... dashed forward and she kneeled to scoop him into her arms, although he was quite an armful for her.

"He's precious, Hayden! When did you get him ... or her?"

"Yesterday, it's a he and his name is Dash."

"Dash! That's a perfect name for him because border collies are so fast. He's a little butterball isn't he? This is a wonderful surprise. I love it. Now you won't be lonely here all by yourself."

Hayden winked at her. "That's right. I was lonely, here all alone."

Dash whimpered and wiggled as Naomi set him down and he made his way to the perennial garden to answer the call of nature. They both laughed as the pup smiled the entire time.

"I expected a puddle considering the length of time he's been in the house, but it looks like he's already trained."

When Dash was finished with the flowers and after briefly chasing a bee, all three went into the cool interior of the house. Hayden poured tall glasses of lemonade for Naomi and himself. Dash padded over to his blanket by the sofa, lay down and started to work at the blanket binding with his needle-sharp teeth.

The rest of the day was idyllic, despite the fact it had gotten off to a difficult start. It seemed that Naomi was none the worse for wear for her ordeal in the barn, or indeed her escape. He told her he'd be able to repair the broken barn boards with no problem. He was just glad she hadn't been harmed, except for her dignity.

They did saddle up for an early evening ride along the river. It was spectacular, the heat beginning to level off now that the sun was preparing for departure, the crickets in full concert. The air was ripe with the sweet scent of fresh-cut hay. The deep pink blossoms on the wild rose bushes now in shadows on the riverbank, had never looked more beautiful.

Hayden had put her on his gelding, Aries, while he rode the stallion, holding the pup in front of him on the saddle. Dash was going to be part of his life, and that meant not only did he get to go everywhere in the truck with his master, but he would also ride atop the horse until he was old enough to follow along behind.

The last light of the day had just begun to fade when they returned, and together put the horses away. They shovelled anything that needed shovelling and walked up to the house arm in arm. They decided to watch a movie, opting for a western, a genre they both enjoyed, and settled down in the big old comfy sofa snuggled together under a blanket. They both fell asleep before the movie was even halfway over, comfortable in each other's arms, Dash curled up on the floor beside them.

It was shortly after two-thirty in the morning when loud knocking startled them awake, the pup also fussing.

Hayden hurried to the back door where two Mounties stood. He stepped outside to talk to them in case Naomi wanted to go back to sleep.

"Are those your pastures about a quarter mile down the road from here, same side?" the older officer asked him without preamble.

Hayden ran a hand through his hair, still sleep dishevelled, his shirt unbuttoned. "Yes, they belong to the Summer Vale Ranch, why?"

"We caught two men cutting fence posts. They'd already got quite a few of them."

Hayden thought of his new fence posts and what they had cost him. "How many?"

"A couple of dozen at least, maybe more. It's hard to tell the full extent of the damage in the dark. We'll have someone come out in the morning to take pictures. We didn't see any cattle in that pasture unless they're out somewhere...."

"No, what cattle I didn't sell off I moved over to the south pasture. The one you're talking about is empty at the moment, but I'm having fifty head delivered day after tomorrow and that's where I was going to put them. I can use the front pasture for the time being though until I can get those fence posts replaced. Did you get the guys who did it by any chance, or did they get away?"

The officer hooked his thumbs into his utility belt before he spoke. "No, we got them. Lucky for us one of them got tangled in the wire, and his friend came back to try to help him. They're out in the car right now. They said they don't know you, but both of them were in a talkative mood after we placed them under arrest. They also admitted to letting your cattle out that night, opening gates and doing other mischief on your ranch. They were apparently being paid to do it."

Hayden sighed. "Brian Sutherlyn."

"He owns the next ranch over doesn't he? The Triple S?"

"Yep, that's the one, and what you're saying doesn't surprise me. These guys were working for him?"

"Something like that," said the other uniform, Auxiliary Constable his shoulder patch read, which meant he was a volunteer. The other man was a full-fledged police officer.

Hayden folded his arms. "This ranch goes back to the original land grant, it's been in my family for generations but the Sutherlyns have always been trying to get their hands on it. My grandfather died in May and Brian Sutherlyn didn't waste any time making his move. He's not going to get it though because I own it now and that's the way it's going to stay. All of this stuff that's been happening is just payback, pure and simple. I guess he should have hired smarter people to do his dirty work."

The officer, nodded intermittently as he listened intently. "We're taking them in and they'll both be charged."

"What about Sutherlyn?" asked Hayden. "Is he going to skate away from all of this untouched?"

"We'll be talking to him too. Anyway, we just wanted to let you know that your pasture fence was down in case you had to move some cattle. We'll be in touch."

Hayden watched as they turned their vehicle and left. He knew Walt was going to be upset when he told him about this latest episode. Sutherlyn hiring lowlifes to do his dirty work in the middle of the night when they thought no one would be around. They weren't counting on two sharp-eyed Mounties though. He'd like to have Brian Sutherlyn in the room with him for just a few minutes. That's all he'd need. That wouldn't solve anything of course other than to get himself in trouble. No, Sutherlyn had turned up the heat. Let him stew in his own juice. He'd always known the Sutherlyns were difficult, but he had found out up close and personal just how bad they were when he'd gotten in the way of them wanting Summer Vale. He knew it could have been a lot worse too, and probably would have continued to escalate if they hadn't been stopped. Not much wonder his grandfather had been so furious when Hayden had not only consorted with the enemy, but he'd also married one of them.

It burned his ass when he thought about some of his lovely new fence posts lying in pieces, any of them, because repairs would have to be made at his own cost and he was already just breaking even. He'd spent a lot of money on those posts and putting them in, not to mention the time and work involved. He thought again about how his grandfather

345

must have felt the night he'd told him about Mary Rae. If he'd brought her over she'd have strutted around the place like she owned it. At least he'd spared him that, but maybe his grandfather had believed at that point it would only be a matter of time before the Sutherlyns upped the ante on him, thanks to his grandson. What a blow it must have been, the whole thing thrown right in his face.

Funny how the past and the present eventually ended up at the same dance, he mused. His grandfather had acted out of anger when he'd told him to go and not look back, but would he be any different if he'd felt as betrayed as his grandfather had? He had to admit he might have reacted in exactly the same way. In the end it had probably only been their stupid pride that had kept them apart. If he and his grandfather were face to face right now, here tonight, he knew in his heart their rift would be healed. That realization provided immeasurable peace. He was also thankful to his wonderful mother who had talked him into swallowing his pride and contacting Naomi again. Now she was back in his life. There had been plenty of bad, but lots of good too, the best part of it all lying asleep inside on the sofa.

He went over to the veranda swing to sit down, maybe cool off a little more before he went back inside. He didn't want to be angry when he went back in the house. She didn't need to be involved in all of this crap; they had enough on their plate just recovering from their past.

He thought about what Mary Rae had done to her down there on the walking trail today. Naomi could very well have been run over by that fractious horse of Mary Rae's. Silver Dollar might have a little age on him, but he could be a handful and his ex-wife knew how to get the most out of that gelding. He didn't blame the horse. He was only picking up on Mary Rae's agitation. If Naomi had stumbled in front of that big animal it might have been a much different story. And then to purposefully lock her in the hay barn and leave her stuck there in that heat. She likely would have gone back and let her out after a few hours but still.... He had a mind that Mary Rae knew she was getting off easy with what she did, because she very easily could have been charged for what she'd done. Thank God Naomi had managed to break her way out of there and gotten home.

He thought of Naomi, all warm and soft and toasty and waiting for him under the blanket and that made him smile. He started to get up to go back to her when he heard the door open and she came to sit beside him on the swing.

"Is everything all right, Hayden?"

He sighed, putting his arm around her, bringing her closer. "More trouble from the Sutherlyns. The police caught someone cutting down my new fence."

Her breath caught. "No! Hadn't you just finished installing that a short while ago? You and Walt?"

"That's right. They said they'd cut quite a few but we won't know until morning how many."

"I'm so sorry that happened to you, Hayden. All of this has got to be so hard to deal with. You say the police got who did it?"

"They did, two men from Franklin. They're going to be charged. They said they were working for Brian Sutherlyn."

"Your former brother-in-law?"

"Yep, my former brother-in-law. They'll probably charge him too unless he manages to squirm his way out of it like he does everything else. People like him think they're above the law because they've got money."

He kissed the top of her head as he continued to hold her close. "It's still warm out, nice night. Listen to the crickets."

They were both silent for a few minutes. "There's nothing like a country night, is there?" she asked softly. "The sounds, the smells ... just so sweet and gentle."

"Unless you live next door to the Sutherlyns that is," added Hayden sardonically. "Then the sounds and smells are not so sweet and gentle. Like fence posts being cut down....."

She chuckled. "You know what I mean. I know I'm from the city but I love it here in the country. There's just something about it that soothes my soul, makes me feel refreshed ... energized."

Her face was resting against his bare chest, his cheek on the top of her head. Her hair smelled like summer flowers, fresh and clean. Daisies. There were plenty of them in the fields right now, no wonder she felt so much at home.

They sat there together in the gentle embrace of the warm night air before she broke the silence. "I suppose I must get on the road, Hayden. I didn't plan to spend the night."

He chuckled. "I know, sweetheart, but it looks like you did anyway. It has to be almost four in the morning and look, the sky is already starting to get light. The night is gone and we spent it together. We're already a few hours into a new day."

She snuggled deliciously against him. "I do have to go home though because I never brought an overnight bag, you know, a change of clothes."

"How about you stay and we'll watch the sunrise together then I'll make breakfast and you can go back to Franklin. Change and do what you need to do and then come back up and we'll spend the day together. We kind of got cheated out of yesterday. I'd like to go up to Walt and Alice's and say hello, reintroduce you, that kind of thing. I know they'd love to see you again."

Naomi was silent for a moment. "Sure, why not? If I was home I'd probably spend it in the nature park, but I'd rather spend it with you."

"It's a deal then. I love us sitting here and holding each other. I'll never get tired of doing that."

"Me either," she said on a long satisfied sigh.

They listened to the last of the night birds; the quieting of the crickets, resting now under a cool blanket of early-morning dew, and watched the full glory of a purple and peach dawn breaking around them.

Hayden shifted. "Naomi, my heart is beating like a trip hammer right now because there's something I want to say to you, okay? Please try to keep an open mind."

"All right," she agreed, wonderment in her voice. "I'll keep an open mind."

He cleared his throat. "Okay, here it goes. Naomi, I want us to get married. I've tried to think of a clever way to ask you to be my wife, different from the original proposal I mean. Now I'm about to say it, it sounds cliché. So I'll just be honest and say what's on my mind. The truth is I love you, Naomi. I always have and I'll say it a million more times. I got off track and ruined everything between us, but I hope I haven't done a permanent job of it. So do you think you could give me another chance to get it right this time?"

He realized she was crying about halfway through his speech and his heart sank. Now he'd gone and done it, reminded her of their broken engagement. At least he'd tried, but now that he was back on the ranch, he just couldn't imagine calling it home without Naomi by his side.

"I'm sorry. I made you cry and I didn't mean to. I know we said we were going to take it slow but I love you, baby. Naomi, are you all right?"

She sniffed. "Hayden Barlowe, was that a marriage proposal I just heard?"

"Yes. It was."

"Then I accept. I love you, Hayden, and ditto for me, all of it. Maybe we'll both treat our love for each other with more respect this time around."

Hayden let out a loud "woohoo" which the neighbours, if any of them heard, could interpret any way they liked. Getting to his feet he pulled Naomi up off the swing and they danced an impromptu waltz around the veranda before he sat her back down.

"Wait here, I'll be right back," he told her before disappearing inside.

Within minutes he was back, slightly out of breath, but wearing a broad, satisfied smile. Taking her hand in his he slipped a diamond ring on her finger. Perfect fit.

She held it up, aghast, and there were tears in her eyes again. "Hayden, that's the diamond you gave me before."

"You gave it back to me, and I put it away. For some reason I just couldn't see returning it and getting my money back. But if you don't want it, we'll go and get a new one. Maybe you think it's tacky giving you the old ring."

"Not at all! This is the one I want. I know how long you saved for this ring, and it's beautiful. I loved it then and I love it even more now. And I loved you then and I love you even more now."

"Naomi," he said, a few tears in his own eyes. "We're going to be so good together. This time we're going to get it right."

# Epilogue

One Week Later

Grandmother Bridger welcomed Hayden back into the family with open arms. She told him she wanted their first born if it was a boy, to be named Robert after Grandfather Bridger, and Sylvia, after her, if it was a girl.

Brian Sutherlyn entered a plea of not guilty as to his involvement in the mischief and damage caused at the Summer Vale Ranch. A trial date was set. The other two suspects, both men in their twenties and residents of Franklin south, pleaded guilty to carrying out a number of acts of mischief at the ranch; being paid by Sutherlyn to do so. With a promise of leniency, Brian Sutherlyn was counselled to change his plea and so all three were awaiting sentencing.

Two Weeks Later

Peggy Barlowe-Snow and her husband, Barry, arrived from Maryland for a visit at Summer Vale, and both were impressed with the upgrades Hayden had carried out on the ranch so far. They were also delighted to see Naomi and Hayden together again. It was a very happy reunion, especially when Peggy shared the most-welcome news with them that she had actually managed to quit smoking. She had enrolled in a smoking cessation program at a clinic in her town in order to break her long-standing tobacco habit. She now had four smoke-free weeks to her credit. Hayden said he'd just then realized there hadn't been any smoke rings during their recent conversations, and hugged his mother, thanking her for making the effort.

One Month Later

Hayden and Naomi were married in a small ceremony in Walt and Alice's beautiful backyard, a handful of guests present. There wasn't a dry eye there that beautiful August afternoon when the couple repeated their vows to one another. Alice catered, preparing a delicious sit down meal. She also insisted on making their wedding cake, another hobby of hers. She baked and trimmed a gorgeous two-tiered creation, complete with edible garden flowers. Walt served as best man for Hayden, a very pregnant Ginger stood up with Naomi as matron of honour, and Shane was a groomsman. Alexandra attended from Ireland via Zoom as an honorary bridesmaid, and Grandmother Bridger kept everyone entertained at the reception with her dry wit as mistress of ceremonies. Her toast to the couple had everyone in stitches, as did her warning to the groom.

Six Weeks Later

Mary Rae Sutherlyn left for an extended visit with her Great-Uncle Tab and Great-Aunt Marina in Queensland, Australia. When Hayden heard the news he felt a huge sense of relief, although she hadn't come near him, Naomi or the ranch since Hayden had read her the riot act. It had apparently worked.

Three Months Later

Ritchie Jamieson met the girl of his dreams at a family wedding, and both agreed it was love at first sight.

Five Months Later

Ginger and Shane welcomed their first child, Heather Sylvia Elliott. All three were doing well.

One Year Later:

Dash was now fully grown and one of the best cow dogs Hayden and Walt had ever seen. A loving and faithful companion to both Hayden and Naomi, he also had the full respect of the cattle on the Summer Vale Ranch.

If you enjoyed this book, please leave the author a review.

## *Eden Monroe books published by BWL Publishing*

Sudden Turn
Looking for Snowflakes
Sidelined
Dangerous Getaway
Almost Broken
Just Before Sunset
Unforeseen Shadows
Incomplete Truths
Storms in the Valley
Back in the Valley
When Fate Comes Calling
Gold Digger Among Us
Dare to Inherit

Eden Monroe loves giving voice to the endless parade of interesting characters that introduce themselves in her imagination. She writes about real life, real issues and struggles, and triumphing against all odds. A proud east coast Canadian, she enjoys a variety of outdoor activities, her cat, and a good book.

BWL Publishing

bwlpublishing.ca